TAME

COLET ABEDI

Book Design: Shanoff Designs & Nina Grinstead
Photos: Robert Unger
Editing by Christine Estevez

TABEL OF CONTENTS

"God created woman to tame man."
-Voltaire

For my mother, Effat Abedi.
For your strength. Your faith. And love…

PROLOGUE

Fifteen Years Ago

I fell in love with Michael Sinclair when I was eight years old.

I can even remember the exact moment.

After years of being alone after the death of my father, my mother married one of the most eligible bachelors in London - Charles Edward Dalton Sinclair. He was wealthy, had an incredible pedigree, and adored my mother.

What was more, he also happened to have a son who was five years my senior. I was thrilled I was finally going to have a sibling. An older, protective brother. One who would cherish and look out for me. It was something I had dreamt about my whole life and it seemed as though my wish had finally been granted.

But God had a different plan.

My new stepbrother, Davis Sinclair, would quickly become the bane of my adolescent existence. My curse. He was everything but brotherly and caring.

In fact, I quickly became convinced he was the Antichrist.

After our parent's marriage, I soon realized his biggest pleasure in life came from teasing me mercilessly and making me cry. Davis liked to see people suffer. There was a sickening type of joy that came over him when he saw someone's pain. Since I was so young and naïve , I played right into my stepbrother's evil machinations. It wasn't until I was much older that I finally stopped the tears and learned the art of feigning indifference, which in turn, made Davis thankfully leave me alone.

But during my younger years, while I depended on my tears as a source of comfort, Davis' cousin, Michael Sinclair was there to protect me.

I'll never forget the moment he stepped into my life like a knight in shining armor when I was only eight, and he was sixteen.

It was a beautiful summer day in Surrey and I was outside playing with my dolls at my stepfather's country estate.

"Shabby Abby!" Davis screamed at me in a shrill voice as I cried over the injustice of such an awful nickname. "Shabby Abby, are you crying like the flabby baby you are?"

He circled me and stuck out his tongue.

I covered my ears with my hands and tried to block out his tormenting words.

"Leave me alone!" I cried out.

"Shabby Abby!" Davis shouted with glee. "Shabby Abby, you're so flabby! Flabby Shabby Abby! Flabby Shabby Abby!"

Looking back now, I must admit, I *was* on the flabby side.

To my mother's horror, I was a chubby child, so much so, that she had put me on a strict diet. Unfortunately, it ended up backfiring, because it turned me into a closet eater. Chocolate, potato chips and fattening baked goods became my constant companion in the hiding spaces I would sneak off to. I stole food from the pantry whenever no one was paying attention to me, which wasn't so great for my mother's plan, because it just so happened no one ever paid *any* attention to me at all.

So there I was, surrounded by my dolls, remnants of cookie crumbs littered all over my uncomfortably tight pink dress, wishing Davis would somehow magically disappear.

And that's when something even better than his disappearance happened.

"What's going on out here?"

The sun was glaring in my eyes as I squinted up to see who had joined Davis. If it were one of his hideous friends, I was ready to take my dolls and go inside the house for a few hours and hide inside a dressing closet where they wouldn't be able to find me.

"I'm here with Flabby Shabby Abby!" Davis declared proudly as he pointed at me like I was diseased.

There was a break from the bright sunlight as the clouds moved, and it was at that moment I stared into Michael Sinclair's piercing blue eyes for the very first time.

He seemed as tall as the sun. And just as handsome as all the fairy-tale heroes I read about at night.

He leaned down next to me and took in my sad face. He reached out and brushed my cheek with the back of his large hand and gave me a sympathetic smile.

"Are you okay, Abby?"

"Are you Prince Charming?" I asked in awe. "Are you here to save me from my evil stepbrother?"

He smiled at me. "Do you need saving?"

"I do," I told him as I nodded my head. "He's very mean to me."

"He is?" Michael asked sympathetically as I nodded.

"He makes me cry," I admitted softly.

"Shut up, Flabby Abby!" Davis sneered. "You talk too much!"

Michael gave me a sweet smile before standing to his full height and turning his attention to my stepbrother.

"You need to stop teasing our Abby," Michael told him sternly.

I watched Michael with wide eyes, half in love with him already.

"Or what?" Davis sneered at him. "What will *you* do?"

"Punch you in the face," Michael informed him.

Davis shook his head and laughed, then for good measure stepped close to me and leaned in so that his face was only inches from mine.

"Shabby. Flabby. Abby," he taunted me again. Except this time he crossed a line he was warned not to go near.

It happened so fast.

One second Davis was leaning in so close I could feel his breath on my skin and the next he was lifted up away from me and punched soundly in the face.

I watched in happiness as he flew through the sky and landed with a thud on the ground, a good distance away from me.

Michael Sinclair descended, loomed over him like an imposing young demigod and grabbed him angrily by his collar.

"You've been warned, Davis."

Davis was too frightened to move. He could only nod his head in acknowledgment before he ran off like the devil was chasing him.

Michael turned to face me when Davis was gone and gave me the most beautiful smile I had ever seen in my life.

"If he bothers you again, Abigail," he said to me, "I will beat him to a bloody pulp."

And just like that.

I finally had a hero.

I decided right then and there when I grew up I would marry Michael Sinclair.

CHAPTER ONE

"I'd like a tall, half-caff, soy latte with an extra shot, and cream at 120 degrees."

WTF?

120 degrees?

"Did you get the order, Abby?" Ronald, my manager and boss at the coffee shop, asks.

"Yes," I nod, even though I'm not so sure I'm capable of making the customer's order. How does one make sure the coffee is *exactly* at 120 degrees? Is it even possible?

Ronald brushes his bright orange hair away from his pale, freckled face and squints his eyes. He does that a lot when he looks at me, like he's sizing me up and doesn't quite know if I'm capable.

Can I blame him?

Not quite.

Since I started this job a few weeks ago, I've been a complete disaster at it. It's pathetic, really. At the age of twenty-three, this is my first real job—a barista at a coffee shop. And I am completely inept at it. The only reason why I'm still employed is because Ronald feels sorry for me.

"I've got this," I tell him in what I hope is a confident voice.

I hear Paul, the other barista working today, snort, and I fight the urge to throw a scone at him.

I make my way to the counter where all the machines are lined up and grab a cup. Who knew that making a cup of coffee was actually so difficult to do? The new respect I have for baristas is astounding. I promise myself for the thousandth time I will never order an elaborate drink again.

"Maybe Paul should do this one? It's a complicated order,"

Ronald says nervously.

Perfect. My boss thinks I'm an absolute moron.

"If that's what you prefer," I say evenly. I know an impending disaster when I see it. The last thing I want to do is mess up another customer's order.

I need this job.

It's the first time in my life I'm on my own for money.

For better or worse, I've never had to worry about my finances until now. I've been blessed with a well-to-do family and come from a life of privilege. And up until a few months ago, when I broke my engagement with my absurdly wealthy Russian fiancé, I never thought I would have to worry about money.

I try not to think about that moment in my life but as usual, the memories creep up on me, and I find myself reliving what was without a doubt the worst time in my young existence.

My ex-fiancé Dimitri Lobonav-Dostyanevsky was handpicked by my mother to bring an end to, as she so eloquently put, my "lack-adaisical" life. It's not like my mother was far off at the time. After I graduated from St. Andrews University with a degree in history, I had never felt more lost. I didn't know what I wanted to do with my life. All my other schoolmates had clear paths mapped out in their minds, but me, I felt like I had been placed in a super car on a Formula One racetrack and didn't know how to start my engine.

I came home to London after university and moved into the flat my father had left for me when he passed away when I was a baby. My stepfather had given me a monthly allowance, and my mother warned me to find my way. I had tried. I volunteered at different charities and actually enjoyed giving my time to the organizations, but it wasn't enough. Not for my mother, whose sole mission in life was to see me marry well.

Since I wasn't much of a dater, she took it upon herself to find my future husband. Enter Dimitri Lobonav-Dostyanevsky, my rich Russian oligarch. I had tried to like him. I really had. He was pleasant looking enough, was as rich as Midas, and really didn't care what I did or whom I went out with. In fact, he pretty much left me alone, a condition I had grown acutely accustomed to over the years. Dimitri was forty-one and wanted a young wife who would stay home and give him children. My mother convinced me that it was enough. That I didn't need love because if I married him, I would never have to worry about anything again. That my situation couldn't get much better than this. She reminded me that there was a line of women waiting to take my place if I said no. At the time, her advice seemed logical and the right thing to do. So to my great shame, I was foolish enough to go along with it.

I was comforted by the fact that Dimitri felt the same way as me. We were both using each other. Neither of us was in love, we were just looking for a means to an end. And so I naïvely believed it would work.

He proposed with an enormous twenty-five-carat diamond ring that must have cost a small fortune. It was horrifyingly gaudy. I actually cringed when I saw it. It was too much and not my style at all. I only wore it when I would see him, which luckily was only a few times a week.

Dimitri was generous and had opened a bank account for me to buy a new wardrobe and to plan our wedding. He told me to spare no expense and the bigger, louder, and more ostentatious, the happier he would be. I wondered if he even realized that I'd rather run from those three adjectives than toward. My mother, on the other hand, was another story altogether. She had lit up like a Christmas tree when she heard him say those words.

Bigger? Check.

Louder? Check.

Ostentatious? Check.

"Shall we ship in swans and have them running around on the estate?" she had asked me one evening while having dinner at Scott's.

"The wedding is in December," I argued. "And I'm pretty sure swans won't just run around the estate, at least not the way you're picturing in your head. They might even freeze to death. They migrate during the winter months."

My mother waved off my concern.

"We'll have heaters for them," she said. "We take care of our animals, Abigail."

It took all my years of discipline to refrain from rolling my eyes.

In my entire life, I had never even seen my mother change the water for our pets.

Regardless, I realized quickly this was something she could plan in her sleep and would have a ball doing, so I left it all to her. She became immersed in organizing the wedding of the century and thankfully ignored me.

But everything was just moving too fast.

And the only thoughts that kept going through my head were: *Am I making the right choice? Is this my future?*

Is.

This.

It?

But even with all of my reservations and fears, I had pushed all self-doubt out of my mind and blindly forged ahead. It was all fine and dandy, and I had even fooled myself into believing this marriage would be good for me.

And that's when it all went to shit.

The second I was in Provence and had set eyes on Michael Sinclair after not seeing him since I was seventeen years old, everything inside my soul shifted. For years I had tricked myself into believing that it was only a child's crush. That all the moments we shared together meant nothing. That he was an illusion I had conjured up in my head.

But I was so wrong.

Here was the man who had been my first kiss. Who had always

been kind to me. Who was gorgeous beyond words. And who had made my heart race like a mad woman whenever he was near.

He made me feel alive.

And special.

Needed.

And in no way inadequate.

I had tried to push my feelings aside for him, and I had thought I did a good job until the night of a party that my best friend, Georgie, had thrown for me.

I'll never forget it.

Dimitri loved skimpy, revealing clothes. He didn't seem to mind if other men ogled me. In fact, it seemed to please him if his friends found me desirable, like he owned something that others coveted but couldn't have. My brown hair had been curled and primped the way he preferred, and I had a thick layer of makeup on that made me feel like a wax figure at Madam Tussaud's famous museum.

I had tried to be confident. But the face that stared back at me in the mirror was not one I recognized, and from the moment I arrived at the party all I had wanted to do was find a way to cover up my half-naked body. After chatting with a few of our guests, I had escaped into one of Georgie's guest bedrooms.

I shut the door and blocked out the noise from the party, needing to escape from all the suffocating feelings that were slowly choking the life out of me. It wasn't like Dimitri would miss me. He was too busy texting and playing *Candy Crush* on his phone.

I took off the five-inch stiletto heels my stylist had paired with my minidress and found myself laying on the bed, wishing the party to be over. And my life, for that matter.

I didn't know what I was doing with my future.

I felt as though I had lost all direction.

Like I didn't even have a purpose.

And as destiny goes, that's how Michael found me.

I heard the door slowly open, and I was annoyed that someone was about to invade my private moment.

"The room is occupied," I called out without bothering to see who it was. If it was some couple looking to shag, they could bloody well find another place. The place was certainly big enough.

"Shouldn't you be enjoying your party?"

I shot up from the bed when I heard Michael's voice.

I tried not to think about how incredibly handsome he looked in his tailored black suit. He was so beautiful it almost hurt to look at him. Michael Sinclair had movie star good looks. He was tall, well over six feet, with longish, jet black hair that was mussed and always looked as though he had been up to no good in a bedroom. His bright blue eyes were like jewels shining out of his tanned and handsome face. His cheekbones were strong, his lips, full and sensual. His face was angular and masculine, his jawline perfect and his body... God, his body. It was long and lean, with slim hips and broad shoulders and a chest that was made to lick, kiss, or do any other type of dirty deed one could think of.

My blue eyes focused on his sensuous lips. I knew what they tasted like, considering he had been my very first make-out session. It was a moment he probably didn't even recall since he had been so smashed.

But not me.

Me. I remembered every minute of it. Every detail. My back pushed up against a wall, his hands on either side of my face, his tall, hard body leaning down close to mine as he tasted what I willingly offered. The memory of that kiss had been my companion on many lonely nights.

And now—

This.

Michael Sinclair here. Right now. To torture me more.

It was unfair for him to have so much raw sex appeal.

He oozed it.

I was hit with a surge of pure, white-hot lust. God, I imagined he'd be great in bed. The beautiful way he moved, like some exotic cat, the strength I could see in his hands and body. I didn't need to be a Nobel Prize winner to come to that conclusion.

"I just needed a moment," I told him as I pushed the forbidden thoughts out of my mind and tried to tuck my very naked legs underneath my minidress, which was virtually impossible. I was exposed in every way.

"It's a party for your upcoming wedding," he pointed out the obvious.

"Thank you for the clarification," I replied, annoyed that he had to be here right now when so many conflicting emotions were racing through my head.

Michael's inscrutable gaze studied me.

"Dimitri seems…" He waited a moment like he was searching for the right word. "Pleasant."

I could hear his disapproval, and it infuriated me. This was not something I wanted to deal with at the moment.

But still, I found the need to defend my fiancé.

"He's wonderful," I told him.

"Of course," Michael replied politely. "And you love him."

Love him?

That was rich. I *wished* I did. I knew I should have agreed with Michael. It was the proper thing to do. But I couldn't utter the lie. For some reason saying the words, *yes, I love Dimitri*, made me feel like the sky would open above my head, and I'd be struck by lightning.

Especially professing the lie to him.

So instead, there was an uncomfortable silence.

"Don't you?" Michael pushed as his keen gaze searched for the truth.

"What's it to you?" I asked flippantly.

He watched me like a hawk.

"I'm curious."

"You shouldn't be," I responded. "I'm marrying him, aren't I?"

Michael stepped forward and his lips curled in disdain.

"I never took you for a woman who would marry for money."

"I'm not," I said angrily, genuinely hurt by his accusation. Even though I had basically just insinuated I didn't love Dimitri, I was horrified that he actually thought I'd marry him, or any man for that matter, only for money. Yes, Dimitri was wealthy, but if he weren't nice, I wouldn't have agreed to marry him. It was a flimsy defense, I knew, but in that moment I didn't have the time or the inclination to analyze it further.

"Then what is it?" Michael replied, his eyes watching me.

My mind raced as I tried to remember all of Dimitri's pleasant attributes.

Candy Crush.

What?

What was that? Why did that come to mind?

Well, he is extraordinarily good at it, Abigail.

"Is it the sex?"

I was shocked into silence.

"Is that it, Abby?" Michael went on, his voice low and almost husky. "Does he know how to fuck you?"

My body pulsed in excitement as he robbed me of the ability to breathe.

Did he really just say those words to me?

"I'm not discussing my intimate relationship with my fiancé with you," I finally said. "And I'm appalled you'd even ask."

"Appalled?" Michael said with amusement. His lips curled into a smile as he studied my face.

"I'd venture to guess he can't even make you come," Michael went on to my mortification. "You don't have the look of a woman who's satisfied in bed."

Holy shit.

He guessed right.

But I'd never admit it.

"Are you finished?" I asked coolly, trying to downplay the conversation and what he was making me feel.

Michael continued to stare me down in that toe-curling way of his, unnerving every inch of me—inside and out. He was too confident and cocksure.

And he had every right to be.

"Why are you hiding up here?" Michael ignored my question and asked another of his own.

"Hiding?" My eyes rounded. "I'm just taking a break from the party."

"You should be basking in love, glued to his side," he told me as he took a step toward the bed. "Nothing is adding up here, Abby, and I'm trying my best to figure it out."

The room suddenly felt so small. His presence seemed to take up every inch. And his words. The insinuations. The truth in them was something I couldn't deny.

"There is nothing to figure out," I finally said. "I *am* basking."

In what feels like acute misery.

He raised a brow. I knew he didn't believe me.

And then Michael's gaze moved from my face to my naked legs and my practically exposed chest. I could feel the heat burn my skin and I was shamefully turned on beyond belief. The fire in his eyes nearly took my breath away.

"Neither the dress nor makeup suit you," he finally said.

I felt the air leave my lungs as I insecurely brushed back my hair. Why was he doing this to me? Turning me into a hot mess at my own engagement party?

Goddamn him and his sinful good looks.

I decided I hated him at that moment.

"It seems your travels around the world have caused a memory lapse in proper manners," I said coldly. "You've forgotten how to speak to a lady, Michael."

"You don't look like a lady."

I sputtered in outrage.

He took another step closer to the bed, holding my gaze as his eyes glimmered with something I couldn't decipher.

"I thought you might want to know."

"A real gentleman—" I began in a huff.

"Whatever gave you the impression I was a real gentleman?" Michael asked quietly, interrupting me.

Right.

He wasn't.

In so many ways he was the furthest thing from the word.

He was the enigma of the Sinclair family. The one who threw out women the way one would do to trash. The one who reveled in a good pub brawl. The one who flew around the world, chasing humanitarian causes. The one who everyone in our social circle said could never *ever* be tamed.

A man I so desperately desired.

Even now.

I had to get away from him.

Michael Sinclair was my weakness. An addiction I had never been able to shed since I was a child. I could resist chocolate, but I could not resist this man. I scooted off the bed as elegantly as possible, trying my best to keep my short dress in place and not give him even more of a view than necessary.

"I guess I was mistaken," I told him as I reached for my stilettos.

"You were," was his taut reply.

I could feel his hot eyes on my body.

I wondered if he was judging me. Like I was some foolish child incapable of making a decision on her own. I couldn't stand it.

"Is there a reason you came in here? Did you intentionally seek me out to insult me?" I let him hear how annoyed I was. "Or let me guess, you're meeting a lover for a quick shag? If that's the case, there are plenty of other rooms that are empty."

"I'm not meeting a lover," Michael replied quickly.

The relief I felt from his words was staggering.

And not the type of reaction a woman who was about to get married should have for a man other than her fiancé.

"Not yet, at least," he went on.

Right.

I fought the urge to throw my high heel at his handsome face.

"Well then," I said with false bravado. "I'll leave you to it. The night is still young, and I know there are plenty of women out there who are just dying to become another notch on your belt."

"Know of anyone I should look out for?" Michael asked with a raised brow, the look on his face sinful.

Bastard.

I ignored his question, standing up and wishing more than anything my feet weren't hurting so badly so I could walk out of the room without looking as if I was in acute pain.

"If you'll excuse me," I said as I tried to make my way past him.

He grabbed hold of my arm and the surge of desire I felt from that single touch was astounding. My entire body was burning with longing.

Why, God?

Why did *he* have to make me feel this way?

"I haven't said you could leave," he growled.

A shiver of nervous energy shot down my spine. I looked up and met his stormy gaze and wondered why he seemed so angry.

"I don't recall needing your permission," I replied.

His blue eyes narrowed.

"You don't need a husband, Abby. You need a keeper."

"A keeper? How medieval of you. But thank you, I'll be sure to take your opinion into consideration." I rolled my eyes, smirking. "Now please let go of me."

I felt his hand loosen its grip as his finger lightly brushed my arm. My entire body was on hyper alert. I couldn't think properly, let alone make my legs move. My breath was frozen. My insides were highly aware of the sexy man standing so painfully close. I could feel the goose bumps appear on my skin and I hated myself for reacting.

"Are you sure that's what you want?" Michael's voice was rough, hypnotic, as his cerulean eyes met my gaze.

I tried to look away. But I felt trapped. Was that desire I saw? Or was my mind playing tricks on me?

"Completely." My voice was breathless. I couldn't help it. I was turned on. Like want-to-rip-off-his-clothes-and-jump-into-bed-with-him-turned on.

Michael broke my gaze for a brief second before hitting me head-on with his intensity.

"I think I read somewhere that it's custom for the bride to receive a kiss from someone other than her fiancé before she's sent off for marriage." Michael's gaze flicked to my lips then back to my eyes.

My heart leaped out of my chest.

"Whose custom would that be?" I asked shakily.

Michael shrugged.

"Must be someone's."

I tried to laugh it off, but when I saw the look on his face, my eyes widened in fear. If he kissed me, I was done.

"Michael—"

"Abigail—"

I didn't stand a chance.

In a second, he looped his arm around my waist and pulled me toward him as his lips began to descend upon mine.

"What are you doing?" I put up a half-hearted fight. The kiss was exactly what I wanted.

"Something I'll probably regret," he said enigmatically. "But then, I think I'll regret it more if I don't do it."

I wasn't given a chance to argue. Or to push him away. His lips were on mine before I could even think of a proper reply.

And at the second of impact, I knew I wouldn't have stopped his onslaught if I could.

Michael Sinclair didn't just kiss.

He devoured.

He consumed.

He owned my soul with a single brush of his sensuous lips. He showed me just how good it would be if I were lucky enough to fall into bed with him. He knew what he was doing. What he made me feel. He was a master at seduction, and I was so willing to be schooled by him. His strong hand pulled me up against his taut body as his lips slammed into mine and took every inch of my soul.

It wasn't just a kiss.

It was mouth-fucking at its best.

His lips coaxed mine as his other hand wrapped itself in my hair, pulling me toward him so that he could have deeper access and control. I was unable to stop myself from wrapping my arms around his neck and pulling him in. This was the man I dreamed of my whole life. And he was giving me exactly what I continually fantasized about.

His tongue swept into my mouth as he deepened the kiss. His fingers moved from waist to my ass, cupping it, as he pulled me against his hard cock. I was soaking wet within seconds. If possible, he deepened the kiss, ravaging my mouth, claiming me, *owning me* in the way no other man had in my entire life. He was all that I wanted.

Needed.

My knight in shining armor come to life.

It was so wrong.

I was about to be married.

I was supposed to be the happy bride-to-be. But *this* kiss, *this* man, proved me wrong in more ways than I ever knew. He pulled his lips from mine as he grazed my neck with his teeth, marking me first, then placing soft kisses on my skin. I grabbed hold of his head, ran my hands through his thick hair and pulled his mouth back to mine, as I sucked on his tongue, melded my lips to his and unleashed all the passion I had for him.

Within seconds he ripped himself away from me and stared down at my flushed face. I was panting with need. Longing. I would sleep with him right then and there—propriety, the fact that I was supposed to be getting married next week—all of it be damned. All he had to do was ask. Make one move, even.

But he didn't.

His eyes were dark and wild as he pulled away from me, creating distance between us.

"Jesus," he panted. "Who the hell are you?"

It was a fight or flight moment.

I chose to fly.

Because at that moment, I had no idea who I was.

CHAPTER TWO

"The bagel, Abby!" Ronald hisses as he pulls the blackened bread from the toaster.

Crap. I burnt it.

"You've got to pay attention! I saw you staring off into space again."

"I know," I admit guiltily. "I'm so sorry."

Ronald must be tired of hearing me say the words.

"You keep saying the words but your actions…" He lets out an exasperated sigh.

"Maybe this isn't for you."

"It is!" I rush out in fear of getting fired. "I'll stay late to learn how to work the machines and I'll figure things out. I'll do whatever it takes. I need this job. Please. I promise I won't mess up again."

Ronald doesn't look like he believes me.

"Swear," I nod earnestly. "I won't let you down again."

"Just work the cash register," he mumbles. "You can handle that without too many missteps."

I choose not to answer and turn to stand in front of the register as someone comes up to place an order.

I plaster the fake smile on my face before I look up.

"Good morning," I say. "What can I get you?"

It is unfortunate Ronald didn't let me continue burning bagels.

Fuck.

Me.

It's Michael bloody Sinclair.

Standing right in front of me in all of his magnificent glory. Unexpected desire shoots through my body as I smile awkwardly and try to straighten out the green apron I'm wearing. I'm immensely grateful I'm wearing the company hat today. I'm hoping it covers up my flushed cheeks.

If he's surprised to see me working as a barista at the popular coffee shop it doesn't show. I realize the last time I came this close to him was months ago at his younger brother William's funeral when he was overcome with grief. We had barely exchanged three words.

Now, this.

Not exactly how I hoped I'd look or what I'd be wearing when I saw him again.

Mortifying!

"Abigail." His voice is like velvet.

Rich. Delectable.

Heavenly.

Fuckable.

I look up at his ruggedly handsome face and suck in my breath. Good Lord, he is perfect.

He has a bit of stubble, and his blue eyes practically beam out of his face as he stares at me with the Sinclair intensity. He's dressed casually in a thermal black shirt that stretches out over his broad chest, a puffer vest, and blue jeans. His black hair is longer than usual and held back with a hair band.

He looks delicious and dangerously appealing. Like one of those high-calorie, mouth-watering Frappucinos I'm forced to make every day and use all my willpower not to consume.

"Michael," I give him a big smile, pretending like working at a coffee shop is the most normal thing in the world for me. "Nice to see you."

"You too."

"So what can I get you?" I know my voice sounds awkward. I really wish the ground would open up and swallow me whole.

"Just this," he says as he hands me a bottle of water.

"It's on me," I tell him with a fake smile.

He hands me a hundred pound note.

"Take it," he says.

"No," I shake my head. "I insist. We're family, after all."

I know my face must be the color of a tomato with how embarrassed I feel. As if my life can't get any more depressing.

Michael's keen gaze meets mine for a long moment.

"Thank you," he says then proceeds to drop the hundred pound note in the tip jar.

I see the gesture for what it's meant to be.

Charity.

Michael feels sorry for me and this is his way to give back to someone in need. Exactly the way he does with his company—The Michael Sinclair Foundation. He runs one of the world's largest charitable foundations—doing everything from helping children around the world have clean water, saving endangered animals, wildlife and marine conservation, researching climate change and fighting for Indigenous rights. Did he just add me to his list of those he needs to help?

To say I'm mortified is the understatement of the century.

But more than that, I'm angry.

Furious, actually.

I keep my smile plastered on my face, reaching into the tip jar to pull out the note to hand it right back to him.

"I think you made a mistake," I tell him.

"I didn't," he tells me, raising an eyebrow like he's chastising me. "It's yours... *cousin*."

Now I know my face has really changed color. I can hear the innuendo in the word. Like he knows it makes me uncomfortable as hell. I see the way his eyes flicker to my lips. Teasing me. Turning me on.

The image of his mouth on mine comes to mind.

Kissing cousins.

That's what we are.

It's not like we're blood-related.

I'll have to talk myself off a ledge in no time thanks to this man.

"It's actually *ours*," Ronald says in excitement as he comes up to stand next to me. He's obviously been listening in on our conversation. "We split tips. Wait. You guys are cousins?"

I want to scream and tell Ronald it's none of his bloody business but I can't—I need this godforsaken job.

"Through marriage," I tell him quickly, and to my horror, I hear Michael actually laugh.

I turn to him.

"Great to see you, *cousin*."

Michael gives me a mocking grin and doesn't bloody move.

"When do you have your next break?" he asks instead.

"Now," Ronald quickly answers before I can lie.

"No," I shake my head at the red-haired devil. "I've still got a ways to go—"

"You're off the clock," he interrupts me, smiling at Michael like he's enamored. "Go and grab something to eat with your cousin."

"Wonderful," Michael smiles charmingly and meets my gaze, almost challenging. He knows damn well how uncomfortable I am. "Let me take you to lunch, Abigail."

I hate it when he calls me Abigail. Like he's admonishing me for bad behavior.

"You don't have to," I say.

"I know that," he returns. "But I want to."

And I want to do so much more with you…

"Just give me a minute," I say to him after a long second, knowing I don't have much of a choice. "I'll see you out front."

I leave the cash register and walk to a room in the back of the shop where we keep our belongings. I pull off my apron and hat and turn to look at myself in the mirror. I gasp when I see the image that stares back at me.

Oh, my Lord.

My long brown hair is in wild mess around my pale face. The heat from the coffee must have melted my mascara because it's running down my cheeks like I've spent the morning crying, or worse, doing some type of illicit drug I've only read about.

I can't help it.

I burst out laughing.

Like the crazy kind of laughter that tends to scare people off.

But look at me. Abigail Mary Walters. Once, a refined lady about to marry one of England's richest bachelors—now, a hot mess.

I pull back my hair into a ponytail, smooth out my white shirt over my fitted jeans, and do my best to clean up the mess under my eyes.

I sigh as I take in my sad appearance. Unfortunately, it's really not going to get much better than this. But what can I do? Michael already saw what I looked like. He *is* forcing me to have lunch with him. I might as well make him suffer through staring at the walking disaster I've become.

I grab my handbag and head out to face my lifelong crush. A shiver of excitement races down my spine as my traitorous heart pounds in my chest. It takes all my willpower to stay the course and meet him out front. For a moment I debate walking out the back door and ignoring him altogether, but I have a feeling that would not go over very well with him.

I make my way out of the coffee shop and find Michael standing outside with his hands in his pockets, waiting for me. When I reach his side, I feel especially small with him towering over me.

The look on his face is indecipherable.

"Sushi?" he asks as he studies me.

I really hope I got all the mascara out from under my eyes.

"Italian?" Michael goes on. "What would you like?"

"Indian." My response is fast. "I've been craving it for some time. Unless you don't care for it?"

Michael looks surprised.

"I love Indian," he says.

"I know a great place that's close by," I tell him. "It's a bit of a hole in the wall, but the food makes up for the lack of ambiance."

"I'll follow your lead." He motions toward the sidewalk.

"It's not far," I reply as I start walking.

Michael falls into step next to me.

His arm brushes against mine, and I feel as though I've been burned by the gods of lust. I put a bit of distance between us since the last thing I need to be doing is rubbing up against this man in any way. It's not at all safe for my sanity or my libido.

"So how have you been?" I finally ask in what I hope is my calm voice. "How are your parents doing?"

"As well as can be expected." His response is curt.

There's a long silence between us. I can imagine his brother William's death is not a topic he wants to discuss. I don't blame him at all, but I felt obliged to ask.

"How is Clayton?" I ask softly as I sneak a peek at him.

I've become email pen pals with Sophie, Clayton's American girlfriend, who I met at my "almost wedding" to Dimitri. I really liked her, and we stayed in touch after she left London. I know Clayton's been staying out with her in Los Angeles and from the sound of things, it seems like they're both doing really well.

I'm happy for my cousin. Even when he was younger, he was always rigid and almost unapproachable, but since Sophie's come into his life, he's slowly become a whole new man.

"He sounds like he's doing well," Michael says. "But I'll know for sure when I go out and visit him."

"Do you have a trip planned to Los Angeles?" I ask.

"Maybe," Michael shrugs and looks over at me. "I guess it depends on how much longer my brother will be staying out there."

"Well, it sounds like he's doing well and I'm very happy for him," I say. And I mean it.

"Me too," Michael admits then turns to me and laughs. "There's hope for me yet, Abby."

"Hope?" I question.

"Maybe I'll get lucky and find a woman to change me too."

My heart sinks in dread at the thought of any woman other than me reforming Michael.

"Watch where you're going!" Michael calls out as he grabs hold of my arm and pulls me out of the way of the telephone pole I'm an inch away from plastering my face into.

"Thanks," I stammer, pulling myself out of his grip.

I'm angry at myself for being annoyed at the possibility of Michael settling down. He is *not* my boyfriend. Nor has he *ever* been. And besides that, I should want him to be happy. He deserves the best because he is a good man. He deserves to find love.

But can't he find all that with you? My inner voice asks the question that's plagued me from the first moment I set eyes on him.

We reach the entrance to the Indian restaurant, and I'm thankful for the distraction.

"We're here," I tell him.

We walk in the small family-owned restaurant, and since there are only a few tables, we seat ourselves in the intimate space. Pictures of famous views in India and a collection of off-season fairy lights have been hung up but other than that the décor is pretty bare. The smell of Indian spices fills the air and my stomach growls in anticipation. Michael looks around and shakes his head.

"Do you come here often?" he asks in disbelief.

"I do," I admit, noticing the startled look on his face. "Why do you ask? You seem surprised."

"I am," he admits slowly. "This is just not the kind of place I'd picture you eating at."

"What do you mean?"

"You're a Sloanie."

My back stiffens.

"Come on, Abby," Michael laughs as he takes in the look on my face. "If there were a picture of proper in the dictionary, it would be yours. Can you deny you spent your teens in and out of high-end retail stores, running around in A-list social circles, all while hoping to make the match of the century? A husband to outdo all other husbands?"

"Is that what you think of me?" I'm horrified even though his observation about my life isn't far from the truth. The only thing I didn't do from his list is the search for the match of the century. That was a duty I left to my mother.

Michael pins his gaze on me.

"Am I wrong?"

"I'd like to think my life has had a bit more meaning," I return curtly and try my hardest not to let on that I'm hurt by his words. "And I'm not always so proper."

The waitress comes to stand next to our table.

"I'll have a green tea," I say without missing a beat. She nods and looks over at Michael.

"I'll take whatever beer on tap you have." I watch as the woman's eyes light up when she looks at Michael. I try not to roll my eyes. It's annoying that no female seems to be immune to his charms.

"And we'll just need a minute to look over the menu," he continues as he gives her a charming smile.

The second she turns and leaves us, Michael's hand reaches out and grabs mine. The single gesture sends a surge of electricity through my body. I try to pull my hand back, but he won't let me.

"I apologize if I hurt your feelings," he says sincerely. "It wasn't intentional."

"I'm fine," I shrug and do my best to keep eye contact.

"Are you?" he asks, studying my face.

"Perfect."

We stare at each other for a long time, and I wonder if Michael Sinclair can see into my soul. If he can see all my insecurities, fears and doubts. Because he's absolutely right.

I am not fine.

I am the opposite of fine.

And I don't know how to fix it.

I tug my hand and this time he lets me pull away. I pick up the menu and stare blindly at the items.

"What do you recommend?" he asks after a moment.

"Everything is really good here. You can't go wrong."

"Then I'll let you order," he says to my surprise as he leans back in his chair.

The waitress brings our drinks, and I order a few of my favorite items. When she leaves us, I take a nervous sip of my tea and try not to openly gawk at his gorgeousness.

"So how's work treating you?" Michael asks, lifting his beer to his lips.

I watch the way his bicep flexes against the thin material of his shirt when he brings the drink to his mouth. Oh dear. I hope I'm not drooling. Now that would not be very proper of me.

"It's great," I shrug indifferently.

"How long have you been working there?"

"A little over three weeks."

"I can't say I'm not surprised," Michael says.

"That I'm actually working or that I'm a barista?" I'm sure he can hear the annoyance in my voice.

"By both."

"Aren't you just full of compliments this morning," I remark sarcastically.

"Abby," Michael leans forward and stares at me with those sexy eyes of his. "Come on. Your current predicament is a far cry from being the fiancé of a Russian oligarch."

"Things change."

"Things don't change," Michael says firmly. "People do."

"Then I guess I'm different now," I say defiantly.

It annoys me, really.

Michael thinks he knows me so well. But he doesn't. He only knows a picture. A facade that I carefully put up through all the years. An image for people to see. It's a far cry from the real Abby.

Unfortunately, I don't even know who that woman is yet. I'm still trying to figure that part out, and sometimes I wonder if I'll ever really know. But at least I feel like I'm finally on the right road.

My own path.

In charge of my destiny.

Finally.

"Why did you break off the wedding?" I'm not surprised when he asks.

"It's not something I'd like to discuss." It's my go-to answer for anyone who asks the obvious question. And it's the truth.

"I'm curious."

"Sorry to disappoint you," I say. "But I don't want to talk about it."

"Was he unfaithful?"

"No."

"Did he hurt you?" His tone is protective, and it touches me.

"No," I shake my head. "He did not."

"So there's no need me for me to avenge your honor?" He sounds serious.

"You can put the pistols away," I tell him with a laugh. "I'm fine. He's fine. We're both better off, and I'm sure he sees that now. It's a chapter I've closed in my life that I don't ever wish to revisit or even discuss. It's over. That's all there is to know."

"So you say," he says as he leans back in his chair, his face impassive.

I hope he's satisfied with my answer.

"I can only assume your mother didn't take the news too well?" he says, half joking.

"Not at all," I try to laugh it off, hoping I don't come across like

I care. Even though I do. No matter her flaws, she's the only mother I have, and it hurts to know that I've disappointed her.

"She wasn't thrilled with my decision," I say to him. "To be honest, she's barely speaking to me."

"I can't say that I'm surprised," Michael admits, looking at me with concern. "Has it been hard for you?"

I can feel my body tense at his words. The only person who ever asks how I'm doing is Georgie.

It's nice to hear someone worry about me.

Especially him.

"It was at first," I admit to him with a shrug. "But then, I got used to it. It's not like I'm surprised by her behavior."

"You should be." Michael's voice is harsh. "She's your mother."

He's right, I know. But then, he didn't grow up with her.

"It's all right," I wave my hand dismissively. "I'm resigned to the fact that I can't ever seem to make her happy."

"You shouldn't worry about making anyone but yourself happy, Abby. That's all that matters. Trust me."

The genuine concern and empathy I hear in his voice is nearly my undoing.

"Well, you can rest assured that I'm happy with my decision," I tell him with as much composure as I can muster. "And I really have no regrets."

"That's good to hear," he murmurs before his eyes flicker to my lips, causing my thoughts to drift away from my mother and enter into a more sinful zone.

"If you'll humor me," he says softly, "I just have one last question for you."

"What's that?" I ask, hoping I sound calm.

"I'm really hoping you'll answer this time," his voice lowers seductively.

"This time?" I all but whisper back.

Michael tilts his head and gazes at me.

"Was he good in bed?"

Unfortunately, it just so happens I'm taking a sip of my green tea when he asks that question. I spit the liquid out clear across the table. Remarkable really, how far my spit flies. Michael has a good chuckle before busying himself with wiping away my mortifying mess while I gasp for breath and try to think of a suitable reply.

"That's quite a response," he says with a smirk.

"That was quite a question," I reply indignantly.

"I'm trying to understand why you'd agree to marry him."

"That question is still as completely inappropriate as it was the last time you asked!" I growl, crossing my arms.

Memories of the kiss we shared at my engagement party flood my mind. How good would it feel to have those strong hands of his all over my body right now? It's shocking really, just how turned on I am in a matter of seconds.

"Then why would you want to stay with him?" he prods, completely unaware of the turmoil he's causing.

"People can make mistakes."

Michael watches me intently.

"They can," he agrees. "But you. You've always been in control. So wound up—"

"Wound up?" I interrupt in surprise.

"Very," Michael's smile is slow, seductive. "That's why I've been so curious to know if Dimitri was able to break that perfect composure of yours..."

In bed.

I know that's what he's implying.

It's almost impossible for me to get my thoughts under control. It's not fair how fast Michael always ends up making me feel so confused.

"That wasn't very proper of me, was it?" He lifts a brow with a mischievous grin, and now I know he's playing with me.

"It's fun breaking the rules," he goes on. "You should try it sometime."

I don't even know how to respond to him. Is he just teasing me? Is it just fun for him to see how far he can push me?

I can feel the heat rush to my face as his penetrating gaze continues to study me.

"What?" I finally say after I can't bear the silence any longer.

"Am I making you uncomfortable?" He grins teasingly.

"Absolutely not," I lie with as much bravado as I can muster.

Michael throws back his head and laughs.

"I think you're lying," he tells me.

"I think your ego would prefer I was," I counter.

He shrugs and gives me a sexy smile.

"Maybe."

I can feel my heart pound in my chest. My only hope is that he can't tell what he's doing to me. How thoroughly turned on I am.

Wet.

Literally.

Wet.

I wonder how much more of this torture I can take.

"So if this is the new and improved Abby," Michael says after a moment, "come and work for me."

My world stops.

"What?"

Is he serious?

"You're not a very good barista," Michael points out the obvious. "And I don't mean to be insulting because I'm only telling you what the entire line of customers were witness to."

He has the audacity to deliver that insult with another one of his sexy smiles. I should be offended, but instead, my libido goes into overdrive.

"I'm still trying to get the hang of it," I finally manage to say as it dawns on me that his opinion of me might not be very high.

I want to tell him he's wrong.

But the odds are stacked against me.

I'm a grown woman who's never had a job. Who can't manage to make a proper cup of coffee on her own and who was willingly engaged to a man she didn't love.

What an attractive package I must appear to him.

"Come and work for me, Abigail." Michael's voice is forceful.

"You're serious."

"Quite," Michael watches me with an unreadable look. "My PA has left me and I need to replace her. You need the money. It's actually a perfect situation."

Perfect?

Becoming Michael Sinclair's PA is not exactly what I picture for my future. Not that being a piss-poor barista is, but still, at least I'm in charge of my destiny. Calling the shots. Answering to a boss that doesn't know a thing about my old life or self, who only knows me as I am now. Who only judges me based on my skills or lack thereof...

"And besides, we're family."

I can feel my heart pound in my chest.

Family.

I don't like the way his words make me feel.

"It's a generous offer," I tell him slowly. "But I'll have to decline."

"Why?" Michael demands. "And this time look me in the eyes when you answer the question."

My blood simmers as I meet his gaze dead-on and feel the familiar rush move through my body. Damn him. And damn this undeniable attraction I have always had for him. The desire to jump across the table and rip his clothes off and lick every inch of his tanned body. I wonder if I'll ever be free of it.

I'm pretty sure the odds are very unlikely.

"I don't think I like your tone," I finally say.

"Well I don't like your answer," he returns.

"Because you always get your way?"

His silence is telling.

"It's a generous offer," I say appreciatively. "But you and I both know, I'm not right for the job."

"If I didn't think you were right for it, I wouldn't have asked."

"Michael—"

"Do you think you're *right* at being a barista?"

It's hard not to miss the sarcasm in his voice.

"I'm learning."

"Come and learn from me." Michael's tone changes. It's almost seductive. "I know I can teach you a few things. And I promise you'll enjoy every minute of it."

My stomach does a somersault, then a high kick, as I am undoubtedly sure he can teach me *many* things.

But what I'd like him to teach me and what he has in mind are two completely different areas of expertise.

"Take a chance, Abby," Michael goes on. "We'll have fun together."

Fun?

Together?

For a moment I'm tempted, but then a picture comes to mind… me sitting outside his office door behind a desk taking calls from all the women in his life. Setting lunch dates. Dinner dates. Travel plans. I wouldn't be able to run from it, pretend it wasn't happening because I'd know exactly where he was and *who* he was doing it with at all times.

"No," I reply sharply, realizing I wouldn't be able to handle working for him in this capacity. "My answer is no."

"Why?" Michael frowns as he leans forward and crowds the table with his energy. I move back in my chair and try to keep as much distance from him as I can.

"Stop asking why. I don't have to give you a reason. I can just say no."

"I'll pay you well," he continues forcefully. "You won't have to worry about money."

If anything that makes me want to refuse the job even more.

"It's still no."

I almost cringe when I see the hard glint in his eyes.

"Are you afraid?" Michael asks in a low voice.

"What?" For a moment I think he knows exactly why I want to keep as much distance as I can from him.

"Are you afraid I'll be hard on you?"

Oh, Michael, I'd love for you to be hard inside me… That's the fundamental problem here.

"No, of course not."

"Aren't you up for the challenge? Something different?" Michael continues. "The adventure."

Adventure.

Wouldn't that be lovely?

The idea of an adventure is too enticing for words.

To be honest, at this very moment in my life, adventure sounds like everything I need. Unfortunately, I know it's not a safe bet with Michael since it will only serve to turn my life into more of a crazy mess.

"My answer still stands."

I can't tell what he's thinking. He's too good at masking his thoughts.

"All right," he finally says, sounding disappointed. "But if you change your mind—"

"I won't."

Michael actually smiles.

"We'll see."

"Is that a warning?"

"It's a statement of fact," he says.

"Have you always been so arrogant?" The words come out before I can stop them.

Michael bursts out laughing.

"Probably."

Before I can give him a proper letdown, the server brings our food.

"Smells delicious," Michael says as he looks at the assortment of Indian cuisine.

He serves me a generous portion before helping himself.

"Eat up, Abby," he orders. "I think your lunch break is almost up. I wouldn't want to be the reason you get fired."

***

When I open the door to my two-bedroom flat later that evening, I'm mentally and physically exhausted. Ronald couldn't have been nicer when I returned to work. I gathered it was because of Michael's more than generous tip. Whatever it was, I'd take it if it meant he'd be less irritated with me.

My apartment, a quintessential Victorian, is my sanctuary. It was the last gift my father had left for me, and one I'm eternally grateful for. He purchased it when he was a bachelor, right before he met my mother in America. We had updated it through the years, but I really wanted to keep the bones the way my father found it.

It makes me feel closer to him.

With high ceilings and a generous view of Hyde Park, it's the perfect space. My taste in furniture is very English and traditional. I inherited all of my father's historic art and antiques, pieces that have been in the family forever. Mixed in with modern furniture I've purchased, it makes my home feel both cozy and up-to-date. I'm a fan of neutral color themes, crèmes and whites with velvet and floral cushions placed on the couches. My friends tell me I have an eye for interior design, and I must admit, I did enjoy putting my home together.

Since my mother believed I would be marrying Dimitri, no

expense had been spared. I wonder if she now regrets being so extravagant.

"*Enfin te voila*!" I hear my best friend, Georges de Banville, in his thick French accent calling out to me from my kitchen. "You're late."

I walk to the kitchen and find Georgie—which he prefers to go by—opening a bottle of champagne. I smile when I take in his appearance.

He's always dressed in designer clothes from head to toe. The cost of one of his outfits could feed a family of four for a month. And not only that, but his looks also fit the part as well.

Georgie has dark olive colored skin and a face that should have been in fashion magazines. He's beautiful. I've always thought he looked like an underwear model. Like an ad you'd see for Calvin Klein.

Georgie pours the champagne into two glasses and hands me one.

"Abby," he begins as he takes in my appearance and shakes his head in dismay as he dramatically motions to my outfit. "We need a spa day. It's an emergency situation for you. Look at those nails!"

"Like the good old times," I tell him drolly. I take a sip of the champagne and sigh in pleasure. "This is delicious. And so needed after the afternoon I've had."

"*Oui*," he says. "Now tell me, was he as beautiful as ever?"

After Michael walked me back to the coffee shop, I had immediately texted Georgie and told him the news. He wrote back instantly, and since he carries a spare key, he told me he would meet me at my apartment that evening.

So here he is.

Waiting to hear all the details.

I don't leave anything out. And I do go on for a while about how ridiculously beautiful Michael looked. Sometimes I think Georgie is as obsessed with Michael as I am.

"Abby!" Georgie says, when I'm finally done with my story.

We are sitting on the couches now, with our feet propped up on the fluffy ottoman.

"If you don't take the job with Michael, I might," Georgie says in excitement. "I can't think of anything more enticing than seeing that perfect specimen every day."

"I can see it now," I laugh just picturing the image of Georgie bringing Michael a coffee in the morning. I doubt he's ever even toasted a slice of bread. He has a full staff that takes care of his every need. Georgie is a trust fund baby, and what his parents failed to provide in the emotional department they made up for financially, ensuring he will never have to work a day in his life.

"Tell me again so I can understand," Georgie says as he takes a piece of cheese off the plate I had put together and pops it in his mouth. "Why on earth did you turn him down?"

"I can't work for him."

"Why not?"

"It's a recipe for disaster."

"It's a recipe to finally get you into bed with him," he counters. "Sex, Abby! Think about the office sex you can have with him. On his desk. Servicing him under his desk. On his couch. Against a door. How sordid and wonderful, and just what you need."

"Georgie!" I can feel myself blush as I try to admonish him, but the picture that comes to mind from his words excites me.

Tempts me.

"I speak only the truth," he says. "And I am only verbalizing the thoughts and words that lie dormant in your heart. I really dare you to deny it."

"I won't," I counter. "But whatever the case, we both know that I cannot work for him."

"Cannot?" Georgie says with a cocked brow. "*Non, ma belle...* you *will not*."

"Imagine if I have to set dates with women—" I argue.

"You will. Undoubtedly, that will happen," Georgie agrees quickly. "But then you will be the master of his domain."

"What?"

"You will hold the keys to his kingdom, Abby," Georgie says with a great deal of gusto. "Think about it."

"I'm not following—"

"You can finally see him for who he is," Georgie continues as if I haven't spoken. "You will get to live with him in his world. See every part of his personality. Maybe he isn't what you think, maybe, you will finally rid yourself of this dreadful crush."

"Dreadful?"

"It has handicapped you in many ways," he points out the obvious. "You've lived your life pining after him, even when you were in a relationship with other men. You've compared every man to him. Everything has always come down to Michael Sinclair."

"That's not fair," I argue.

"How many nights have we spent talking about him?" Georgie counters. "How many nights have we spent dissecting his words, his actions, his looks even?"

"Some…" I shrug defensively.

"Some?" Georgie raises a brow in disdain. "Most. We have searched the internet for him. We have found pictures of the women he dated and picked them apart. We have gone to restaurants, clubs, and pubs, that you believed he might be at so that you might *casually* run into him."

"All right—" I try to stop Georgie from speaking any more.

"Not only that, *ma belle*," he continues dramatically, sounding almost horrified. "We have stalked him like common criminals. *I, Comte Georges de Banville,* have been an accomplice to your insanity!"

"Georgie!" I gasp. Just hearing him paint the picture makes me seem almost—

"*Oui*, Abby," my friend says as if he can read my mind. "He makes you crazy. What is more, I feel that unstable, *Single White Female* alter ego of yours has the potential to rear her ugly head at any time. All because you are hoping that one day he will turn to you and admit his true feelings."

It's really sad that I can't deny his words.

"I'm not that bad," I argue.

Georgie's look stops me from saying any more.

"I think of this as your chance," Georgie says with a wave of his hand. "You can test the waters in an opportunity that was never given to you before. It's not like seeing him two times a year and briefly flirting and dreaming about that flirtation for the next six months of your life. You will be with him every day, Abby."

Every day.

I can't deny it. The thought thrills me.

"You will see him for who he is. You will know him in every way. And you will finally be given a chance to see if he is as attracted to you as you are to him. Or sadly, if you are just crazy and cursed with an overactive imagination."

Georgie smiles at me.

"I wouldn't say no to his generous offer just yet."

CHAPTER THREE

"You're fired."

To be fair, Ronald looks grossly uncomfortable as he tells me the words I had a distinct feeling would be coming for me.

"But—" I begin quickly, ready to put up a fight.

Ronald holds up his hand to stop me from talking.

"Abby," he says. "Please don't make this any harder on either one of us. You are not good at being a barista. You should never be one again. Ever. Like really, *ever*. Go find something that suits you. In retail, maybe? You seem to have a good fashion sense."

Ronald doesn't seem convinced by his suggestion.

"I need this job." My voice sounds small.

"I'm sorry, Abby," Ronald shakes his head. "But you'll just have to find another. I need someone here that knows what they're doing. And it's not just that—the other staff has been complaining about you not pulling your weight."

"I'm trying," I insist.

"It shouldn't be so hard."

"I can stay late—" I'm practically begging now.

"No," Ronald shakes his head. "It's over. I can pay you out for the week, but that's it. I'm sorry."

Ronald leaves me in the employee room, and I feel the sudden urge to either cry uncontrollably or shop myself to death. The problem is, I don't have the money to do the latter.

I pick up my bag with as much dignity as I can muster and leave through the back exit. I don't want to run into any of the other employees, and I know there really isn't anyone who'll be sorry to see me go. I welcome the cold air and rain when I'm outside and pull out my phone from my purse.

"*Oui?*" I hear Georgie's familiar voice.

"I was sacked," I tell him.

"Ahh," he doesn't sound surprised at all.

"Aren't you going to ask why? Or defend me?" I prod.

"*Non*," Georgie replies, sounding bored. "There is a reason why I avoid that coffee shop now."

"Georgie!"

"*Ma chère*, being a barista is not your calling." His voice is firm. "Now call Michael, who is a much better choice. He needs a PA and you now need a job. See how perfect it is?"

"It's not perfect," I counter. "It's dangerous."

"*Oui*. There is a possibility it will be difficult for your heart," Georgie agrees. "But *c'est la vie*. Take a chance, *ma chère*. It's the perfect time in your life to try it out. Think about all the changes you've been making. All the chances you're taking. This is just another one."

The way Georgie lays out his argument gives me a glimmer of hope.

And possibility.

"I'm hanging up now," Georgie continues. "Call me after you speak to him. I'll take you to dinner to celebrate."

He hangs up before I can respond.

I stare at my phone for a long minute.

Take a chance, Abby.

I know if I give myself time to think about it, I'll come up with a million reasons why I shouldn't take the job, so I make my decision.

My heart beats a mile a minute at the thought of even calling Michael. Of hearing his voice. It's pathetic really, how giddy I am over the possibility. I walk into the closest café and sit down at an empty table. My phone and I have a stare-off for a long minute before I throw caution to the wind and just go for it.

Since I can't bring myself to actually *call* him, I text instead.

ME: Good morning, Michael. I hope you had a wonderful

evening. It's Abby, in case you're wondering.

I press send and immediately feel hives begin to form at the thought of him not responding. I will die if I don't hear back from him. Like crawl-in-a-fetal-position-under-my-dining-table-and-cry-myself-silly die.

Luckily, my phone pings a second later.

MICHAEL: I know who it is. I trust you're well.

It's like I can hear his mocking voice as he types the words. I know my text was stiff and formal—*proper* as he would say—but I didn't know how else to begin. Then the thrill of texting with him for the first time washes over me, intermingled with my nerves, and I find myself trying to hide a goofy smile.

ME: I am, thank you.

MICHAEL: Is everything good?

ME: Yes.

Just ask the damn question, Abby, my mind shouts out in anger.

Now or never. I type away.

ME: This might come as a surprise, but I was wondering if the job is still available?

I don't have to wait long for a text back as my phone immediately begins to ring. My heart is in my throat when I answer.

"Hi," I say shyly.

"Where are you?" Michael demands in that sexy voice of his.

"Out shopping," I lie.

"The job is still available," he tells me.

My heart thumps against my chest.

"Can you come by my office?" he asks quickly.

Vanity kicks in and I think about what I'm wearing. Black jeans, boots, and a matching sweater. Is it cute enough? Sexy? I run a hand through my freshly washed brown hair.

You're going in for a job interview, Abby, not to be his girlfriend.

"What time?" I ask throwing caution to the wind.

"Now."

I'm surprised he has the time to see me so fast.

"I think I can make it work," I force myself to speak. "Can I get your address?"

"I'll text it to you," he says quickly. "I'll be waiting."

He hangs up and I'm left reeling.

I'm going to see Michael Sinclair.

I'm actually going to take a job with my lifelong crush. What the bloody hell just happened? A few days ago, I couldn't say no fast enough. Today... well, today I was fired, and now it's a matter of survival, I tell myself almost defensively.

First things first. In order to calm my nerves, I'm going to need something fattening and sugary. I get up and stand in line at the cafe and order a large hot chocolate and a blueberry scone and instantly feel a calm sense of peace wash over me.

Food.

I love it.

Every part of it. It's a constant battle with me to refrain from giving in and eating everything my heart and stomach desires. If my body could take it, I would. But God forbid, if I ever hear the words Flabby Abby again, I think I'll die.

The hot chocolate and scone work like magic, and when I hail a cab to Michael's office, I'm feeling infinitely better. My optimism stays with me until I get out of the taxi and reach the glass double doors that lead into headquarters of The Michael Sinclair Foundation. The building is eight stories high and crystal clear. It's sleek and modern, just like the man whose name resides on the front door. I move through the crowd of people and reach a security desk, where two men are sitting.

"Can I help you, ma'am?" the silver-haired security guard asks with a smile.

"Yes," I reply. "My name is Abigail Walters, and I'm here to see Michael Sinclair."

"Of course. Please have a seat, Miss Walters, and someone will be with you shortly," the man says as he motions toward a large waiting area with brown leather couches and rustic tables.

I walk over and sit down as I study my surroundings. The décor is a mix of modern and industrial. The open-air plan creates a raw and edgy atmosphere. It only takes a few minutes before a twenty-something pretty blonde comes over to greet me. She's dressed casually in jeans and a sweater.

"Abigail?" she says in an American accent.

"Yes," I reply, standing.

"My name is Jessica, and I'm one of Mr. Sinclair's interns. I'll take you up to his office."

"Wonderful."

I follow Jessica into the glass elevator and feel myself begin to sweat as we ascend. And that's when the panic slowly takes hold.

What am I doing here?

I can't work for Mr. Tall, Dark and Gorgeous! Am I crazy?

The elevator comes to a stop at the top floor, and I catch Jessica staring at me with a look I can't quite decipher. As if she's sizing me up like I'm some sort of competition.

"This way," she says coolly.

I try my best to calm my nerves, following her out of the elevator through the office floor. The ground is cement and large industrial desks form a circle around an enormous exotic-looking indoor plant.

The employees are busy working, talking amongst each other: all look young and hip.

"This is the Think Tank," Jessica tells me as we walk through the large room. "This is where we brainstorm and come up with new and innovative ideas to help the Foundation's outreach."

I nod in acknowledgment as we continue to walk to the end of the room where we come to a panel of dark tinted glass windows that you can't see through. Jessica knocks before pushing the glass door open and motions for me to go inside. She stays outside as I walk in and she shuts the door behind me. And then I find myself walking into Michael Sinclair's lair for the first time.

I am not surprised by what greets me.

The room is enormous and stares out onto the River Thames. He has a sizeable sitting area with plush brown leather couches and a large wooden table in the center with hardcover books placed neatly on top. A large glass caddy with what looks to be a full bar is placed next to the sitting area. Michael's desk is simple with a huge glass top and round metal legs, resembling a piece of art. A brown leather chair is behind it along with a wall filled with black and white photos of animals and different places around the world.

My gaze finally moves from the photographs on the wall to the owner of the company.

Michael has been expecting me.

He's leaning against his desk with his arms crossed, staring at me in silence. My pulse goes into hyperdrive at the sight of him. He's wearing jeans, a navy sweater, and scruffy looking brown boots. His longish black hair is down and messy and all I want to do is run my fingers through it and pull those lips of his onto mine. God, what I wouldn't do to have him.

If only just once.

I watch his brow lift and for a panic-filled moment, I wonder if he can read my mind. *Calm down, Abby*, I tell myself. *Just breathe.*

The silence is unbearable.

I look away from his knowing look and stare out at the Thames.

"Nice view," I finally say as I gather my wits and try to calm my treacherous nerves.

"It is." His voice is low and sexy and I can practically feel his gaze touching my face. "I'm enjoying it."

I meet his sizzling gaze and try to act unaffected by his words. I try not to read into anything. God, it's hard, especially when he continues to watch me in that smoldering way of his, turning me into Jell-O pudding with his silence.

I grip my purse.

"So you know why I'm here," I say lamely as I ramble on. "I know it must be surprising, considering how vehemently I originally opposed the idea."

"Actually I wasn't surprised at all," he replies arrogantly.

He continues to lean and stare in that toe-curling way of his. I shuffle uncomfortably.

"I was fired."

I blurt the words out before I can help myself. Now I know my face is on fire. Why the hell did I just say that? Talk about TMI!

Michael finally smiles.

"I gathered as much."

"Did you?" I whisper, horrified.

Michael shrugs, and I have the distinct feeling he's trying hard not to laugh in my face.

"Well, I was," I go on to my complete and utter mortification. Like I'm possessed by Abby's evil twin sister who's hell-bent on blurting out those truths that are better left unsaid. The mortifying ones like when you walked from one end of the campus to the other with your skirt hiked up underneath your backpack with your bum naked as the day you were born, all while a group of guys was behind you taking pictures the whole time.

Yes, it happened to me.

Yes, I might still need therapy because of it.

"Fired. This morning, actually," I continue talking. "So I don't have any references. And I've never done this sort of work before, so there is a good possibility I might be a complete mess at it."

"Are you trying to make me regret offering you a job?" Michael's grin is wicked.

"I'm just being honest." My tone is defensive. "I want you to know what to expect."

"A mess?" he asks.

"Possibly." I shrug.

Way to sell yourself, Abby.

"You don't seem to have a very high opinion of yourself."

"That's not the case at all. I'm just—I just want to disclose everything so you know up front," I say, flushing with embarrassment even though he has every right to come to that conclusion.

He watches me silently.

"I'm perfectly capable. I think you should know I'm just new at this sort of thing," I rush out to say.

"Working?"

I don't miss the sarcasm in his voice.

"On second thought, maybe this isn't such a good idea," I frown, crossing my arms. The last thing I want is to be subjected to comments intended to make me feel less adequate. He has every right to think them, but to actually voice them, now that's a whole other story.

"I apologize," Michael covers quickly. "I was only joking with you. It seems you've lost your sense of humor. We'll have to work on getting that back."

I force myself to meet his warm stare.

And it happens just like that. The ache below my belly. The lust that shoots through my veins. God, he's hot. Just leaning there against a table, dressed casually and acting like he has no care in the world. He's just too good to be true.

The air around us shifts.

"When can you begin?" His voice is low.

"When do you need me?" I reply.

"Now."

My heart stops. There's something about his voice. The urgency I hear that makes me dare to believe he's as turned on as I am. That there's more to this job offer than meets the eye.

Lord, I just can't help it.

But I *so* want to believe it.

"Tomorrow, maybe." My throat starts to close up, and I have the sudden urge to put some distance between us. "I can't today."

He watches me evenly. I think I see a flicker of disappointment, but I can't be sure.

"Tomorrow it is," he concedes.

"Wonderful."

Michael tilts his head to the side and his eyes narrow as he watches me pensively.

"You haven't asked me any questions about the job," he says. "What it's like to be my PA. What I expect."

"I know you're very busy and just assumed you'll have someone train me," I tell him with a shrug. "We both know why you offered me the job."

"Why did I offer you the job?" he asks in a silky voice.

"Because I'm family," I answer quickly.

"No."

"No?" I ask in confusion.

"That would be a reason why I would refrain from hiring you," he explains.

His response makes me laugh.

"Then why did you hire me?"

"Because I like you."

God.

The way he says it. The way he looks at me—like he's the Big Bad Wolf and I'm as tempting as Little Red Riding Hood.

"Oh." I can barely speak.

His gaze is sizzling.

"And you're wrong about one more thing," he goes on.

"About what?" I ask.

"I'll be training you myself," he says as he studies me. "That way you'll know exactly what I want and how I like it."

I have the distinct feeling we're not talking about the usual job duties of a PA.

"I want you to know how to please me," he continues, his voice almost husky.

"Please you?" My mouth has gone completely dry—the lower half of my body, the exact opposite.

"Yes," he smiles. "You'll find that by making me happy, I'll reciprocate. And you'll be happy."

My stomach drops through the floor straight to Middle Earth.

"I don't need you to make me happy," I all but croak out. "I just need a job."

He pushes away from the desk and comes to stand right in front of me. His large body towers over mine. I have to tilt my head back to keep his gaze.

"I'm good at it."

Holy cow.

"I'm sorry?" I practically whisper.

"Pleasure," he traces the pad of his thumb over my bottom lip.

My body shivers in lust, instinctually reacting to his touch.

"I like to reward good behavior. You'll find me to be very generous."

It takes all of my power to step away from him as heat flushes my cheeks and nether regions.

"Your lack of humility is astounding," I say in a shaky voice.

His grin is wicked.

"You and I are going to have fun together."

Oh. My. God.

What am I getting myself into?

"Lots of it," he continues on.

Before I can even think of how to respond, there's a knock on the door. Michael keeps my gaze when he calls out.

"Come in."

It's Jessica again.

"The car is here," she says coldly. I can feel her gaze move over the two of us and I know I must be the color of a tomato.

"I'll be right down." Michael says, dismissively.

Jessica lingers for a moment before she leaves us alone again.

"I'll see you tomorrow then," Michael tells me in a no-nonsense voice as if nothing had just transpired between us. "Nine o'clock. Human Resources will go over pay and benefits with you. I'll also need you to sign an NDA."

"Of course," I say hoping my face doesn't betray my desire for him.

If there's one thing I can be sure of it's that I'm completely turned on. Like need-to-pleasure-myself-when-I-get-home turned on.

Use your feet, Abby. And walk the hell out before you throw yourself at him!

"Thank you," I say, backing away and heading for the door.

"I'll walk you down," he stops me from fleeing the scene. "I'm leaving for an appointment."

I remain silent and wait for him to grab his coat from the back of his chair. He walks me to the door and opens it. His physique, his height, his smell even—everything about him makes me feel so incredibly female.

We walk in silence through the office and I can feel a dozen curious eyes flicker over us. The elevator doors slide open as soon as Michael hits the button and we step inside. I move to the farthest corner, trying to put as much space between the two of us as I can.

Michael watches me with an amused look on his face. Like he knows he has me on edge. I watch his muscles bunch together as he slips on his coat.

"Where are you headed?" he asks.

Going home to masturbate, I think to myself.

"I have plans to see Georgie," I lie to him instead. "We were going to grab something to eat."

"How is Georgie?" Michael asks.

"Perfect as always."

"I'll drop you off."

"No!" I blurt out fast. "There's really no need. I'll just grab a cab."

The last thing I want is to sit next to him in an enclosed space. My hormones are raging and I might not be responsible for what I'll do.

The elevator door swishes open as Michael chuckles.

"I'm driving you. There's no need for you to grab a cab." His voice is firm. "Don't be ridiculous."

Since I know there really is no other choice for me, I nod in agreement and mumble a thank you. We head outside where a driver waits by a black Range Rover. He holds the door open for us.

"Thank you, Simon," Michael says to the older gentleman, who is dressed in casual gray pants and a top.

I step into the car and glue my body to the opposite door. Michael gets in behind me and swallows up all the space in the car. He stretches his legs out and his knee actually rubs up against mine. I keep my face pressed against the window as I fight for control.

"What's Georgie's address?"

"If you don't mind, I think I'm going to stop off at home first to freshen up," I say as I give him my home address. Simon takes off and Michael fiddles with the music and turns on Peter Gabriel.

Wonderful. As if it can get any worse.

Love ballads play the whole way to my house. I do my best and try to ignore Michael by keeping my gaze glued out the window.

"Who knew the view of the city streets could be so fascinating after so many years?" Michael's mocking voice finally breaks the silence.

I give him an embarrassed smile.

"Just lost in thought," I try to cover.

He raises a brow and smirks. Like he can see right through the lie.

"Would you like to be found?" he asks softly.

I laugh nervously and shrug. Luckily the traffic isn't bad and we get to my home in record time. The car pulls up in front of my flat, and I can't get out fast enough. Simon jumps out and opens the door before I can and to my surprise Michael gets out, turning to his driver and asking him to wait.

"You don't have to see me up," I argue.

"I insist." He gives me that irresistible smile of his. "And to be honest, I'm curious to see your place."

"It's just a regular home," I say.

Michael shrugs. "I'd still like to see it," he tells me, then gives me a teasing smile. "Shouldn't you be inviting me up for tea? After all, I am family and now happen to be your boss."

"I thought you had an appointment," I defend myself.

"It can wait."

"Then by all means, please come in and have some tea," I offer politely.

And just like that, my dream lover comes up to my home for the first time.

I think I might have heart failure.

CHAPTER FOUR

Having a man you fantasize about on a pretty regular basis in your flat for the first time is definitely a bucket list moment.

The moment would be even sweeter if the reason he was standing in here was because he was about to have his way with me in every corner of my home.

A girl can dream.

I watch Michael from the corner of my eye as he walks through my place and lingers over family photos, mementos I've put up, and the artwork I've collected over the years. After what feels like an eternity, he turns to me with a smile.

"Your home is beautiful, Abby. You have impeccable taste."

"Thank you."

Why I'm so happy he likes my taste is beyond me. But his compliment has filled with me such pleasure that you'd think he just asked me to marry him.

"Can I bring you a coffee or tea?" I ask him. "Something to eat? I have to go shopping, but I think I have some cheese and crackers."

"I'm fine," Michael says as he shakes his head and looks down at his watch. "I was teasing you downstairs. I just had to satisfy my curiosity. I have to leave for my meeting."

"Of course." I nod in understanding. I can't lie. I *am* disappointed that he has to leave so soon. I stand in the center of my living room and wait.

"But you haven't shown me the rest of your place," he tells me as he looks around the room.

"The rest?" I ask, feeling my heart pick up its pace.

"The bedrooms." His eyes are hooded.

How did I know he was going to ask?

"You don't mind, do you?" He cocks his head to the side, his gaze inscrutable.

"No," I practically gasp out. "The bedrooms are this way."

I motion toward the wide hall that veers off toward the guest bedroom, then my own room. I can hear Michael's footsteps behind me. *Act cool, Abigail,* I tell myself as my body warms up.

My heart beats fast.

I can feel myself begin to perspire.

Everywhere.

I can barely walk like a normal person.

All because the walking sex god, who haunts my every dream, is literally two steps behind me.

Right about to walk into my bedroom.

Is this what an anxiety attack feels like?

"Here's my bedroom." My throat is parched. "Simple, really."

It's the only thing I can think to say.

Michael comes up right next to me and stands in front of my four-poster oak bed and crosses his arms. I look at my room as if I'm seeing it for the first time. White linens and a white quilt, with a pale blue throw and matching pillows. An ivory fainting couch sits by the large French window that stares out onto the park. A round metal table is next to it, the book I've been reading sitting on top. The artwork in my room only consists of two modern pieces above both antique side tables next to my bed. I have a framed picture of my father and me when I was just born on one of the nightstands next to a matching pale blue lamp.

And on the other, my...

Vibrator!

Holy. Shit.

My eyes are glued to the mortifying hot pink pleasure toy that sits so innocently on my nightstand.

I would like to die now, God.

Quickly.

Like now.

I know the moment Michael's gaze finds the offending object.

I can't even bring myself to look at him. It's like all the oxygen is sucked out of the room and breathing will never be an option again. He inhales so quickly that if I weren't so in tune with his every movement, I wouldn't have heard the noise.

He's looking at it, I think to myself.

Oh. My. God.

I tell myself over and over that it's not a big deal. I'm a grown woman. Masturbation is a healthy activity. It's completely normal.

And it's not like this is the first vibrator he's ever seen!

When I finally gain the confidence to look at Michael, I'm surprised by what I see.

I was fully expecting him to tease me.

To have to bear through his mocking, sexy grin.

But it's actually quite the opposite.

His eyes are cold.

His jaw tight as he exhales and his blue eyes darken as they skim over my face.

"I have to go," he says abruptly. "I'll see you at the office tomorrow."

He turns quickly and walks out of my room, down the hall, to my front door. I barely have time to catch up to him. He opens the door and steps out, standing tall before he reaches the elevator.

"I'm confident I'll keep you satisfied."

"I'm sorry?" I feel my cheeks heat at the innuendo.

"Your new position," he says as he turns his sizzling gaze to mine.

I can't read his expression.

And I don't understand if he's playing some sort of game with me, or if I'm reading into everything. But I am one hundred percent positive something about seeing my vibrator has dampened his mood.

"With me," Michael continues.

"I don't doubt it," I hold his gaze, wondering if he can hear the longing in my voice.

If he realizes how I'm so turned on I can't wait for him to leave. If he knows I want to run back to my room and put myself out of my misery with that vibrator he seems to dislike immensely—the vibrator that happens to be my new best friend.

"See you tomorrow." He smirks at me. "Have an eventful evening."

Right.

There's no doubt to what he's referring to.

I watch his tall frame walk to the elevator and force myself to shut the door. I fall against it and listen to the elevator door ding. Once I know Michael's gone, I let out a breath.

I am *so* in trouble.

Just how the hell am I going to survive working with that man every day?

***

"You have an hour for lunch," Mrs. Lions, the pleasant woman who heads up Human Resources, tells me as she gives me a tour of the office.

I follow Mrs. Lions as she zips through the office.

For my first day on the job, I'm wearing a navy, knee-length pencil skirt, matching sweater, with fitted over-the-knee brown suede high-heeled boots. I pulled my long hair back into a low bun and wore minimal makeup. I feel like I look the part and I want Michael to see me as responsible and ready to take on my new position. And not think I'm trying too hard.

"This way, Abby," Mrs. Lions says as she takes me up another elevator from the second-floor Human Resource office.

Mrs. Lions is in her late forties and extremely helpful. She couldn't be nicer, patiently listening to all my questions and going out of her way to assure me that Mr. Sinclair would not have hired me if he didn't believe I could do the job. What she doesn't know is that my objections and lack of faith come from my secret fear of not being able to handle the raw sex appeal that my new boss embodies.

When Michael left my flat yesterday, I ordered a pizza, opened a bottle of wine and spent the rest of the day and night panicking over my new predicament. How was I going to survive living in a state of perpetual arousal? How was I going to start dating when I'd be around him *every single day*?! After my fifth helping of pizza—I should have stopped at two slices—I came up with the only logical solution that could work. Stay at this job for a few months, learn as much as I can and then find another more appropriate place to be employed. Once I gain more experience under my belt, I'll be able to find something much easier.

Simple. Easy.

A foolproof plan.

In the interim, I told myself, I'd just have to figure out a way to survive it. I'd just have to pretend that Michael is married and off-limits.

My confidence worked until I got to the office and became immersed in Michael's world.

And then everything seemed to fly out the window.

It's astounding how quickly I learned he didn't have a girlfriend.

Apparently, not even dating anyone.

At least that's what I heard some of the interns whispering about when I went to the commissary for a coffee in the morning. And that's another thing—it seems that I'm not the only female in the building that is insanely attracted to him. Any breathing and single male or female employee seems to suffer from the same problem I do.

At least I'm not alone…

Who am I kidding?

I want Michael for myself. Just me. And now I secretly view the rest of the women in the office as competition. And as Georgie pointed out so eloquently a few nights earlier, the crazy female in me who is apparently a nudge away from rearing her ugly head just might decide to take center stage.

At any moment. The thought is chilling.

I think about my competition.

There is the young American, Jessica—the intern with the perfect body who's quite aware of this genetic blessing of hers. Her jeans and tops couldn't be any tighter. And today I noticed she's wearing a full face of diva fuck-me-hard makeup.

Jessica's best friend in the office is Marina, an intern from Madrid, who I learned from Mrs. Lions is here for course credit for her university. Of course, she's also equally blessed in the looks department and has a chest that you can't help but stare at in awe. I have never been self-conscious about my breasts because they are pretty amazing but compared to Marina…

And that's it.

The problem.

I haven't been on the job for even a day and I'm already comparing myself to every single woman here. I'm unconsciously narrowing down my competition, potential females who Michael might be attracted to.

Georgie was right, all my crazy alter ego ever needed was a nudge, and she would be awakened in all her frightening glory.

"You will be Mr. Sinclair's number one," Mrs. Lions tells me as we make our way back to my desk.

"Number one?" I ask in confusion.

"I thought Mr. Sinclair might have mentioned this to you earlier, but I guess not."

"No," I shake my head.

"Mr. Sinclair has two PA's," she explains. "His number one sits outside his office, and number two takes any calls that number one misses and takes care of personal business matters."

"Where is number two?" I ask feeling foolish referring to someone as a number and not a name.

"I'm taking you to her now. Danielle has been with Mr. Sinclair for five years. She is now his longest lasting PA. Wanda, who just left, was his number one before."

"Forgive me for asking, but why is Danielle not his number one?" I ask the obvious. "Wouldn't it make more sense for me to be number two?"

I would so much more prefer that. Not having to sit directly outside his office, being able to hide away somewhere in the back of the office—talk about the ideal situation for me.

"It was Mr. Sinclair's decision." Mrs. Lions face does not betray what she's thinking.

We walk to an office that is located at the far end of Michael's. The doors are glass, and I can see a pretty dark haired woman who I think is in her early thirties sitting behind a glass desk facing a giant desktop.

Mrs. Lions knocks on the door and the woman nods welcomingly. We enter her pristine office.

"Danielle, I'd like you to meet Abby," Mrs. Lions says as she motions toward me.

"Nice to meet you, Abby," Danielle says with a wide, welcoming smile. I can't say I'm not surprised to see it. I thought she might be resentful that I had usurped her number one position. I wouldn't blame her—I probably would be after five years.

Up close, Danielle isn't just pretty. She's beautiful. Her face is soft and quite stunning. She reminds me of the actress Zoe Saldana.

"Please, have a seat," she offers politely.

"Can I leave you to it?" Mrs. Lions asks, looking at her watch. "My schedule is packed this morning. I've given Abby a general overview of the company and how things work, but thought you might be best suited to talk to her about Mr. Sinclair's needs."

"Of course," Danielle smiles graciously.

"Wonderful. I'll be seeing you, Abby. Welcome to the company."

"Thank you for showing me around, Mrs. Lions," I tell her gratefully. I like her. She seems very nice.

Plus, she's happily married.

I'm so *not* crazy.

Mrs. Lions leaves Danielle and me alone. As Danielle studies me, I can't help but shuffle uncomfortably.

"We're excited to have you here with us, Abby."

"Thank you," I reply. "I'm really grateful to be here and want to do a good job for Mich... Mr. Sinclair."

Danielle smiles as she catches my slip.

"I know you guys are cousins," she tells me. "Michael filled me in when I saw him last night."

My stomach drops to the floor. *He saw her last night?* I wouldn't be surprised if he were dating this bombshell.

"I just got engaged," she goes on to tell me. To my great relief as she shows me her sparkly ring. "I had my party last night, and Michael's one of my best mates from school. I am so grateful you're starting now and can take away some of the pressure off of me since I'm planning my wedding and all. It's been a little overwhelming trying to handle all of this on my own."

"I was just there," I tell her with sympathy. "I completely under-stand how crazy a wedding can get."

Danielle seems surprised as her gaze flickers to my wedding finger and lack of a ring.

"You're married?"

"No," I shake my head awkwardly. "We broke up before the day actually arrived."

"Ahh," Danielle says knowingly as she meets my gaze. "Do you want to talk about it?"

"Not really."

"Understandable. So I'll just go over some quick things with you."

For the next hour, she goes over my job duties with me. From what I understand I'll be scheduling Michael's meetings and running his personal life. Everything Danielle explains to me is pretty straightforward and seems fairly easy to do. Once I find my rhythm, it shouldn't be so bad. From what I understand, Danielle works on the more business related tasks for Michael. Keeping his deals in order. His appearances at events that will garner money for a charity and meetings in other countries with important dignitaries, or CEOs of companies. Also, if I miss a call, it is forwarded along to Danielle's desk. From what I gather from Danielle, Michael is a pretty laid-back boss as long as things are getting done.

After she's done filling me in, she gets up and walks me to my new space. It's directly in front of Michael's office. My glass desk faces the center room I walked through the day before where the Think Tank is set up. There is a large desktop computer and a phone. There's also a leather-bound day calendar because, according to Danielle, Michael likes to have a hard copy backup with his schedule in it in case the computer system goes down.

"So here you are," Danielle says with a kind smile. " I think you're going to do just fine here. I'm going to leave you to it to fiddle around on the system and become acclimated. Here are the instructions for setting up your voicemail and you've got your password for the computer. IT has come by already and synched Michael's personal email to your account so you can start familiarizing yourself with his life."

"Personal email?" I ask.

"Yes, Abby," she says matter-of-factly. "That was his request. We both have access to his emails. Lyle from IT will be around shortly to answer any questions and help you navigate the system."

"Great. Do you know when I should be expecting him?"

"I believe he'll be in later this afternoon, which should give you plenty of time to get comfortable."

I'm actually relieved I get to immerse myself in the job without Michael around to unnerve me. Danielle leaves me a short while later and before I can even turn my computer on, Lyle, the young IT guy, is there to go over passwords and protocol with me. He gives me a company cell phone, a personal laptop, and shows me how to use the network. It's all fairly easy to navigate, and within no time I am up and running.

He opens Michael's inbox on my computer and loads his personal contacts into my hard drive, and I'm good to go. The thought of going through Michael's personal emails still feels strange. I avoid looking at his inbox and instead choose to read the resource book about the company that Mrs. Lions gave me earlier. I'm quickly impressed with all the work the foundation has done around the world. Michael's really helped make a difference in people's lives and for the planet itself.

I end up working straight through lunch and am reading up on company protocol when Michael finally shows up.

It's after three o'clock when I hear his voice echoing through the room. I glance up from my reading material and see him standing next to the Think Tank chatting with Jessica. She assumes the instinctual flirtatious stance with him. Hip tilted to the side, hands on her narrow waist, finger twirling a strand of her hair.

It's so obvious it practically induces vomit.

I have no right to be annoyed, I tell myself.

No right at all.

I hear her frilly little laugh and roll my eyes.

"Vulgar," I mutter under my breath and flip through a page in the book.

I stare blindly down at the words and try to block out everything around me. *You're going to have to get used to this*, I tell myself. This is going to be your life for the foreseeable future.

Demoralizing.

I reach for my cell phone, desperately needing to text Georgie for a power drink after work but stop when I feel someone walk behind my desk.

It's Michael.

Standing directly behind my chair and essentially trapping me to the desk. He places his hand on the glass counter next to where mine rests frozen over my phone.

He leans down over my shoulder, his lips a breath away from my ear, his cologne invading my every sensory skill, his muscular body burning mine even though he isn't even touching me.

I am so in trouble.

"What are you reading?" Michael's voice is low and husky, his breath tickles my skin.

All I have to do...

All I have to do is turn my head and my lips will be right on his. For a moment I think about doing it... but then sanity...

Keep the crazy under control, Abigail.

Don't let her out.

"Protocol," I manage to croak out.

I hear Michael sigh as I remain utterly still.

"The rules, you mean?" he whispers.

"Yes."

"What do you think of them?" I swear his lips are practically touching my ear and I know his gaze is on my flushed face. I can feel my nipples harden.

I am so turned on I don't know what to do with myself.

"They seem good." My voice is practically a whisper.

"What's your favorite so far?"

The man is insane.

"I can't remember."

His wicked laughter in my ear wakes me up.

"No fraternization with the employees," I blurt out.

I don't even know if it's a rule. But I have to say it, especially because somehow I know he's doing this to me on purpose. And I still don't understand how to play his game.

"Do you usually follow all the rules?" There's almost a primal look in his eyes when he asks the question.

"I do."

"That's a shame." Michael sounds disappointed.

And just like that, I'm robbed of his presence. He steps away from my desk and walks into his office.

"I'd like to speak to you for a moment in here," he calls out over his shoulder before he disappears into his office.

I'm left panting with desire. Completely turned on. My entire body is on fire, and I wonder if I even have the energy to walk into his office. To face him this time.

See that mocking look in his eyes.

It's too much.

Breathe, Abby. Just breathe.

Is this some sort of fun torturous game for him, I wonder? What is he doing to me? Flirting, turning me on…

And now he's my boss.

My phone rings for the first time. It jolts me out of what could have been a quick spiral into fantasyland, a dangerous place that I know can only serve to further torture me.

"Michael Sinclair's office," I will my voice to be calm and professional.

"I'm waiting." The sound of his sexy voice on the line jolts me right to my core.

My boss.

My tormentor.

My fantasy lover.

I put the phone down, pick up his calendar, and make my way to his office. I walk inside and try to leave the door open, but he stops me.

"Shut it."

Lord.

I do as he says and stand next to the leather couch he's sprawled on. His arms are stretched out over the top of the couch and the look on his face is playful.

"Have a seat."

I sink into the chair opposite him.

"How has your day been?" he asks politely.

"Wonderful," I return easily. "Mrs. Lions and Danielle couldn't be more helpful. And I have to say, what you're doing here is pretty impressive. You should be proud of the work you've accomplished."

"There's still so much that needs to be done," Michael returns.

"But you're helping make a change," I tell him. "That's a step in the right direction."

"Are you complimenting me?" Michael gives me a teasing smile.

"Yes, I am."

"Thank you," he says softly. "It means a lot coming from you."

It does?

"Have you had lunch?" Michael suddenly asks, changing the topic.

"Actually, I haven't had a chance yet," I shake my head. "Time flew by and I completely forgot. I wanted to acclimate myself with everything before you got here."

Before I know what he's doing, Michael picks up his cell phone and makes a quick call.

"I'd like a club sandwich and Caesar salad brought to my office," he orders into the phone.

"That's totally unnecessary," I argue, but I'm touched by his thoughtfulness.

"It's my job to keep you satisfied."

I think my stomach flips over.

Michael throws the phone on the couch and folds his arms. I can't decipher his look.

"How was your night?" I don't miss the mocking tone in his

voice.

"Fine, thank you," I barely manage as I think about how he saw my vibrator last night. Talk about a giant elephant in the room. A vibrating one at that. I grip his calendar in one hand and click my pen hoping he'll keep things professional and ask me to write something down.

"And yours?" I ask politely.

"Unsatisfactory."

Don't ask, Abby!

"Why?" Clearly, I'm glutton for punishment.

"I find myself to be in a state of acute frustration," he tells me quietly. "It's a feeling I don't particularly enjoy."

"Are you in the middle of a deal?"

"Fortunately, I closed the deal," he says as his eyes blaze into mine. "I'm just working out the terms. It's always the most tedious part of any negotiation."

"Should I be familiar with it?" I ask him.

"You will be."

The way he says that… it's almost like he's about to be in control of something.

Or someone.

"In fact, it will probably take up most of your time." His voice is commanding.

"Is there any reading material you can give me?" I'm trying to keep our conversation as professional as possible. "I can take it home with me tonight and get up to speed."

"You're not ready yet," he tells me, his eyes settling on my mouth, causing it to go dry. "But soon. Very soon."

I think I hear a warning in his voice, but I can't be sure. His gaze flicks down to the calendar I'm clutching.

"I take it Danielle filled you in on your job requirements."

"Yes," I'm happy he has changed the subject to something that feels safe.

"What did she tell you?"

"That I'll be scheduling your meetings and seeing to your personal needs—"

Did that even come out right?

"I mean—" I stutter. "I'm taking care of whatever you might need outside the office."

Michael grins.

"My extracurricular activities, you mean?"

"Yes." I look down at the book again. I wonder if discussing his personal life will ever get easier with time. "Setting your dinner dates, making sure your life is in order. The usual duties of a PA."

"And how are you feeling about everything?" Michael continues his cross-examination.

"Fine," I say, plastering a smile on my face as I meet his gaze. "And appreciative, of course. Thank you again for giving me this chance."

"Don't thank me," Michael says cryptically. "I never do anything I don't want."

"Still." I know my voice sounds nervous. "I'm happy to be here, and I'm just looking forward to diving in."

Michael watches me for a moment before a broad smile sweeps across his face.

"Perfect," he says. "Then let's get to it."

CHAPTER FIVE

The next couple of weeks go by in a blur.

After a few hiccups my first few days, I finally begin to understand how Michael likes things done and what a force of nature he is. His mind goes at warp speed, jumping from one project to another, it's a wonder he can keep up with the fast pace of his life and remember everything that's going on.

But he does.

His days are spent in and out of meetings with heads of companies he targets for his non-profit work, and on nonstop daily conference calls. I find myself growing more respect for him as the days go by. He is genuinely passionate about all the causes he puts his name, money, and time behind. I also quickly learn his employees respect him deeply and speak very highly of him. Anytime I've happened to overhear a conversation about him, someone is usually singing his praises about some miracle he's been able to get done even with the odds stacked against him. The respect he's managed to garner from his employees is a testament to who he is as a man and only makes him that much more attractive to me.

I thought the job would just be that—a job, where I'd clock in and out and not get invested in anything going on around me. But that hasn't been the case at all. I've found myself reading more about the causes the Foundation has put so much into. I've become invested in what's going on and gone through the whole gamut of emotions Danielle told me I might experience when I started—the outrage, the sadness, and the hope that we're part of something bigger, something that's actually making a change.

Since I had never been part of a team before and am an introvert by nature, I thought I'd be on my own. But it's been the opposite of what I expected. Danielle has taken me under her wing and has become my constant companion here at the job. She is a godsend, and we've grown close in the short time I've been at the company.

She patiently answers any question I might have and has helped me navigate my way through my new job. She's looped me in on office gossip, included me on coffee runs, lunches, and has really gone out of her way to make me feel welcome. What's more, through Danielle, I've learned bits and pieces about my enigmatic boss/cousin through marriage.

Apparently, the last steady girlfriend Michael had was over a year ago and was an actress I've actually heard of.

I've never really been a fan of her work, and I swear it has nothing to do with that fact that she dated Michael. I swear!

Since he ended it with her, there hasn't been anyone significant. For the most part, Michael's known as a serial dater and playboy. Danielle also confirmed my suspicions about the women in the office being as obsessed with him as I am, and as far as she knows he's never dated anyone who works for him.

Cue the sad music.

Other than the first day when we had the strange energy between us, there have been no other overt sexual teases thrown my way by Michael.

I'd be lying if I say I'm relieved by it.

"So what do you think of this for our centerpieces?" Danielle asks me as we sit in her office on a Friday and share a late lunch.

Danielle is the bride I should have been when I was going to marry Dimitri. She's thoroughly engrossed in every detail and wants everything to be perfect. A bit of bridezilla peeks out every so often, but it's nothing too dramatic. Seeing her enthusiasm for her impending nuptials only reinforces the fact that I made the right decision.

She shows me a few pictures of different flower arrangements and I point at the one I like best.

"This is my favorite," I tell her, choosing the simple white flower display.

"Mine too! It's a bit more than we wanted to spend but I feel like if I'm going to splurge on any day, this should be it."

"You should choose whatever makes you happy," I tell her as I take in a spoon full of my pea soup.

"You're right, it's *my* day." She puts the pictures away into one of her many wedding folders and digs into her pasta. She has a whole color coordinated system going for her wedding that I find pretty damn impressive.

"God, Abby, I'm going to have to start my wedding diet soon. But the problem I'm having is that my nerves are making me want to eat more."

"What?" I laugh in disbelief. "Trust me, you don't have anything to worry about. You don't need to diet. Your body is perfect."

"You haven't seen me with my clothes off."

"You're crazy." I shake my head.

"Regardless of whether I'm crazy or not, it's what all the brides do. A bride is supposed to look emaciated on her wedding day."

I burst out laughing. "Who says?"

"My mother," Danielle tells me, rolling her eyes. "Now, if there's one thing that's driving me crazy about this wedding, it's my mother. It's like she's possessed or something."

"I can't tell you how relieved I am to hear you say that."

"Why?"

"It's good to know I'm not the only one who's cursed with an overbearing mother," I commiserate with Danielle. "For years I thought I was all alone."

"Was yours a nightmare when you were planning your wedding?"

"Nightmare doesn't even begin to describe what she put me through." I cringe at the horrible memories coming back to me. "She was the absolute *worst*."

We share another laugh.

"So I'm going to have to go there and ask," Danielle says after a moment of silence. "How long has it been since you broke it off?"

"Five months." I can't believe it's only been that long. It seems like a lifetime ago.

"Can I ask why you broke it off?" Danielle's voice is cautious.

"I wasn't happy," I reply honestly.

Danielle has such good energy that it's so easy to let my guard down with her. When I was growing up, I didn't have many girl-friends I could relate to or felt like I could really confide in. And when I was going through all of my misgivings about Dimitri, there was no woman in my social circle that I could talk to because they all believed I found the perfect match.

It's nice to talk to a woman who has her life together. And who comes from a world where love trumps pedigree.

"Well that's a reason if there ever is one," Danielle agrees. "Happiness should always be your first priority."

"I just couldn't see how I would ever be fulfilled with him—if I'm being honest, we didn't share any love or passion between us—and I couldn't imagine that being my life forever." I can feel the suffocating feelings come over me just by remembering that time in my life.

"I just couldn't go through with it. Not even when I thought about what it would mean for my future or who it would hurt. I had to be selfish."

"I don't see what you did as being selfish."

"Not everyone would agree with you." I smile ruefully. "My mother and a lot of friends think I'm crazy for leaving him."

"I can't say anything about your mother because I think it's just inevitable for them to always think they know what's best for you," Danielle says. "But your friends—they're supposed to support you no matter what."

Her words ring true and for once I feel happiness that someone gets me—understands how I feel and is on my side.

"So when did you know?" Danielle continues to prod.

"From the moment I got engaged," I say my truth out loud for the first time.

"Holy shit, Abby." Danielle can't contain her surprise. "Why did you say yes in the first place?"

"Family pressure," I tell her with an embarrassed smile.

Danielle stares at me in silence

"Sounds crazy, right?" I say.

"Not at all," Danielle says, shaking her head. "Everyone has that in some way or another. Yours is still a bit old-fashioned and extreme..."

"He was the ideal candidate on paper," I go on to explain how I arrived in my situation in the first place.

Danielle remains quiet so I rush on to explain.

"I don't want to put him down in any way because I know he'll be perfect for someone else. He had many great qualities going for him. He just wasn't for me."

Danielle digests my words.

"Well, I think it was incredibly brave of you." Danielle's voice carries a great deal of respect. "I don't know if I would have been able to cut it off so close to the date."

I shrug off her comment.

"You'd be surprised."

"So you're a bit of a rebel, Abby," Danielle says with a bit of awe. "You're like the real-life *Runaway Bride*."

"I'm not like," I tell her with a smile. "I *am*."

We both burst out laughing.

"Are you dating anyone now?" Danielle continues on after a moment.

"No," I shake my head. "No one."

"We'll have to set you up. I love playing Cupid." Her eyes glow in excitement. "Tom, my fiancé, has some really great single friends. When you're ready, of course—are you?"

"Ready?" I question, meeting her gaze.

I think about finally going out with someone. Sharing a first kiss. Holding hands. Feeling cherished and loved.

I long for that kind of companionship. A real relationship.

"I am more than ready." I'm sure she can hear the longing in my voice. "It's time."

"How long has it been?"

"Since I've been with a man?" I ask her with a playful smile. "Too damn long, Danielle. Too bloody damn long."

I watch Danielle's smile freeze on her face as her gaze moves over my shoulder and settles on whoever is standing right behind me.

My heart sinks in dread.

"Michael," Danielle says. "Can I help you with something?"

Lord.

He's standing in the doorway? *Right now?* Behind me?

"Ladies." I hear his sultry voice.

Did he hear that last bit about me needing a man?

"I'm sorry to interrupt your lunch, but I was hoping I could steal Abby for a minute or two."

I slowly turn around and shamelessly stare at his tall body. He usually dresses casually at the office in jeans and T-shirts or long sleeved thermal tops. Today he's wearing a fitted dark navy blue suit that looks like it was made for his body. My stomach clenches as I admire the way he looks.

"I didn't think you'd be in today," I tell him as my heart races. I'm surprised to see him since he had me block off the entire day.

"Change of plans." His eyes are guarded. "When you finish up in here I'd like you to meet me in my office."

He leaves us quickly and I let out a breath when he's gone.

"Strange," Danielle says, staring after him.

"Must be important," I tell her as I gather my things together.

"Must be," Danielle says as she continues to eat. "IM when you're back at your desk."

"Will do." I get up and make my way down the hall to his office. I knock once before entering.

"Come in."

The door slides open and I find Michael standing by the floor-to-ceiling windows staring out on the river. I shut the door and wait in bated breath.

"That perfume you wear…" His voice is low and almost husky.

I put a self-conscious hand on my neck and wonder how he can smell the scent clear across the room.

"It's like fresh flowers on a spring day. It lingers in a room after you leave."

He turns and faces me, and I'm hit with the full force of his intensity. I try to think of a clever response, but before I can, he pulls the rug right out from underneath me.

"I like it."

My mouth goes dry. My gaze meets his and for a second I see a glimpse of the fire lurking behind the shadows. And then I know. It's not in my head. It's not just my wishful thinking. There *is* something between us. I don't know exactly what it is, but it's there—an underlying sexual tension and it's not just coming from me, I feel it oozing from him as well.

He's attracted to me.

And that knowledge fills me with such pleasure that, if I could, I'd dance around the room and do a million cartwheels.

"So how can I help you?" I ignore his compliment and ask the question as soon as I'm able to breathe normally again.

Michael gives me a knowing smile before crossing his arms.

"Do you have plans tonight?"

"Plans?" I shake my head thinking he needs me to stay late for work. "No plans."

"On a Friday night?" Michael's voice is curious.

"No plans." There's a defensive edge to my voice. "I didn't have time to make any. I've just been too busy here."

"Perfect." I think I hear a sigh of relief. "I need a date."

"A date?"

For a moment I wonder if wants me to go through his black book of ladies and pick someone for him to go out with.

Over my dead body—

"So I'll pick you up at eight?" His lips curl into a cocky smile, and I feel as though I'm a tennis ball that's being struck back and forth on a court.

What is going on here? Have we just crossed a line and entered a grey zone?

"Umm, sure," I finally manage to say. "What's the occasion?"

"I'm having dinner with an old friend and I thought you might like to join."

"Is it business related?" I ask in confusion.

"It usually ends up going there with Jack and me," Michael replies smoothly.

But he hasn't really answered the question. So is it a real date or business? I can't be sure.

"I'll join if you need me to." I hope I don't sound too eager. Or stunned.

Or both.

"I need you to," he replies politely.

I continue to stand there, probably looking like I've just gone through electroshock therapy.

"Is there anything else I can help you with?" I finally find my voice.

"I think that covers it for today," he tells me with a slow, knowing smile.

***

I find that alcohol and courage go hand in hand.

Truly. It's one of life's greatest miracles.

I left the office earlier than I usually do and rushed home to get ready for my "date" with Michael. The first executive decision I made was to shave my legs. I told myself it was a precautionary move and it had to be done anyway, so what was the harm in doing it before my "date"?

It didn't mean anything.

Yes, I know. Sometimes I find it's easier to lie to yourself rather than face the truth.

I showered quickly, tried on three different outfits and finally settled on a simple sleeveless black fitted dress that falls right to my knees. I paired the dress with a pair of Gucci suede black heels, left my long hair down around my shoulders and got in two full glasses of champagne before Michael had even arrived.

Hence the newfound confidence.

Now, I'm feeling good.

When the phone rings to let Michael up to my flat, I have a healthy buzz going that has done wonders for my state of mind.

He knocks on my door faster than I expect.

My heart is in my throat and I don't know if I feel nauseous or am just in desperate need of taking him to my bedroom and having my way with him. All that separates me from my fantasy come to life is one door.

Calm down, Abby. You've got this.

Just remember, you're shaved, locked, and loaded.

I take another sip of champagne needing a bit more liquid courage and finally open the door.

My mouth goes dry when I see him.

He looks really good.

Michael is still wearing the suit from earlier today, but now the top few buttons of his white shirt are open, exposing some of that tanned, muscular chest I've pretty much fantasized about my whole life. After I'm finished checking him out, I watch him take his turn. I try to remain unaffected, but it's hard when the look on his face can melt steel.

"You look beautiful."

His compliment works like an aphrodisiac.

"Thank you," I reply shyly.

Michael's gaze comes to rest on the champagne glass I'm still holding in my hand before flicking up to my face.

"Liquid courage?" His smile is sinful.

"Hardly." I hope my voice sounds calm. "Would you like a glass?"

"We don't have time." He sounds disappointed. "Maybe after. You can invite me up for a nightcap."

I don't miss the innuendo in his voice.

My senses reel. I want him.

So badly.

So badly that I'm tempted to tell him to forget about the dinner and ask if he'd like to have that nightcap right now.

Maybe the alcohol on an empty stomach combined with my nerves wasn't such a good idea after all...

Or maybe it's exactly what I need to get to where I've wanted to be my whole life.

In Michael's Sinclair's bed.

Or him in mine. Whatever scenario works out faster.

"Are you ready?" Michael's voice is gruff.

"Yes." I put my champagne flute down, reaching for my camel colored coat.

He stands by the door and waits for me to exit before shutting it behind me.

Dinner is actually really fun and conversation flows easily.

Michael's friend Jack reminds me of the guys I went to school with.

He went to Eton with Michael and now works for a tech company that specializes in social media. He has a pleasant demeanor and is a lot of fun. I especially like the way he dotes over his girlfriend

Jennifer, who's in town from Hong Kong for the week. Seeing couples in love always gives me hope. Jennifer tells me the two have had a long distance relationship for over a year and that it hasn't been easy, but they plan on moving in together in the coming year.

"I'm surprised I've never met you before," Jack says to me as the waiter pours us another glass of wine. My glass has not been empty since we sat down to dinner hours ago and I'm immensely grateful for it because the alcohol has only helped loosen me up.

"You being family with Michael and all."

Jack studies my face as he continues.

"But I have to say, you do look very familiar to me."

"You've probably seen me out over the years." I take a sip of my wine. "I'm sure we've been to some of the same places."

Jack leans back in his chair and brushes his blond hair away from his eyes.

"I never forget a face," he says, furrowing his brow. "It's going to come to me, I know it."

"You're making her nervous," Michael says as he looks over at me with sympathy. "Don't mind him, Abby. He's harmless."

"I'm fine." I laugh.

"So you're working for Michael now?" Jennifer intervenes with a gentle smile as she reaches over and takes Jack's hand in hers.

"Yes, it's been just a few weeks now."

"How do you like it?"

Jack interrupts our conversation. "Is he a slave driver?"

"Hardly," I reply acutely aware of Michael's eyes on me. "He's a great boss."

Jack bursts out laughing and looks over at Michael.

"You train them well, my friend."

"No training here." I'm sure Jack can hear the irritation in my voice. "I'm not afraid to speak the truth."

"If he were an ass you'd tell him?" Jack's smile is devilish.

"Absolutely."

Michael bursts out laughing.

"There, you see," Michael says, putting an arm on the back of my chair. His long fingers brush up against my neck, causing goose bumps to make their way up my body. "I can't be so bad if she's not afraid to call me an ass."

"I like you, Abby," Jack says. "You're brave."

"You have no idea," Michael agrees.

I shrug in embarrassment and look down at my plate of half-eaten soufflé. What I wouldn't give to eat the whole thing…

Flabby Abby.

Right. Scratch that. Not going to touch the rest of that dessert.

"It just came to me!" Jack claps his hands together in realization. "Where I've seen you, Abby."

I wait for Jack to continue.

"Were you engaged to that wealthy Russian?" Jack asks curiously. "Dimitri something or other?"

My stomach drops in dread, but I keep a smile plastered on my face. Michael's body tenses beside me.

"I was." I bite my lip, not supplying any other information.

"And you broke it off rather dramatically if my memory serves me well," Jack continues on as if we're discussing something as trivial as the weather.

"Jack…" Michael intervenes quickly to my relief. "This isn't a topic Abby wants to discuss."

"She doesn't?" Jack asks innocently.

"No, she doesn't," I interject, shaking my head. "She really doesn't."

Jack meets my gaze with an apologetic grin.

"I'm sorry, Abby," he says earnestly. "I've had a lot to drink and sometimes I forget my manners."

"It's all right." I look down into my lap feeling embarrassed.

"Jack is really good at putting his foot in his mouth," Jennifer rushes out to say to me as she shakes her head. "Trust me, I know from previous experiences."

I can't help but laugh.

"So now that I've completely managed to make a mess of what was an absolutely lovely dinner, where should we go?" Jack asks the group with a sheepish smile.

"It's late—" Michael begins as he glances over at me, the look in his eyes protective.

"It's Friday night and we haven't gone out in ages." It doesn't sound like Jack will take no for an answer. "And Jennifer is here from out of town. And now I've got to make up my blunder with Abby and show her a good time. Come on. You must. I insist."

Michael fixes his brilliant blue gaze on me, and I feel his finger brush up against my shoulder.

"What do you think?"

I'm not thinking. I can't. Not with all the wine I've had and the way he keeps touching me and wreaking havoc on my senses.

"I'm up for it."

He lifts a brow, questioning.

"You're sure?"

"Why wouldn't I be?"

Michael's grin is wicked. My toes curl in my shoes, and I want to lean into him so badly it's a challenge to remain still.

If Jack and Jennifer notice any of the tension between us, they cover it well.

"So there," Jack interrupts our stare off. "It's settled then. Let's go dancing."

***

Over the years, I used to fantasize about running into Michael at one of the clubs I used to frequent. I had every scenario mapped out in my head. Of course, they all always ended the same way—with Michael and me in bed together having the best sex of our lives.

Georgie spoke the truth when he said I dragged him to different clubs and bars I thought Michael might be at. Unfortunately, all of my endless stalkings never produced any results, and I always missed him.

And now…

Now here I am at one of London's most popular clubs as his date. I still don't know what the parameters are between us, what is really going on, but a buzzed Abby is happy to test out the waters in any way she can.

The owner knew who Michael was the moment we entered and rolled out the red carpet for him. They ushered us through the crowds back to a VIP section where we settled into a booth in one of the darkest corners of the club. They placed a few bottles of hard liquor on the table and Michael gave orders for them to bring wine and champagne as well.

With the music thumping around us, and the alcohol warming my body I feel myself get a second wind. I can't remember the last time it was when I let my hair down and had fun. I've been so consumed by the drama that I forgot about this part of life that we all need every so often.

Like just have a bloody good time.

I haven't felt this free in forever.

Jack pours four shots of tequila in the small shot glasses that were placed on the table. He passes them around.

"I don't know…" I shout above the music as I shake my head. "This might not be safe…"

"Nonsense!" Jack sounds inebriated. "What's not safe about tequila?"

Let me count the ways.

Michael is sitting just opposite me in the booth and Jennifer and Jack are standing up with their shots swaying to the music. I steal a look at him as he takes his shot and lifts it in the air. His gaze crashes into mine.

"To a wonderful night!" Jack says with a bit too much enthusiasm.

Michael's brilliant blue eyes are glued to mine and we both take the shot at the same time. The liquid burns down my throat and into my stomach.

God! That stuff is strong!

"Let's go dance, beautiful!" Jack grabs hold of Jennifer and takes her out to join the crowded dance floor.

And then there were two.

Michael stretches out in the booth like he owns the place, his face partially hidden because of the dark lighting in the club. I can't see his eyes now, but I know he's watching me. I can practically feel his gaze, like he's reaching out and touching me. The music pulses through my body. All around us are people dancing and drinking away, but it feels like we are the only two people in the world.

"Come closer."

Said the Wolf to Red Riding Hood.

"Why?" Tequila makes me brave.

"Why not?" I can hear the challenge in his voice. "Are you scared?"

Scared?

Excited would be the better adjective to use.

I think I threw my sanity out the door when I took the shot of tequila because in the next second I scoot around the curve of the booth and settle in about a foot or so away from Michael's lean body. The small distance between us makes me feel like I am still in control even though I'm well aware I'm not the one in the driver's seat.

Michael ends that brief sense of safety when he reaches out and takes a piece of my hair in his hand. He rubs it together like it's fine silk.

The intimate gesture wreaks havoc on my nerves.

"I like your hair down," he tells me.

I promise I will wear my hair down for the rest of my life. And yes, I am fully aware that my lack of humility is astounding.

"Thank you."

"Thank you," he mimics back.

"Are you back to making fun of me?" Clearly, the alcohol has given me a crazy amount of courage.

"Are you back to being proper?" he counters.

"What do you mean?"

"I thought that last shot of tequila might have helped shed some of that armor you wear."

"I don't wear any armor." I cross my arms and legs defensively.

"No?" He doesn't sound like he believes me. "When was the last time you did something like this? Go out and just have fun?"

"I can't remember," I reply honestly. "But that doesn't mean I'm wearing armor."

He laughs.

"The way you say it, it's like I implied you're physically dressed like some medieval knight." He smirks. "You're not understanding me."

"Then please explain."

"When was the last time you let go of your inhibitions and just lived in the moment?"

I'm silent as my thoughts drift over my life.

"When was the last time you just did what you've always wanted to do?"

Michael places his hands over my heart and I know he can feel how erratic the beat is.

Because of him.

"I'm talking about this."

I feel like I'm playing a chess game with a master.

"And what is this?" I'm happy my voice sounds calm even though I'm anything but.

"This?" Michael's grin is wicked. "This thing between us?"

His admission that there is an "us" thrills me.

"This energy we have. The attraction…" he continues, hypnotizing me with his words. "It's exciting. And risky. Dangerous. But it's fun."

His gaze flicks from my eyes to my mouth and back up to my eyes again. My mind races as I look away and stare blindly out onto the dance floor.

He grabs hold of my chin and pulls my gaze back to his.

"What do *you* think this is?" His sparkling blue eyes pin mine.

Now or never.

I love you, Alcohol.

"I honestly don't know." My voice is strong.

"You don't?" There's no mistaking the primal look in his eyes.

"I've never really known." I finally admit the truth.

His hand begins to caress my jawline right before the pad of his thumb comes up to rub my lower lip.

"What do you want it to be?" I can hear the desire in his sexy voice.

Since I can't find the words, I show him instead.

My tongue brushes up against his finger that rests on my lip.

Michael reacts as though he's been burned by fire. He drops his hand and moves it through his hair. I take a calculated breath of my own as I wait for his next move.

Now he knows.

I want him.

CHAPTER SIX

"I don't play games."

Michael says this to me right before Jack and Jennifer make their way back to our table. Jack is now hammered and Jennifer looks as though she is on her way. They fall into the booth in each other's arms, laughing and stealing kisses.

I want to scream out in frustration.

Talk about an interruption at the worst possible time! I've waited a lifetime for this moment, and now I'm going to be forced to wait even longer to understand what he means by that last comment.

I intend to find out as soon as we are alone again.

"Shots?" Jack yells out again as he stands up and begins to pour another round.

Don't mind if I do...

I gladly take the glass out of Jack's hand and down the drink as soon as I can. It burns again but not as bad as it did the first round. I know I should probably take it easy considering the amount of alcohol I've already consumed, but I can't seem to stop myself. From the corner of my eye, I see Michael do the same. Before I can contemplate my next move, Michael grabs hold of my hand.

"Dance with me."

He doesn't ask. He commands.

He pulls me out of the booth and holds onto my hand as he takes me out onto the dance floor. Within seconds he's navigated his way to the middle of the crowd and with a remix of Marian Hill's "Are you Down", I let all my inhibitions go and start moving my body to the music.

The song is sexy, her voice sultry and my hips sway to the music like I was born to move to it. Michael's lithe body slides up against mine. His hands reach out and take hold of my hips, pulling me close as he rubs up against me in a way I've dreamed about my whole life, causing my body to pulse with electricity. My head tilts back and I look up and lock eyes with his steely blue gaze. His eyes darken and an almost animalistic energy seems to emanate from him as he leans into my body, turning me into a fiery mess of longing.

And anticipation.

My hands move up his muscled chest to his shoulders and I allow myself free reign to touch him here, now, with a crowd of people surrounding us, their presence making my sinful action feel safe. Our eyes remain locked and the heat that moves between us could light the place on fire. Michael's hands move from my hips up to my waist, over my back and through my hair until he tugs on the thick strands and moves his face down to mine.

We breathe each other in.

We both stop moving.

The club around us, the people, the music—all of it seems to stand still.

Our bodies speak to each other in a way we've never been able to communicate before. The years of desire we've both felt crashes down around us like the powerful surge of a waterfall. My heart gives a wild kick and I'm completely overcome by the moment, the intensity of my feelings for him.

His lips brush up against mine, teasing me, his tongue moves across my lower lip and before I can respond his mouth moves to my ear.

"I want you." Michael's husky voice is like music to my ears.

If he weren't holding onto me, I would crumble to the floor.

I don't just want him. I *need* him.

"Come home with me tonight." His voice commands me as his hands run down my bare arms until he's gripping my waist again, pulling me up against his impressive erection.

"*Please.*"

Holy. Shit.

The moment I have been waiting for my whole life. Dreamed about. Fantasized about. Hoped for.

Now.

It's happening.

Now.

His tongue trails up my neck to my ear, driving me insane with longing, like he's trying to make sure there is no way I will say no. I can turn him down. Be proper like he always says or I can throw caution to the wind and take a chance.

A dangerous one.

But one I want more than anything else in the world.

My hips rub up against his erection answering his request before I can form the words. I hear his hiss of desire before his strong hand envelopes mine and he leads me off the dance floor.

Is he taking me to his place?

The faces around me are blurred together as he pulls me through the club.

"Can we get my coat…" I remember my things, asking him to stop to get them. "My purse…"

He ignores my words as he expertly navigates his way through the club until we're down a dark hallway that is practically devoid of people. Before I know what's coming he pushes me up against the wall, lifts my hands over my head and his beautiful mouth, those gorgeous lips I remember so well, come crashing down onto mine.

The instant his lips touch mine all the pent-up desire I've had for him over the years unleashes like an exploding dam. I open my mouth as his tongue sweeps in possessively and gives me life. He groans into me, his hands reach down and cup my ass as he grinds his erection into my core. I move against him, wanting to feel more, wanting him to be inside me more than I've ever wanted anything in life. My emotions are wild and unsure but my body—my body knows exactly what it wants.

And it's him.

I tug on his hair and move my lips over his. My tongue mates with his as he explores every crevice, brushing against the inside of my mouth. I'm swollen, wet with desire, an insatiable fire that only Michael can appease. He drives his hardness against me, rubbing slowly and I groan with need. I push my breasts against his chest, my nipples hardening in reaction, my body primed and ready to go.

Michael rips his lips away from mine and as he presses kisses on the side of my face, my neck, any piece of unclothed skin he can find.

"Abby…" His voice is heavy with need. "You taste too good."

I move my mouth to his neck, reciprocating the action. His skin tastes like heaven to me, that heady masculine smell of his overwhelming any grip on sanity I might have. My hands brush over his wide back, and I revel in the pleasure from finally being able to touch him.

I want him naked.

I want to explore that beautiful body of his freely.

And I want him inside me.

"I want to go home with you." The words sound like they've been ripped from my soul.

I feel his entire body tense when he hears my words, and he pulls away from me so he can stare down at me in hunger.

God.

Just to see this look in his eyes. To know it's just for me gives me a sense of power I've never felt before in my life. My fingers move to my lips and they feel raw and swollen. I want more.

"We're leaving," Michael says as he looks over my face possessively.

"Yes."

He takes my hand in his and leads me back through the club. We pass people in the hall who were probably witness to our display of carnal lust, but I feel no shame in it. This is it.

Finally.

We make it back to the booth and I'm relieved Jack and Jennifer are not there. I assume they went back to the dance floor, but I don't even care. Michael flags down the VIP waitress and hands her his credit card while I grab my jacket and handbag.

Michael's gaze finds mine and my body trembles in anticipation at the hungry look he gives me.

The waitress comes back with the bill and Michael signs for it quickly. He holds out his hand for me and I gladly take it.

"Ready?" he asks.

You have no idea.

"Yes."

We walk through the club and when we pass the ladies room, I tug on his hand. Michael looks down at me.

"I need a moment," I tell him shyly.

"I'll wait right over here."

I run into the restroom and make my way to one of the empty stalls. When I push the door open and sway my way inside, I realize the last shot of tequila might have been overkill. Oh well! I pull up my dress, sit down, and take out my cell phone from my purse.

I text as fast as I can and send off the message to Georgie.

ME: OMG!

He writes back fast.

Georgie: I'm afraid to ask.

I giggle out loud.

ME: You're going to die!

I watch the bubble come up as Georgie types.

Georgie: I'm waiting...

ME: Michael.

Georgie: Please tell me you're not stalking him at some dinner date you had to schedule :/

I shake my head like he's in front of me but then remember I'm in the bathroom stall. Since typing is taking a lot of effort, I decide it's a good idea to FaceTime him.

Georgie is bare-chested and in bed when he answers. I'm smiling like a lunatic when his face finally comes into focus.

The tequila is definitely doing its job.

"You're smashed," Georgie says as he takes in the scenario. "And you're on the toilet, Abby."

I wave him off. I think my hand is moving in slow motion, but I really can't be sure.

"It's tequila," I admit.

"Do I need to send a car for you?" Georgie asks and I burst out laughing when I watch him lift a glass of champagne off his dresser and take a sip. "Have you thrown up yet?"

"I don't throw up!" I sputter in outrage.

"You might." Georgie's voice is knowing.

"That's for amateurs," I tell him like I'm some seasoned tequila drinker—which I'm not by the way.

Georgie doesn't look like he believes me.

"So what is so important that you felt the need to text me at twelve thirty in the morning?"

"Is that how late it is?" I ask in horror.

"Yes," Georgie replies then moves the phone so I can see a very naked man lying in bed next to him. "You're lucky Stefan is passed out."

"He looks hot," I say, staring at Stefan's impressive muscles.

Georgie really does have good taste.

"Of course he is." Georgie sighs as if that should be a given. "Now tell me before I hang up on you. I was about to wake Stefan up again and take part in that good deed you haven't had for a very long time, *ma chère*, and probably don't even remember how to do."

"That's so nice." I hope my smile isn't too goofy. "But I'm about to go there."

"Go where?"

"To bed with Michael," I whisper.

"Jesus, Abby," Georgie says with a laugh. "I think the whole restroom might have heard that."

"I know. But it doesn't matter. Did *you* hear me?"

"How? When?" Georgie rushes out. *"How?"*

"He asked me out on a date... I think I forgot to tell you that part." I start to ramble and tell him the story in what I hope is a linear way.

When I'm done, Georgie is laughing.

"Finalement!" he shouts in joy and I hear Stefan mumble something next to him.

"Right?" I tell him, nodding my head in happiness.

"Oui," Georgie says. "Go get to it, my love. I'll be waiting anxiously in the morning for all the details."

"I love you!" I think I shout that part again, but I don't care.

We hang up, and I finish up in the bathroom and make my way to the mirror to freshen up as fast as I can. I hope I haven't been gone for too long.

The face that looks back at me is one I haven't seen in a long while. My blue eyes are bright with desire, my lips swollen from Michael's wild kisses, and my skin has a healthy flush that only passion brings. I run a hand through my disheveled hair and put on some lipgloss, even though I know it's bound to be kissed away in the very near future. The thought thrills me.

Am I about to be another notch on Michael's belt? *Possibly.*

Do I care at this moment? *Not really.*

When I'm done, I take a steadying breath and walk out of the bathroom expecting to see Michael waiting for me, but he's nowhere to be found. I walk through a crowd of people and when I still can't find him I move back closer to where the restroom is, hoping I'll spot him.

Unfortunately, he's not who I find.

"I didn't believe Clive when he said it was you."

Talk about buzzkill.

My stepbrother Davis is standing in front of me with that god-awful shit-eating grin of his that I can't stand. He looks terrible and completely worn out. His receding hairline and potbelly don't help the situation at all.

"It's me," I reply coldly.

Davis and I barely speak to each other. In fact, the last time I saw him was before my almost wedding. The God's honest truth is that I'd be happy if I never saw him again. His slimy friend Clive comes to stand next to him. I don't appreciate the way he looks me up and down, like I'm some tasty piece of meat he's about to have a piece of.

He's always given me the creeps.

"Abby," Clive leers.

"Clive," I force myself to respond to him.

"I told you it was her," Clive says to my stepbrother. "I could recognize that hot little bum of hers from a lineup."

"Wonderful," I say coldly. "Now if you'll excuse me and my bum—"

Davis reaches out and grabs my arm before I can make my exit.

"Are you fucking Michael Sinclair?"

I react as though I've been slapped and jerk my arm out of Davis' grasp.

"How dare you speak to me that way," I hiss at him as Clive continues to smile at me with bloodshot eyes.

Davis grabs hold of my arm again and yanks on it.

"Answer the question, little sister," he says in disgust. "Are you another one of his girls? Have you been Sinclaired?"

"Sinclaired?" I repeat in horror.

"Fucked by a Sinclair," Clive enlightens me with that piece of information.

"That question is absolutely none of your business," I tell him and try to tug my arm out of his painful grip. " Now let go of me!"

"We saw you on the dance floor," Clive chimes in, looking at me in a way that makes my skin crawl. "Acting like a whore. Funny, I never took you for one."

Even though what these two think of me is the last thing I should care about, I feel my flush of embarrassment.

I'm mortified they saw us in such an intimate way.

It's unfortunate how sobriety likes to kick in at the most inopportune times.

"If you think you can hurt me, you're sadly mistaken."

Davis' grip on my arm tightens as his eyes narrow in anger.

"I asked you to let go of me." I meet Davis' gaze head-on. "What I do is none of your business."

"It is my business when you keep making a fool of yourself," Davis sneers. "You're dragging the family name through the mud with all of your antics."

"The last time I checked my name is Walters, not Sinclair," I remind him.

"Semantics. Isn't one embarrassing relationship enough for you?" Davis ignores my words and continues on with his jabs. "At least the Russian was going to marry you. Michael is just going to use you until he's bored."

I shouldn't care.

I shouldn't care what he thinks. Or says.

But his jab hurts because the fear of it actually becoming a reality is too much to bear. The truth is, my horrible brother could be right.

"Well that's just my choice, isn't it?" I reply coldly.

"I never thought you would stoop to this level," Davis continues harshly. "But someone is going to have to stop you from embarrassing yourself any further."

"Spare me the fake brotherly devotion." I roll my eyes. "I don't need you or anyone else telling me what I can do or who I can see."

"And how would your lovely mother feel about that?"

His comment makes me laugh. Like really, laugh.

"If you think after everything I've been through I actually care you're a bigger moron than I took you for." I smile at him in disbelief.

After everything, I can't believe he really thinks her opinion matters to me.

"Now let me go before I scream bloody murder," I tell him harshly.

Davis takes my warning to heart and finally releases my arm, but being the giant ass that he is, shoves me away with such force I would have lost my balance and hit the floor if it wasn't for the rock-solid chest that I fall into instead. Strong arms wrap around my waist to keep me steady.

"What's going on here?" I hear Michael's voice.

Of course it's him. Just my luck.

I turn slightly and grip his arms as they tighten around me.

I don't have to turn around to know he's angry. I can feel it on him. His muscles are taut, the energy coming from him, volatile.

"Nothing," I rush to tell him.

I turn in his arms and cringe when I see the furious look on his face.

Since childhood, Michael and Davis have never got on and it all stemmed from the moment Michael defended me by punching Davis in the face. Since that time the two have always hated one another.

"We just ran into each other," I say, putting my hands on his chest. I can feel his heart pulsing rhythmically. There is a fierce, possessive intensity in his eyes when he looks down at me and I'm not going to lie, it gives me a rush. It makes me feel safe.

And protected.

"Are you planning on ruining Abby's reputation even more?" Davis sneers at Michael to my horror.

"Excuse me?" There's a warning in Michael's voice.

But Davis doesn't seem to notice or care.

"She's already fucked up her reputation enough as it is because of that fiancé of hers," he continues on to my dismay, his words sounding slurred. "Leaving him at the altar, like she did. And now *you*. Sleeping with you won't help what's left of it."

I close my eyes when I hear Davis' words. I wish I could beat him to a bloody pulp. Why does he always have to be so cruel and say the most hurtful things?

More importantly, why does he have to be here right now?

Here in the moment that should be the most exciting of my life.

I suffered through an entire childhood with him torturing me, wasn't that enough for a lifetime? I promise myself I'm going to have some words with God once I can think clearly.

In the meantime, I hold on to Michael like my life depends on it. The last thing I want is for him to get into a brawl with my hideous stepbrother.

But I can tell he has a different idea.

He starts to peel my hands off his body.

"Step aside, Abby." His voice is so cold, so filled with rage, that I almost feel sorry for Davis.

Almost.

"Please," I beg him as I stare up at him. "Don't do this. He's not worth it. He's *so* not worth it."

He ignores my words, grabs hold of my hands and forcefully pushes me behind his back. I close my eyes in dread when I watch him walk up to Davis and Clive with a rage I've never seen before in my life. He ignores Clive like he's some meaningless ant and grabs hold of Davis by the neck and shoves him right up against the wall.

A crowd begins to form around us.

"If you ever, *ever*, put your hands on Abby again, I'll kill you," Michael hisses the words at my stepbrother, holding on to his choke grip for a moment longer before shoving him against the wall one more time and then letting him go as if he's diseased.

His gaze then moves to Clive and the look he gives him scares me.

Not one word is exchanged but Clive knows.

The message is for him as well.

"Michael," I call out, wanting to get his volatile energy away from my spineless stepbrother. I want to tell him that Davis has done much worse to me in the past and this is really not a big deal, but I have a feeling it will only serve to exasperate the situation.

I look at him and can feel him trying to control his emotions.

Like he's some boxer about to rip his opponent to shreds.

I've never seen him like this before.

"What's going on here?" A giant security guard finally makes his way to us and walks over to stand next to Michael. "Mr. Sinclair?"

It takes a full minute before Michael finally answers.

"We're good, Jimmy," Michael says to the security guard, who he obviously knows. "My cousin and I just had to come to an understanding."

"You need me to take care of anything?" Jimmy asks, staring at Davis in an intimidating way.

My stepbrother looks scared. I can't help but smile. It feels good to see him feeling so panicked. The bully finally having the tables turned on him.

"No," Michael says. "We're good."

Michael turns around then and makes his way over to me. He grabs hold of my hand and all but drags me out of the club. I can feel the aggression oozing from him. He's still angry and I'm pretty sure he really wanted to punch my stepbrother soundly in the face. I would have enjoyed seeing it, but not at the expense of Michael ending up in trouble, or worse, hurt.

I remain silent as Michael grabs his cell phone from his pocket and dials a number.

"We're finished here, Simon. Pick us up in the back," he barks out the order and shoves his phone back in his front pocket.

He leads me to the back alleyway of the club where I assume

we'll be waiting for Simon and before I know what's coming, he spins me around and pulls me up against his body so his lips can devour mine.

Fuck. Me.

He clutches me tightly as his tongue dives hard into my mouth. His hand wraps around my hair and he pulls my face up to his, while his other hand cups my ass and lifts me off the ground so that his hips can grind up against mine. My nipples harden as my breasts press up against his sinewy chest. I'm moaning in no time. My hands are clutching his hair, pulling him in closer so I can drink from the well he's offering.

"Fuck!" he hisses before ripping his lips away.

I'm in a daze of desire and it takes me a minute to realize he saw the headlights from Simon's car coming straight for us.

"You make me forget myself." His tone is almost accusatory.

The Range Rover rolls right up to us and Michael opens the door for me.

I glance up at him before I get in and notice how he still looks pretty furious. And completely turned on.

A lethal combination.

Immense satisfaction comes over me knowing that it was my fingers that messed up his hair.

I get inside the car and move to the far end to make room for Michael, but he doesn't get in the back with me.

To my surprise, he sits up front with Simon.

"You remember how to get to Abby's house," Michael says to Simon.

What. Is. Going. On.

I don't understand.

I thought we were going back to his place? What has just happened here? Did Davis just manage to ruin yet another thing in my life for me?

Since I'm now confident in knowing that Michael wants me just as badly, I decide to test the waters.

"Michael?" I know he can hear the confusion in my voice.

He turns quickly and pins me with his stormy gaze.

"The night is done."

And just like that, all my dreams are crushed.

CHAPTER SEVEN

To say I cried my way through the weekend would be the understatement of the century.

Not only did I wallow in self-pity over what I now saw as a disastrous Friday night date with Michael, but I also consumed enough calories in two days to feed a family of five. Postmates had become my new best friend and I had gone to town ordering food at every hour and allowing myself to gorge on anything my heart desired.

But I didn't care. Food was the only comfort I had at this moment in my life.

I wished I had never called Georgie in my drunken stupor from the bathroom at the club because he called and texted all weekend long, wanting to hear all the details. I had not wanted to share the sad news with him. Instead, I texted him that everything was good and I would call him on Monday. He hadn't been thrilled with my response, but I was sure he just assumed I was staying over at Michael's having the best time—aka sex—of my life.

Too bad that hadn't been the case.

There were a lot of hard truths I had to come to face in my time alone in those forty-eight hours of hell.

One.

I despised Davis. Like wished-his-body-would-be-consumed-by-a-tribe-of-cannibals despised.

Two.

Michael Sinclair had magically achieved the impossible without even being my boyfriend—breaking my heart. Shattering it, to be exact. His rejection of me was one that would live vividly in my mind for years to come.

When he had seen me up to my flat without so much as a kiss on the cheek goodbye, I had stood there by my door for a long while trying to comprehend the change of events—and the change in his feelings. The only logical conclusion I could come up with was he had been so smashed at the club that he hadn't realized what he had been doing.

Every perceived look, touch, glance... all of that had obviously been in my head and wishful thinking on my part. My delusional self —probably a third personality that I had been unaware of until now —had tricked rational Abby into believing, *hoping* that there was something more between us.

Nothing else made any sense.

Three.

I was going to quit my new job.

Surprisingly, I was upset about having to do this for reasons that were not just about my feelings for Michael, but because I was genuinely starting to enjoy being part of the non-profit work. But what choice did I have? How could I torture myself by working for him?

Especially now?

I didn't even know how I was going to face him.

So I had my plan, and instead of obsessing about how I would react when I saw him on Monday morning, I chose to stick my face in a gallon of chocolate gelato and let the sugar do its magic trick.

***

Why didn't I bring the flask to work like I originally planned?

I ponder this question for the thousandth time when I walk through the office on Monday morning, bloated and ready for what-ever was going to come my way. For my first order of business, I knock on Mrs. Lions' office door.

"May I come in?" I ask, motioning to the seat across from her.

She nods. "Please."

I decide not to mince words.

"I'm quitting."

Mrs. Lions looks at me in complete shock.

"What?" she says, shaking her head in disbelief. "You just started. And you seemed to be doing so well. I thought you and Danielle got on really well."

"It's not Danielle."

"Then what is it?"

"It's Michael," I admit. "Mr. Sinclair. We're just not a right fit."

I'm impressed by my boldness, but then, what do I have to lose at this point? I'm quitting, and this job will be but a fleeting moment in my life.

From the look on Mrs. Lions' face, it seems she's just as surprised as I am by my comment.

"I see," she says when she's finally able to speak.

"I know you'll have to talk to Mr. Sinclair about it and I'm pretty sure he won't disagree. He might even be relieved."

Mrs. Lions can't seem to find the words to reply, so I continue.

"Of course, I'd like to stay a few days to help Danielle out in any way I can."

Danielle has been nothing but nice and helpful to me since I arrived, and I consider her a friend. The last thing I want to do is add more stress to her plate.

Regardless, I'm pretty sure she won't take me leaving too well.

"I see," Mrs. Lions says again.

I wait for something more, but she continues to stare at me in uncomfortable silence.

"I guess I should thank you for your candor, Abigail."

I smile awkwardly.

"So what's the next step?" I ask anxiously. "Do I need to sign anything?"

"I'll have a talk with Mr. Sinclair and then get back to you sometime today," Mrs. Lions says. "I don't believe he's in yet."

"He's not. He has a few morning meetings but should be here by noon."

Right when I'll be taking my lunch.

Not that I'll be eating anything but ice chips after the weekend I had, but still, I am going to do the best I can to avoid him for the rest of the time I'm here.

And the rest of my life, for that matter.

"All right then." Mrs. Lions sighs and then gives me a stern look. "Let's reconvene at five o'clock after Mr. Sinclair and I have talked."

"Perfect."

I leave Mrs. Lions and walk over to the commissary to grab a cup of coffee. After I'm done there, I make my way to Danielle to say hello and ask if she'd like to have lunch so I can break the news to her on my own, before I finally make my way back to my desk.

Michael's door is open.

My heart takes off at warp speed. I quickly try to calm myself.

It's still way too early for him to be in yet. And he *never* cancels a meeting. It must be the cleaning crew or IT.

I walk over to see who's inside.

"Tell me exactly what she said, Mrs. Lions."

I hear his voice bark from outside the office.

I freeze.

My heart rate starts thumping so fast I'm pretty sure I could be on the verge of a coronary attack. I look over at the clock. It's half past ten! He shouldn't be in for at least another two hours!

Fuck.

Fuck.

Fuck.

I immediately turn around in a panic and start walking in the opposite direction as everything blurs around me. Where should I hide? The bathroom? Downstairs? I can go for a cigarette break even though I don't smoke and just sit out there for a while.

No one will think to look for me there.

I tell myself I just need a minute to gather my senses—that it has nothing to do with actually being afraid to face Michael.

Liar, my inner voice says as she chooses that moment to make another untimely appearance.

My face begins to perspire, my breathing has become erratic and I find myself looking for the nearest exit. I just need to go and sit somewhere and take in some deep calming breaths before I face my tormentor.

"Abigail!" Michael's bellow echoes through the room.

Every single person who works in the godforsaken Think Tank looks up in shock. Like they just heard Parliament has declared war.

Clearly, this is something out of the ordinary.

I stop walking. And turn ever so slightly to look at him.

He's wearing scuffed up jeans that fall low on his waist and an inappropriately tight T-shirt that stretches out over that beautiful chest of his. Does he have to intentionally draw attention to himself?

And why do I even have to notice?

Then I notice a few other things—like how he hasn't shaved and how he looks so tired.

And mad.

Really, *really* mad.

"Inside my office," he barks at me as I face the fire shooting out of his cerulean eyes. "Now!"

There is a collective gasp in the room.

I'm mortified so many people are witness to my humiliation.

Lucky me.

I look over at the group and try to smile as though I'm unaffected, but it's really hard. And I'm pretty sure I've failed miserably at it. Michael turns around and walks inside his office before I reach his door.

I stop at my desk to grab his calendar before I go in, but I'm stopped by another shout.

"You don't need the damn calendar!"

I'm pretty sure everyone hears that order as well. I rush into his office before he can bark out another order.

"Shut the door." His voice is cold.

He's standing with his back to me, facing the window.

I do as he says and it takes all my willpower to try to remain unaffected by his anger or the embarrassing way he just spoke to me in front of his employees. When he finally turns to face me I'm shocked by the rage I see in his eyes.

What did I do to deserve that look from him?

He is the one who is so in the wrong here, not me.

I was only trying to rectify what would surely become a very toxic situation.

I realize two things very quickly. I can either play the hurt, snubbed girl pining away after his affection—*which I am*—or I can be my cool, unaffected self. The exterior persona I've worn almost my whole life.

I choose the latter.

"Has someone died?" I bite out sharply.

My question seems to take some of the wind out of his sails.

"I'm sorry?"

"Died," I repeat.

"No." He shakes his head. "No one has died."

"Have I ruined a deal for you?"

"What?" Michael seems confused then shakes his head again. "No."

"Then what reason would you have to ever speak to me like that in front of your employees?" I ask him icily. "What can *I* have possibly done to deserve that treatment?"

His eyes flicker down, and I think he might be apologetic about his behavior, but then he looks back up at me with an indecipherable look on his face.

And the shift in power comes again.

"I see the Ice Princess has reared her ugly head."

"Excuse me?" I lift a brow and stare at his handsome face.

"The proper, *icy* Abigail."

My hands ball in fists at my sides.

"You have no right to call me names!"

"I can do as I damn well please," he responds arrogantly.

I count to ten before I speak.

"Just what is going on here? What was that about out there, Michael?"

"You saw Mrs. Lions."

"And?"

"And?" He approaches me and stops so close, I can feel the heat coming from his body.

"You want to quit."

"Yes, I do." I raise my chin in defiance.

"The answer is no," he growls. "I don't accept your resignation."

"I don't think you have a choice." *What the hell?*

"Actually, you're wrong. I do have a choice." The smile he gives me doesn't quite reach his eyes. "You signed a lot of paperwork when you began working for me."

"And?"

"My PA needs one month's notice to terminate the job unless, of course, I fire her."

The wind leaves my sails.

Why didn't I read the fine print? What the hell was I thinking?

"How convenient for you," I finally manage to mutter.

"Yes, it is. So if you feel the same way thirty days from now, we can have this discussion again."

"I know I will feel the same way, so there is no discussion to be had. Consider this my one month's notice."

"We'll see."

If I had my coffee in my hand, I'd probably end up throwing all of the contents on his gorgeous face.

"We will not *see*," I hiss at him. "I know what I want."

"Do you?" His voice is husky when he whispers back at me. He takes another dangerous step closer to my body.

"Don't you dare," I say to him, lifting my hand up in defense. "Don't you dare turn this around on me."

Michael stops and stares at me in that way of his that makes me ache so badly to have him it should be a crime.

"I'm not letting you quit because of the other night."

I hate him.

Hate.

Love.

Him.

"This isn't about the other night," I blatantly lie to his face. I'm pretty sure I'm blushing.

"We kissed. Big deal. It happens."

Hate him.

I hate him.

"Wonderful," I reply as emotionlessly as possible. "Regardless, I'm not going to be your toy. I won't allow you to play games with me. And that's what you're doing. We both know it, and I dare you to deny it to my face."

My words seem to anger him. His eyes become hooded and he takes another step closer to me. I swear we'll be on top of each other in no time.

"I told you I don't play games."

"I think we should just agree to disagree on that point." I let him hear my anger. "Now if you'll excuse me I have work to do."

I try to leave.

I do.

But when he reaches my side and grabs hold of my arm and I feel that touch of his, I can't move.

I don't *want* to move.

"Abby…" His voice sounds just as tortured as I feel. "It's not what you think."

I want to ask what it is then. But I have too much pride. And I already went down that road and it did not end too well for me.

I have to protect myself.

"It doesn't matter, Michael," I tell him, closing my eyes. Feeling defeated.

"Look at me." His voice is forceful.

I slowly open my eyes and stare up into his stormy gaze. I try to mask how hurt I am, but I'm pretty sure he can read it all over my face.

"It matters to me." His voice is husky.

My stomach drops at his unexpected words, and it takes every ounce of my willpower to stay strong. To find that icy shell he accuses me of wearing, and cloak my entire being with it.

"You probably saved us both the other night from making the biggest mistake of our lives." I'm surprised with how calm my voice is despite what I'm feeling inside.

I pull my arm away from his grasp and grab hold of the handle on the door. Michael comes up behind me and crowds my space, not allowing me to open it by putting his arm above my head and leaning down into my body.

I can feel his hard, sinewy length against mine. His face moves to my neck as he breathes me in. The ache for his touch is almost too much to bear.

"God, you smell so good."

His lips brush up against my skin and in less than a second I'm longing for him.

"Please," I practically beg and can feel his body tense up behind mine. He moves his hand around my waist and forcibly turns me around so that I have no other choice but to look up at him.

To see the desire in his eyes.

To feel it hard against my stomach.

His hands move up the waist of my dress and lightly skim over my nipples, and I moan in longing.

Literally, moan.

But when he tries to bring his lips down to mine I turn away.

"Please. Just let me go," I whisper.

And he does.

Just like that.

***

"Here you go. Two Pinot Grigios and a bottle of flat water," the waiter says to Danielle and me as he sets our drinks down at the table.

Once my drink is set down, I pick it up and take a long, satisfying sip.

"So are you going to tell me what the hell happened between you and Michael or am I just going to have to guess and come up with my own deductions?" Danielle asks as we sit across from each other at an Italian restaurant close by the office. "And just so you know, I have a really overactive imagination."

I lift my finger up indicating I need another second to swallow another sip of wine before I answer.

"Careful or you'll be smashed in no time," she warns, picking up her glass of wine.

"And?" I ask her.

"You'll get sacked."

I pick the glass up again and chug the contents before motioning to the waiter that I'd like another.

"Abby!" Danielle cries out in horror.

She pushes a glass of water in my hand.

"Drink this!" she orders me. "And answer my question."

I slump over the table and put my head in my hands. I think about lying, making up some story but then to what end? What's the point?

"I've been in love with Michael my whole life," I confide, wrapping my arms around myself. "And I've just realized this job might be equivalent to Chinese water torture for me. So I need to quit."

Danielle is suspiciously silent, so I look up and find that she doesn't seem at all surprised to hear my words.

"There's more to this story. And I want to hear it all."

So I tell her. Everything. Every detail. Everything.

She knows more than Georgie now.

After I'm done, she watches me with contemplation.

"Well first off, you can't quit."

"I've given him my one month's notice because he said that's what was in my contract."

"That's total rubbish, Abby!" Danielle rolls her eyes. "One month? I've never heard of such a thing."

"What?!"

"He's lying to you." Danielle shakes her head. "But I'd bet my life, he's probably gone in now and added some stipulation in your contract, after the fact, so you'll never know. Did you get a hard copy of it?"

I shake my head in shame.

"He—I just didn't," I tell her lamely. "I told Mrs. Lions to mail it to me sometime. I had no idea I'd ever be in a situation like *this*. Trust me, the lesson is learned."

"Even if you could find a way out, I wouldn't let you go," Danielle says. "Selfishly, I need you... I'm getting married in three months time for fuck's sake. You can't leave me."

It's hard not to smile at Danielle's indignant face.

"I mean, honestly," Danielle mutters. "How could you think to leave me like this? I'm already a nervous wreck as it is, this would only turn me into more of a bridezilla and then Tom might decide to leave me."

"That would never happen."

"Every single time I open one of my wedding folders around him, he leaves the room and says that I'm giving him hives," Danielle says seriously. "I think he might be catching on to how crazy I really am."

I burst out laughing and it doesn't take long before Danielle joins me.

"Okay," she says when she catches her breath. "And it's not just about me, I promise you."

I roll my eyes.

"Too late."

"I'm serious." Danielle laughs. "From everything you've just told me, I think you might be reading this all wrong. With Michael, that is."

"How so?" I ask, picking up my second glass of wine. Danielle's withering look makes me put it right back down.

"Abby, I swear to you… I've never seen him lose his temper like that. Like ever. He's so cool. Even in school. He's never lost it. And over a woman? I never thought it would be possible and honestly, I was starting to worry about him. And with you of all people? You couldn't hurt a fly."

"Maybe I just bring out the worst in him," I mutter.

"No way." She shakes her head. "You know that's not true. There's something between you guys. I swear I've noticed it, but you get so shy and nervous that I didn't want to bring it up to you."

Danielle's words give me hope.

But then I remember Friday night and I quickly squash that emotion.

"Look." I sigh. "It doesn't matter what you think or what I want. He told me what he wants—which is nothing. He basically told me that what happened between us was a mistake."

"That's just boys being stupid."

"Michael is not a boy," I say with another sigh.

Danielle lifts her brow.

"Abby," she says calmly. "All men are boys."

I can't help but laugh.

"That might be the case, but it still doesn't change anything."

"Just give it a minute, Abby," Danielle urges me. "Play it cool. And don't rush into any hasty decisions. You like your job. You like the work and it's a great company. This situation between you two will pass."

Maybe it will pass for him, but I'm another story altogether. I don't voice my thoughts to Danielle because I don't want to disappoint her. She's successfully guilted me into not leaving her right before the wedding.

I'll just have to wait and suffer through my feelings.

"We'll see," I finally say. "I'll stay until you're back from your honeymoon. It will give me time to look for a new job and just give me more experience."

"I'll fight that battle later," Danielle says triumphantly.

She lifts her glass up.

"I have a feeling things are going to get very interesting around the office."

When we get back to the office after our long lunch, I'm relieved to find out that Michael has left.

There is a sticky note on my computer with the following message:

Cancel everything for the week. I'm going offline and can't be reached.

– Michael

I take the note and show Danielle who seems to think that Michael disappearing is a good sign— that he must be confused about what happened between us. I don't know if I believe her, but I am grateful I won't have to face him for a few days.

With Michael's absence, I fall into a rhythm at work. After spilling the beans and revealing my secret crush to Danielle, the two of us have grown closer. We have lunch together every day and go to drinks after work a few times. I like her a lot. She's easy to talk to and carefree and she makes me laugh. Georgie joins us at lunch on one occasion and he and Danielle quickly bond.

Michael doesn't check in with me at all.

I know he's reached out to Danielle a few times because she told me he's been calling in, but he's avoided me at all costs. I've forwarded messages and sent daily email updates, but he hasn't responded. I can't say it doesn't hurt. Danielle thinks he took off to his home in Africa, but she's not sure. He hasn't offered up any information, and she doesn't ask.

I should be happy to have space from him. But I find myself staring at his office door and wishing he was inside to torment me. I find myself longing for our flirtations, for those looks of his that make my heart catch on fire. I find myself craving his energy. Michael's a force of nature, and even though he drives me crazy, I realize how much I like just being in his space. His world.

And at night…

At night I wonder if he's alone.

If he's with a woman.

If he's okay.

And if he misses me as much as I miss him.

CHAPTER EIGHT

"Truth or dare, Abby!" Corinne, my friend from secondary school, shouted at me in a drunken stupor.

I was sitting in a circle of fifteen or so people at a party some university students were throwing. Parents were out of town, and it had quickly become wild and out of control. Kids were partying hard and everyone was having the time of their life.

"Truth," I said shyly.

People from the group started shouting out a list of obscene sexual questions for Corinne to ask me but she waved them off in pleasure.

I waited in dread as she paused for a dramatic effect.

"Who was the last person you hooked up with?"

The room immediately fell silent as all eyes focused on me.

My body burned in humiliation. I knew I should have taken a dare, but I had been too scared about what they might make me do.

"Ummm..." I stalled for some time, thinking about how I should respond.

Secondary school had a way of making you feel insecure about every decision you made in your life. And there was nothing cool about my situation.

"The truth!" Corinne shouted out, riling everyone up.

"Truth! Truth! Truth!" the group began to chant.

The screams grew in a frenzy around me and before I knew what I was doing, I blurted out the truth.

"Never!" I shouted out to the group. "I've never even kissed anyone!"

The room went dead silent. Again.

I couldn't bear the looks of surprise and shock. Or the laughing *gazes of some of the girls who thought it was pathetic I was seven-teen and had never even had my first kiss, even though I was in Sixth Form.*

It was too much.

I ran out of the room and pushed my way through the maze of partygoers.

I made my way to the backyard where there weren't that many people and found a secluded area where I could hide from everyone.

But before I could relive the humiliating experience that I was sure would haunt me for the rest of my days, I heard the sound of a lighter. I turned to find a tall man hidden by the night shadows, standing alone in the darkness smoking a cigar. I hadn't noticed him when I came around the corner.

I was annoyed I wasn't alone and was about to leave before I heard...

"Is that you, Abby?"

My heart froze.

I would recognize that voice anywhere.

"Michael?" I asked in surprise, wiping my sweaty hands on my jeans.

"It's me."

My stomach danced in joy that he was here.

"What are you doing here?"

"I tagged along with some friends." Michael stepped out of the shadows to walk toward me.

He looked too good to be true.

His rugged looks were so much more appealing than any of the guys I went to school with. He was older. Seasoned. With a maturity that made him even better looking. There was a knowing look in his eyes.

About life.

And fun. Everything that was exciting...

Everything I craved.

"Does the smoke bother you?" he asked politely.

I shook my head. My body and brain were in chaos at just the sight of him. I couldn't believe he was actually standing in front of me.

He put out the cigar even though I really didn't mind it, then took a sip out the drink he had in his other hand.

"Is everything all right?" he asked as he studied my face.

"Why wouldn't it be?"

"You seem flustered." He knew me so well and must have been picking up on my energy.

"A little," I admitted the obvious.

"Only a few things could throw you off," he said with a knowing smile. "You've either had too much to drink, which thankfully doesn't seem like the case, or you ran into a guy you like…"

Just now I did, I thought to myself.

"Not quite," I said to him, my voice shy.

"Then?"

"We were playing truth or dare."

Michael's eyes darkened in anger.

"Did something happen?"

"No!" I rushed out. "I opted for a truth question and it was kind of embarrassing, so I had to leave."

"Why embarrassing?"

"I don't really want to talk about it." I bowed my head, not wanting to look him in the eye.

"Now I'm intrigued."

I was so embarrassed yet, my body was humming in excitement because of his close proximity.

"You can say anything to me, Abby." His voice was gentle. "I promise I won't tell anyone your secrets. You know you can trust me."

I looked up at him and the kindness I saw in his eyes was nearly my undoing. Later, when I would relive what happened a million times over in my head, I would remember the telltale signs of him being smashed—signs I should have noticed but had been too blinded to see.

The glassy look in his eyes.

The slight sway in his movements when he stepped closer to me. At the time, I had been too enamored to see it. Too thrilled to be in his company.

All I cared about was being in his world.

"So what truth did they ask you?" he asked again.

"They wanted to know when I had last been intimate with a man," I whispered to him, embarrassed to be repeating it.

My reply threw Michael. Like he couldn't believe someone would even ask me a question that was so sexual in nature.

I watched him take a step back from me. I felt his eyes move over my body as he studied me from head to toe.

Something around us shifted.

Like he was looking at me for the first time.

Not as a child...

But all grown-up.

There was a glimmer in his eyes, like he was intrigued by what he was seeing.

"And what was your answer?"

I looked up at him and watched how his eyes darkened, his gaze roaming over me in a way I had only dreamed about.

"Never."

I should have known.

When he put his cup down, I should have seen the signs but in my innocence, I had no idea what was coming for me.

"It's pathetic, I know."

"Not pathetic," he replied, shaking his head. "It's sweet. And innocent, like you."

I shrugged my shoulders uncomfortably, taken aback by his compliment.

"Would you like it to be different?" His voice was husky.

"What?" I asked, not following his question.

"Your level of experience."

"Of course I would!" I said, hoping I sounded mature and worldly. "But the opportunity has to be there."

"I won't believe you if you tell me you're not popular with the guys." Michael complimented me again as his gaze swept over me appreciatively. "You're too beautiful to go unnoticed."

Michael thought I was beautiful?

I was like a flower blooming under the rays of the sun. I wanted to shout out in joy. Michael Sinclair finding me attractive was everything I had ever wished for.

But I couldn't tell him I found the guys in my form immature. Lacking. Especially when I compared every single one of them to him.

"They're just not my type," I finally said.

"What's your type?"

You, I wanted to tell him. You are my type. But I didn't dare.

"I'll know when I see him," I said instead, staring boldly into his eyes.

Michael watched me for a long moment like he was weighing something in his head. I waited, holding my breath for his next move.

"What would you say if I could solve your problem and give you exactly what you want?" His voice was enigmatic, hypnotizing me.

"You?" I asked in confusion until reality slowly started to dawn on me.

"Yes," he replied as he pulled me close into his body. "Definitely. Me."

I didn't stand a chance.

One second I was the sad girl who'd never been kissed...

And the next, I was a woman awakened to a desire I would long for, crave, for every day after...

His full, sensual lips came down on mine, coaxing them softly, slowly teaching me how to respond to his gentle touch. His arms wrapped around my waist and pulled me against his hard body as continued to kiss me so sweetly.

He slowly pulled his lips away as I clung to his jacket.

It was the best moment of my life.

"That was my first kiss," I whispered innocently to him.

Michael rubbed his cheek against mine, breathing me in, causing butterflies to flutter around in my stomach.

"There's more to it." His voice was possessive, knowing.

"More?"

Whatever it was, I wanted it.

Something about the way I asked the question made him lose whatever control he was holding on to, and within seconds I was introduced to the full force of his passion.

"This. Is. More."

Before I knew what was happening, he lifted me up, pushed me against the brick wall of the pool house and proceeded to show me what sexual desire really meant.

His tongue swept into my mouth. He lifted my hands above my head as his lips captured mine, staking ownership on my soul. His tongue teased me, tormented me, turned my body on in ways I didn't even understand.

"Do you want more?" His words were husky, causing goose bumps to run all over my body as his lips continued to ravage me.

"Yes," I responded, barely able to think.

He took a shuddering breath and finally stepped away, giving us both distance to try to breathe normally again. Michael closed his eyes for a moment, like he was fighting for control.

When he opened them, I couldn't tell what he was thinking.

"Now you know."

Dreaming about Michael Sinclair all weekend does not help my mood come Monday morning. I do everything in my power to block any thoughts about him during the day, but at night when I fall asleep, I'm at the mercy of my free will.

I'm so wound up I decide to go to the office early and work on filling Michael's schedule with meetings and events that will keep him out of the office as much as humanly possible.

Since I'm so early, the office is thankfully empty. I have head-phones in and am listening to Harry Styles' album and am so in the zone, I fail to notice Michael walking into the office and coming straight to my desk.

My heart stops when I look up and find him standing there staring at me.

He looks good.

A bit thinner than normal, but he has a healthy glow, like he spent the week in the sun.

He's dressed in his usual uniform, jeans and a T-shirt.

Delicious.

I wish I didn't care.

But I do.

So do. I take off my headphones and meet his gaze.

"Hi," he says softly.

I think about our last conversation. It didn't end well. I'd like nothing more than to go at him some more. But no matter what happened between us, he's still my boss. And I promised myself I would be mature and rational. I could handle what happened between us. I was an adult. A professional.

"Hi."

"Can I see you in my office?" His voice is neutral, detached almost, and I can't tell what he's thinking.

"Of course," I reply briskly, as I stand up and grab my binder.

My heart races erratically as he follows me into his office. His energy is so tightly wound up I can feel him struggle for control.

He shuts the door as I make my way to stand in front of his desk.

"Have a seat," he tells me.

"If you don't mind, I'd prefer to stand," I reply curtly. I'd like to keep the advantage.

"I'd prefer you to sit," Michael commands, ignoring my wishes.

Of course you do.

I take a deep breath in to force myself not to argue with him. I sit down and wait. My heart gives a wild kick and it takes everything I have to pretend like I'm completely unaffected by him. I pray he can't tell what he's doing to me.

How hurt I am by his rejection.

How devastated I've been since he's been gone.

How sitting across from him now makes me feel like I'm lost and found at the same time.

"How are you?"

How am I? Logically, I know it's the polite way to start a conversation, but the irrational part of me is angry he's asking.

How does he think I am?

"As well as can be expected," I say, meeting his bright blue gaze. "And you?"

"Same."

Wonderful.

"I appreciated your daily updates while I was away," he continues in an emotionless voice. "They were thorough."

"I'm glad you liked them."

There's another uncomfortable silence and Michael sighs.

"Abby," he begins slowly. "I had a lot of time to think…"

My heartbeat picks up its pace.

"And you were right."

I don't think I've ever felt so sick as I wait for him to continue.

"My behavior was inexcusable," he goes on to my shock. "And unprofessional. I apologize if I hurt you."

If anything, his apology makes me feel worse than before. It's like we're having a "let's break up" conversation and we're not even together.

"I need you here this month." Michael's voice is calm as he goes on. "Especially with Danielle's wedding coming up—I'm sure I don't need to tell you how wound up she is over it… but if you want to leave after that, you can. I won't stop you."

I'm surprised by how hurt I am from his words even though he's giving me exactly what I asked for.

The pit in my stomach is almost too much to bear.

"Perfect," I force myself to say as I wait for him to continue and address the rest—the kiss, the intimacy we shared. I fully expect him to go there.

But he doesn't.

"Great," Michael says abruptly as he makes his way to his desk.

I stay seated for a moment.

"You can go back to your desk," Michael says excusing me as he clicks his mouse to look at his computer.

I watch as he runs a rough hand through his hair and it's at that moment that I finally notice how stressed out he actually looks.

And tired.

Even though I'm still angry and hurt by him, I can't stop myself from caring.

"Is everything all right?" I ask as I slowly stand up.

Michael looks up at me and I can't tell what he's thinking.

"Why wouldn't it be?" he returns, making me feel almost foolish for asking.

"I don't know. You seem off, but I guess I'm mistaken. Sorry I asked."

I turn abruptly and make my way to the door, angry that I cared enough to go there with him.

"It's my brother." His voice is low.

I stop, responding to the pain I hear in his voice.

"William?" I say in understanding as I slowly turn to look at him.

"Yes," Michael says with a sad smile. "Sometimes… sometimes his death just hits me hard. For being the youngest, he always seemed to have it all together. More than Clayton and me. We were always so protective of him. We weren't ready for this. "

His ability to express his pain over his brother's loss makes my heart swell in tenderness. It's not an easy thing to do, and I know from first-hand experience.

"Everyone loved him," I tell him. "He was such a good man."

Michael closes his eyes and nods.

"It shouldn't have been him," he finally says, his voice tortured.

"Unfortunately, we're not given a choice," I say softly, understanding the depth of his pain. "It's the worst part about life."

I wish I could walk over and pull him in arms and take away his sadness. I know what loss feels like. I've lived with it my whole life.

"It is," Michael agrees and fixes me with a sympathetic look. "And you know it well."

I feel the familiar lump in my throat whenever someone brings up the fact that I grew up without my father.

"Can I get you anything?" I ask him quietly just wanting to escape the sympathy I see in his eyes.

"I'm all right, thank you," Michael replies politely.

I nod in acknowledgment then turn to leave.

"Abby?" Michael calls out.

I stop when I reach his door.

"There's one more thing…"

"Yes?" I turn around to look at him.

"I don't consider anything that's happened between us a mistake."

***

"What were his exact words?" Danielle asks in excitement as we sit huddled in her office.

"I just told you!" I tell her again as I take a bite of the giant slice of chocolate cake I bought for lunch.

"This is just too good!" she says, shaking her head in happiness.

"How is this good?" I ask in bewilderment, my mouth so full I'm sure Danielle can barely make out my words. "Why would he even say that to me? What is he trying to do… completely ruin my emotional health?"

"Probably," Danielle says as she sets her salad down and gets up.

She presses a button behind her desk and the blinds slide down her office windows so no one can see inside.

I watch her curiously.

"Stand up." Her voice is commanding as she crosses her arms.

"Why?" I ask mid-bite.

"Put that caloric nightmare down and stand up." Danielle shakes her head in admonishment. "For God's sake Abby, women usually can't eat when they're so wound up emotionally! I've never met anyone like you before. It's like you're just the opposite."

"I know," I tell her guiltily. "I like to eat my feelings. It's a real problem."

I put the cake down and slowly stand up.

Danielle gives me the once over and sighs.

"This will not do at all," she finally says.

"What?"

"First, wipe the chocolate crumbs from your lips," she snaps out like a general.

Embarrassed, I quickly do as she says.

"Sorry," I mumble.

"Just stand still and let me work my magic for a second. It won't take much."

Danielle smoothes out my knee-length black fitted skirt, like she's dusting it off for crumbs, then proceeds to unbutton the top three buttons of my white shirt.

"What are you doing?" Embarrassed, I try to cover up my chest.

"Showing off some of your incredible assets," she tells me, swatting my hand away. "It's about time you make yourself known in this office. You're single and available."

"I don't want to be known—" I argue.

"Too bad," she snaps back at me.

For the next fifteen minutes, Danielle proceeds to ignore all my protests and gives me an office makeover. She takes my hair out of the tight bun and brushes the mahogany strands out. Then she pulls out her small makeup bag and proceeds to apply eyeliner, mascara, blush, and lip gloss. More makeup than I usually ever wear to the office.

"You have the most beautiful blue eyes," Danielle compliments me.

"Come on," I argue, rolling my eyes.

"I'm serious," Danielle continues. "You don't know how pretty you are. You've been hiding from yourself for so long, immersed in a little bubble that you've created... it's enough. It's time Abby comes out and joins the rest of the world."

Danielle holds a small mirror up so I can study her handiwork.

I recognize the face that looks back at me.

But I don't.

Danielle didn't overdo it with the makeup, she just lightly accentuated all my features. Made them more pronounced. My blue eyes, more vivid. My lips, more full. My cheekbones look high and full of color.

The top of my blouse, now unbuttoned, only shows a hint of cleavage, just enough to give a man something to think about.

To entice.

And I like it.

"Nothing too extreme," she tells me as she admires her work. "But enough to drive a man wild."

She winks when she says the last bit.

"Now we're going to have some fun."

I was warned.

But I had no idea what Danielle's game was until later in the day.

I leave her office a while later, hungry still because Danielle threw out the rest of my cake, refusing to let me continue my sugar pig-fest. Michael was gone on a long lunch and I was soon too wrapped up in work to really obsess about when he'd be back. Danielle's plan seemed to work.

When I made my way around the office on my usual errands, I noticed the appreciative looks from the men. Lyle from IT, stopped me and struck up a conversation, even an intern named David found an excuse to start talking to me. If anything, the attention gives me confidence, a needed boost to my self-esteem and I'm grateful for it.

It's late in the day when Michael finally comes back to the office. As usual, he stops to chat in the Think Tank before making his way back to his room. I watch him for a moment as he smiles amicably at the group. He exudes confidence and power, demanding respect just by being in the room.

And then there's the other part of him.

The sensitive side that he revealed when speaking to me about his brother. The side that causes him to defend a little girl being bullied by her stepbrother. The part that makes him more human, just like the rest of us. Another facet to his personality that makes the entire package even more appealing.

It takes everything I have to look away and try to focus on my work.

But then I feel that damn pull.

And I know his focus is now directed at me.

As if on cue, I glance up from the computer screen and our eyes lock. For a moment he looks surprised, then it quickly changes to something else. I watch as his gaze smolders in desire, sweeping over me in appreciation, causing chills to race up and down my spine.

My mouth goes dry and I'm longing for him in seconds.

Before I know it, he's standing right in front of my desk, his eyes no longer on my face but on my cleavage that Danielle was so anxious to expose. My breasts take on a mind of their own and act as though he's physically touching me.

My nipples harden.

Lord.

He notices.

I watch Michael's jaw flex before his gaze slowly moves up to rest on my parted lips and finally my eyes.

I hate myself for not being able to hide how I feel about him. To hide what he does to me. To my composure. To my emotions.

To my body.

"Abby." His voice is like sex to my ears. "Any messages?"

"It's been quiet," I tell him, trying to calm my suddenly racing heart.

Before Michael can respond, Danielle comes to stand next to him.

"Hi, Michael," her voice is cheerful as she smiles at the two of us. "How was your lunch meeting with Jim?"

"Boring."

"I can't say I'm surprised. He's always been a bit of a pill," Danielle says with a laugh, then points at me like a proud mother. "So what do you think of Abby's makeover?"

I narrow my eyes at Danielle trying to communicate telepathically not to embarrass me.

"Your handiwork?" Michael lifts a surprised brow at Danielle as she nods on in pleasure.

"Yes." She smiles, winking at me.

Michael turns his gaze back to mine and I try to act like his perusal isn't turning my insides to mush.

"We're meeting Tom and some of his friends tonight at a pub," Danielle tells him to my horror. "I'm trying to get Abby to come out of her shell. Don't you think it's time she gets out there and starts dating? She's too pretty and sweet to be single."

What is she saying?

"Danielle!" I let out an exasperated sigh.

"What?" Danielle gives me an innocent look, but I know better. "Michael's your *cousin*. We're allowed to talk like this. And besides, I'm sure he agrees with me."

I can barely manage to look at him for his reaction.

"Don't you, Michael?" Danielle presses him for a response.

Michael's eyes flicker over me, his jaw tight, before settling on Danielle.

"I'm sure his friends will be enamored," he finally says in a cold voice, his face expressionless. "Now if you'll excuse me, I have work to do."

Danielle watches Michael head into his office and shut the door behind him. When he's safely out of sight, she turns and gives me a devilish smile.

"That'll drive him crazy," she beams.

"You're insane!" I whisper to her. "He doesn't care—"

"Oh, he does," Danielle says knowingly as she stares at his office.

"I think you're wrong. And when did we make any plans for the evening?"

"I did for us," Danielle's voice is sugary sweet. "And I'm not letting you back out. We are going out for drinks with men tonight. Single men."

Danielle walks away from me with that warning and mercifully leaves me alone for the next few hours.

And it's a good thing because Michael doesn't give me a moment to think. He introduces me to a side of him I've never seen before—Mount St. Michael—a volatile volcano that feels like it's on the verge of an explosion at any second. He pulls me into his office and dictates emails to me, then makes me print them out and stand over him, all while he picks apart every section he told me to write.

"This email is for *Miles* Charrington—not Mike!" he barks at me, pointing out my small typo.

"I'll correct it immediately." I use all my willpower to refrain from telling him that he hadn't let me spell-check the email and that I would have noticed it if he hadn't forced me to print it out so fast.

But the sour look on his face stops me from pointing that out to him.

Michael doesn't give me a second to myself, calling me in his office every half-hour, demanding to know what I've gotten done.

Gone is the considerate man I've grown accustomed to, and in his place is a tyrant of a boss, putting me on edge with every snappy question he throws my way. His behavior makes me wonder if the sensitivity he displayed earlier in the day when talking about William had been a figment of my imagination.

By the time the office starts closing down, I'm so tightly wound up that I want nothing more than to drink my sorrows away with Danielle and her friends.

"Going to the pub?"

I spin around and look at Michael, who's now standing outside his door staring at me in a way that makes me so nervous I can feel the sweat begin to form on my chest. I wish I could tell what he's thinking. His biceps flex as he crosses his arms over his chest. My body tightens on its own accord, and I can feel the air crackle with electricity as we stare at one another.

"I was going to, yes." I hate myself for sounding nervous. "Unless you need something?"

He lifts his brow.

"Do you?" I ask when he remains silent.

"Are you ready, Abby?" Danielle calls out, interrupting us as she walks over holding onto her purse.

Michael stares at me for a moment longer before turning to Danielle.

"Where are you going?"

"One of your favorite pubs," Danielle tells him. "The Royal Oak.

Manchester United is playing so we were going to watch the game. Would you like to join?"

My heart slams in my chest as I sneak a peek at him.

"I've got work to do," he quickly declines, and I can't tell if I'm relieved or annoyed he's not coming. "But I'm sure you'll have fun."

"Oh we will," Danielle says with a promise. "Come on, Abby."

***

An hour later, I've taken three shots of some concoction that Tom, Danielle's fiancé, had the bartender make for us. Tom is wonderful and handsome, and so in love with Danielle that I'm beyond thrilled for my friend.

I wonder if she knows how lucky she is.

To have a man that's so crazy in love with her that he doesn't care who can see it. To love so fiercely and be loved in the same way back... it makes me wonder if I'll ever have the same.

Luckily, the buzz from the drinks distracts me from heading down that dark path, and I blissfully choose to ignore my current predicament. And I have to admit, it feels good to be out and not obsessing about Michael at my apartment alone.

Stephen, one of Tom's friends, hasn't left my side from the moment I walked into the pub. Danielle must have told him I'm the single friend because he can't be more attentive. I'm flattered by the attention. Stephen's cute, with his sandy blond hair and brown eyes, and is also very nice. He's a broker at one of the big firms, and his attentiveness is exactly what I need.

"Are you having fun yet?" Danielle whispers loudly into my ear as the guys cheer on the soccer match.

"I am," I tell her gratefully as I take a sip of my cocktail. We're standing around one of the large tables. "I think you realized what I needed more than I did. Thank you for making me come out with you tonight."

"I told you," Danielle replies matter-of-factly, sounding as drunk as I feel. "This will show Michael!"

"Yes, it will!" I agree, lifting my drink to cheers with her.

We clink glasses.

"Oh my," Danielle says in surprise as she looks over my shoulder toward the door to the pub. "I just knew it… but then I didn't really know. But then I kind of did."

"Are you drunk?" I laugh in confusion.

"Undoubtedly, but not drunk enough to be seeing things. Not yet, at least," she says with a happy smile. "Don't look now, Abby. Michael is here."

My heart stops.

He's here?

"I think I might faint," I whisper to her in disbelief.

My stomach starts to do somersaults.

"Me too," Danielle whispers back.

"I'm going to die," I continue on dramatically.

"Don't die just yet," she tells me in a no-nonsense voice before the look on her face changes. She smiles in pleasure as Michael walks over to us.

The energy shifts around me. And the pub suddenly feels too small for the both of us.

"Michael." Danielle's voice is too damn cheerful. "I'm so happy you stopped by. I thought you might."

"I'm sure you did." His voice sounds almost accusatory.

Danielle doesn't seem to notice.

I hate that my heart skips a beat at the sound of his voice.

I hate that my body has gone on high alert.

I hate that he has to be the one to make me feel so alive.

"Your first drink is on me," Danielle says to Michael. "I'll get your favorite whiskey. Keep Abby company for me, will you."

She gives him an insolent pat on the cheek before walking away.

I want to kill her for leaving me alone with him.

Michael's presence invades every part of my senses. I try my best to stay utterly still and ignore him. But he's not having it. His hand rubs my shoulder.

"Abby."

Static.

Electricity.

The kind that jolts you from the dead back to life.

That's the feeling that comes over me from a single touch.

"Michael." I gather the courage to look over at him.

He looks impossibly sexy, wearing a black leather jacket that fits his broad shoulders like butter. I lick my lips nervously and try to act cool. But I can't tell what he's thinking.

"Having fun?" His voice is polite, his eyes hooded.

"Yes," I reply, finishing off my drink.

"I'm glad."

"Are you?" I wonder.

Michael's eyes flicker in surprise.

"Why wouldn't I be?"

Because every time I'm having fun with you, you pull the rug out from underneath me and rob me of my moment of joy.

Before I can answer Stephen takes that moment to walk over to us and hands me a fresh drink.

"I noticed you were running low," he says politely.

I feel Michael's body stiffen next to me.

"Thank you," I reply with a grateful smile then motion toward Michael. "Stephen, have you met Michael Sinclair?"

Stephen's eyes light up in recognition.

"Pleasure to meet you," he says, holding out his hand.

From the look on Michael's face, you'd think he was just asked to eat glass. The look on his face is cold and dismissive. Thankfully, Stephen's either too smashed or to in awe to notice.

Michael shakes his hand but doesn't return the sentiment.

There's an uncomfortable silence.

"I'm a big fan of the work you do," Stephen says with a friendly smile.

"Are you?" Michael replies, shifting his body into mine, effectively trapping me between him and the table.

His stance is territorial.

Stephen's eyes narrow as he takes note, like he's trying to figure out what the story is between us.

"So, you're Danielle and Abby's boss," Stephen continues on, completely unaware of the angry energy Michael is emanating.

"I am." Michael's response is abrupt, rude almost.

"He's also my cousin," I blurt that piece of information out.

My comment seems to appease Stephen… but Michael on the other hand…

His body stiffens.

His mood shifts into something dangerous.

And volatile.

"Then I'm sure you won't mind if I ask her to dance with me," Stephen says as he holds out his hand.

"Of course he won't mind," I say with a laugh trying to make a joke of it. I place my drink down on the table and use the opportunity to push past my tormentor and take Stephen's hand.

I'm too afraid to even look at Michael in the eye.

Stephen leads me out to the makeshift dance floor, and I try my best to pretend Michael isn't there. The combination of good music and alcohol helps because it doesn't take long for me to start enjoying myself. Stephen spins me around, and before I know it, I'm laughing and actually having a good time.

But still.

There's that part of me that knows he's there. I can feel his eyes on me. The female part that knows he's watching my every move.

A slow Irish folk love ballad comes on and Stephen pulls me into his arms and starts singing the words to me, his laughter infectious. If Michael were not in the picture or part of my world, Stephen would definitely pique my interest.

"If you don't mind—" Michael interrupts, breaking up our moment.

If Stephen is as surprised as I am, he covers well.

"Of course," he says graciously, stepping away and leaving me alone to fend for myself.

Michael pulls me into his arms, his hands move down to my sides, to my lower back, brushing up against the top of my ass, holding onto me much too intimately.

Like I belong to him.

My hands come up his chest to push away from him, to give my body and mind the ability to breathe normally, but when my gaze crashes into his, I pause.

"Shit," I swear before I can help myself.

The look in Michael's eyes could light the city on fire.

CHAPTER NINE

"Scared?" he asks with a lift of his arrogant brow.

"Why would I be?" I say. "I've done nothing wrong."

We've stopped moving. I'm just standing in the middle of the dance floor in his arms, and it doesn't look like he's going to let me go anytime soon.

Not that I want him to.

"Haven't you?" His voice is icy.

"I'm not following…"

"Your new admirer," Michael continues. "Stephen."

"What about him?"

"You're using him to make me jealous." He pulls me into his body when he says this, his voice angry.

"You're crazy." I shake my head in disbelief. "I'm not using anyone! And I didn't even invite you here."

"No?" he goes on, his jaw clenched.

"Danielle told you…" I start to argue back, but my sanity kicks in and I lay into him instead. "Why does Stephen even matter to you? You and I are not together. We've never been together. Regardless of what you said in the office today, your actions have made it clear that everything that has happened between us was a mistake. I promise you, I got the message."

"Did you?" His expression is sour.

"I did." I feel humiliated that I'm forced to keep reliving his rejection. "So this back and forth, this, whatever this is… you just need to stop."

I try to move out of his arms, but he holds me tightly in his grip.

"Do I?" His voice is dangerously soft.

"Yes!" And because I can't help myself and have undoubtedly

had too much to drink I continue. "And you know what, Michael?"

"What?" His lips twitch for a moment, and I have the distinct feeling he's suddenly trying really hard not to laugh in my face.

But I don't care. *Why is he even here?*

"You do seem jealous!"

"And what if I am?" he asks to my complete surprise, effectively robbing me of all my anger and all train of thought.

To be fair, he seems a bit floored by this possibility as well.

The mask he has slips, and for a moment he lets me see how conflicted he is.

My mouth instantly dries. I close my eyes and try to fight the small ember of hope that's been lit by his admission.

"Are you?"

Michael's eyes drift to my mouth. My body involuntarily reacts to him. I lean in, waiting for him to respond.

He looks away for a moment, clenching his jaw.

"I don't know what I am." I hear him whisper under his breath.

My heart thumps in my chest.

His confession takes away all of my anger for him.

But still.

"It's not fair what you're doing to me," I tell him honestly.

His body reacts to my admission, pulling me up against his rock hard frame as his hand moves to my hair, tugging my head back.

"Fair?" he practically hisses out as his eyes blaze into mine. "I'll tell you what's not fair. What's not fair is how I have to see you walk around my office every day with that perfect composure of yours, knowing with one touch I can light that fire in your body you've hidden so well from the rest of the world. I have to watch you smile and laugh with the men who work for me. I have to pretend that perfume you wear doesn't drive me crazy."

I close my eyes as his words rush through my soul, fanning that flame of hope that I've been so frightened to feed until now.

"I have to keep my hands to myself," he continues as if the

words are being torn out of his body. "When all I want to do is rip your clothes off and fuck you so hard that you scream out my name as you come again. And again."

My body's reaction to his words is instant.

Raw, primal need rocks me to my core.

A buzz begins to course through my veins.

I can feel the longing between my thighs and my heartbeat roars so loudly in my head that I can't even see straight.

"Have I scared you?" Michael's voice is low and rough as the piercing intensity of his gaze draws me right into his sexual web.

And then the mood around us shifts again and Michael's hands slowly move up, over my arms, his lips brush up erotically against my ear.

"Why did you come here?" I ask him with a ragged sigh.

"Why?" His voice is husky, making me crave his touch, the feel of his lips on mine. A hot ache begins to spread through my body.

"I had to give you something." He pulls away as his eyes move over my face.

Michael takes my hand in his before tugging me off the dance floor.

"Give me what?" I ask, but allow him to pull me away.

Why?

Because I'm more curious than I should be. Because I long to be in his world in any way I can.

Because he wants to fuck me.

Hard.

I should want to run far away from him and all the craziness he invokes inside my soul, but I don't.

I can't.

He leads me through the bar, down a flight of steps and from the way he expertly navigates the place, I know he's been here before.

"Where are we going?" I ask him as we walk down a hall that looks like it's for staff only.

"You'll see."

I don't have to wait long.

He finds the room he's looking for, which happens to be a miscellaneous storage for the pub. There's only a small table in the tiny room that's lined with shelves filled with kitchen supplies.

"What's this?" I ask, spinning around and watching him shut the door.

He locks it.

My heart drops to the floor.

What is going on?

The air is thick around us. Michael's size and presence make the small space seem even more claustrophobic than it already is. He steps toward me as my heart picks up its pace.

"This?" he says as he looks around the room. "This is a closet."

"Why did you lock the door?" I can't help but feel nervous about what's to come.

Michael cocks his head to the side.

"Why do you think?"

I take a step back from him, but there's no room for me to go.

"You... you said you wanted to give me something."

He takes a step closer.

"I do." His voice sounds raspy.

"I don't understand." I hold my hand out, hoping to keep him at bay. My heart races erratically as my stomach clenches.

Michael's hand grabs mine, using it to pull me into his body.

"Let me show you."

And he does.

His mouth crushes mine as his fingers fervently grip my arms, pressing me into his masculine frame. I don't stand a chance. I lose all reason as he begins to kiss my lips and neck, any bit of bare flesh he can find. I'm soaking wet within seconds, longing for release. Michael's hands slide down my shoulders, to the front of my shirt, where he begins to slowly unbutton my top.

"You don't know what you're doing to me." His words are hypnotic as his hands move over my breasts.

I moan into his mouth as his fingers knead my breasts, teasing my nipples until the hot warmth of his touch causes a wildfire to move through my body.

"Abby," he whispers, his mouth trailing kisses down my neck. "You're so beautiful."

His words, his touch... they work like magic.

His hands cup my ass and lift me up, carrying me back until I'm seated on the table. Michael's hands move down my legs to touch my naked calves before sliding back and pushing my skirt up as far it can go.

He moves between my legs, wrapping them around his waist before pushing his erection against my lacy thong, causing me to lose all logical train of thought. The movement drives me wild, and within seconds I want more. I fall back on the table and Michael follows, capturing my mouth, his tongue exploring every crevice it can find.

"So beautiful," he whispers against my lips.

He pushes my bra down, letting my breasts loose, growling low in his throat in appreciation. He palms one of my breasts, his tongue skims a trail down my neck and circles over my nipple. I cry out in pleasure as he sucks and licks, tugging on my swollen flesh until my body is begging him for release.

"Michael!" I cry out.

He ignores my pleas and continues to make love to my breasts. My hands tangle in his hair, and I push my pelvis into his groin, dying for any kind friction. His hand comes to rest on my hip bone, steadying me, before slowly slipping between my thighs. When his fingers barely brush up against me, I think I might explode. My hips buck up to his touch, demanding release.

My body has been craving this from the moment we shared our first kiss.

He slowly pulls down my thong, sliding it along my naked thighs as I shudder in anticipation. His lips find mine again and he slips two fingers inside, blissfully filling me with what I need. I practically scream out in pleasure as his fingers rock into me. They work their magic, rubbing my sensitive nub, moving in and out, throwing me into a haze of pure lust.

"Let me give it to you." His voice is rough and passionate against my mouth.

Yes, I think. *Please.*

I reach the edge.

And when I can't take any more of his sweet torture, I scream out my orgasm. My muscles flex and my body trembles from the force as waves of sweet pleasure rock my core.

It's a long time before I can finally breathe normally again.

Before I can shyly open my eyes.

Michael lifts himself over my body and stares down at me. He lets me see how he feels. The naked desire in his eyes only makes me want more.

Need more.

I try to reach down and reciprocate, but his hand stops me.

"Not yet, Abby," he whispers against my lips. "Not yet."

When? I wonder not realizing I say the words out loud until Michael responds with a soft kiss on my cheek.

"Soon."

***

Not yet.

But soon.

Michael's cryptic words played in my head all night. He successfully managed to ruin another night of sleep for me. I couldn't help but spend the night reliving what was without a doubt the most incredible orgasm of my life. Or what happened after.

When we left the storage closet, Michael had quickly excused himself to go home. He'd kissed me on my cheek and had whispered he'd see me in the morning, and then had just left.

Left.

I, on the other hand, was too shell-shocked to move. In fact, it took me a good ten minutes before I could really come to terms with what happened in the storage closet. In a pub. Filled with people. Employees that could have walked in on us at any time.

But none of that even mattered to me.

Because Michael had given me the most earth-shattering orgasm. And then… just left.

But not without promising more.

But did he?

Did *not yet* mean not yet, but soon? Or *not yet* because he didn't know if it should ever happen? Was it the latter?

There was a good chance I was going to drive myself crazy wondering.

I stayed at the pub until Danielle wanted to leave. Part of me was too stunned to move and the other part just needed the comfort of being surrounded by people. When Danielle asked where Michael and I had been, I told her we had gone to talk. I didn't really want to share the intimate details with her.

So when I finally got home, I sat up in bed for the entire night in confusion.

Not yet.

His words… what happened between us, which I'm equally as responsible for, makes everything even harder.

Because now I know what it's like.

What it's really like to be in his arms.

And it's everything I imagined it would be.

And more.

What I had shared with Danielle, the bits and pieces of what he had said to me leading up to the big O, had thrilled her. She said I was rocking his world, that she'd never seen him so wound up before and that she knew I'd break him soon.

Break Michael Sinclair?

Was that even possible?

It was too dangerous for my emotional well-being to even allow myself the hope.

I'm up before my alarm goes off in the morning and quickly get ready for work. For the first time, I find myself anxious to see what the day will bring. How Michael will act today after what happened between us.

After the emotional roller coaster he's put me through I really don't know what to expect. I know I should probably brace myself for another one of his *"what happened last night was a mistake"* conversations, but a part of me, a small part, has some hope. And I promise myself that if he does actually try to go there, I'll just turn around and walk out of the damn building.

Just as I'm about to leave for the office, I get a text from the man I'm quickly becoming convinced has been put on this earth to torture me.

My insides turn to mush when I see Michael's name flash across my phone. I'm so nervous when I read his message that it takes me a second to focus on the bizarre question.

MICHAEL: Is your passport in order?

The question throws me, but I type back quickly.

ME: Yes, it is.

I wait for him to respond and when he doesn't, I ping him again.

ME: Why are you asking?

MICHAEL: We'll talk about it when you get in this morning. Come and see me when you arrive. I'm already here.

He's at the office?

I don't reply.

I try not to obsess about why he's asking about my passport and just grab my things and head into work. The sooner I get in, the sooner I'll know.

Not long after, I walk into his office and find him sitting behind his desk working. After what happened last night, I don't really know how I'm supposed to act around him.

I try not to think about his mouth on my breasts or the magic of his hands or the most incredible orgasm...

"Good morning." Michael smiles in pleasure as he motions toward the chair in front of his desk.

"Morning." My voice sounds stiff as I take a seat.

"How was the rest of your night?" he asks nonchalantly, his eyes giving nothing away.

For the life of me, I can't tell what he's thinking.

"Fun."

Fun? What the hell kind of response was that, Abby?

His gaze meets mine as he smiles wickedly.

"Not *that* fun, I hope."

There's no missing the innuendo. I can feel the heat rush to my face as sinful images of our night together flood my mind.

"Why did you ask about my passport?" I quickly change the topic.

Michael leans back in his chair and laughs in amusement. My eyes narrow suspiciously.

"We're going on a trip."

If he told me there were pigs flying in the sky, I think I would be less shocked.

"What?"

"To Costa Rica. To my home there. I have some business I need to take care of, and I need you to come along."

On a trip? Alone with Michael? In a country I've never been to and one that has been on my bucket list since the day I knew what a bucket list was.

I don't bloody think so.

"I don't think that would be appropriate—" I argue.

"Appropriate?" Michael's focus settles on my lips before flicking back up to my eyes. My pulse flutters and I lick my lips uncomfortably.

"Given the circumstances—" I begin to say before he cuts me off.

"Last night, you mean?"

Lord.

I bite my bottom lip and nod uncomfortably. I can't even look at him. And I'm pretty sure I'm about twenty-five different shades of red.

"Abby," he murmurs my name, his voice low and seductive. "Look at me."

I can feel the air crackle with electricity as our eyes meet.

"I know you enjoyed yourself." His smile is wicked.

Why Lord?

Why can't the chair just swallow me whole?

Like. Right. Now.

"Didn't you?" he demands to know.

A spark passes between us. And there's so much heat and sexual tension that I have to physically lean back in my chair, needing whatever space I can get.

"Abby."

He wants to hear me say it.

He won't let up until he has his way.

And because there's no way I can deny how much pleasure he gave me, I give him what he wants to hear.

"I did," I whisper.

I see the satisfied glimmer in his eyes, and I hate myself for the way it makes me feel. The high I get from knowing he wanted to please me.

That it mattered to him.

My pleasure.

"Michael," I plead with him, using any logic I can. "I really don't think me coming along is a good idea."

"Why not?" His eyes flicker back down to my lips intentionally wreaking havoc on my sanity.

Because every time we're around each other, we end up doing something you regret and I'm starting to crave more and more.

That's why.

"You know why." I try to keep my voice neutral.

"What do you have against pleasure?" Michael asks curiously, lifting his brow.

"Pleasure?" I have full cotton mouth because of this man.

"Pleasure, Abby." His eyes darken in desire. "Even the word seems to make you uncomfortable."

"We are so not having this conversation," I mutter out loud before I can stop myself.

"But we are," Michael says with a challenge.

"It's completely inappropriate," I snap out in anger. "And you know it. So stop acting like this is a normal conversation between a boss and an employee, unless this is something you're used to..."

"Used to what?"

"Doing with your female employees," I say with an accusatory tone.

"I have never had a relationship with any of my employees." Michael's voice is hard, offended. I can tell he didn't appreciate the insinuation and I can't deny how relieved hearing his admission makes me feel. Even though I knew from the snippets of office gossip I had heard that it was the case, it feels good to hear him actually say it.

"I can tell we're about to go in circles here. And I'm happy to argue the point with you, but the outcome is not about to change. I'm your boss. You're my PA. It's a work trip and I need you to come along with me. So you will. End of story. Nothing else matters."

End of story?

Nothing else matters?

The picture he paints sounds so innocent.

Except it's not.

And he and I both know it.

Not yet.

Soon.

His words ring through my head and my body heats up at the thought.

This will not do.

"Michael," I try again, hoping my voice sounds calm, logical. "I only set meetings for you here and do emails. Danielle does the rest. Honestly, what can you possibly need me for in Costa Rica?"

"Let me worry about what I need from you."

"But—"

He lifts up his hand to silence me.

"I've made up my mind," he says as his blue eyes search mine. "And nothing you say will deter me."

Nothing?

"Have you been before?" Michael tilts his head to the side as he studies me.

"No," I shake my head still reeling from the turn of events. "Never."

My response seems to please him.

"Then I can't wait to show you the country," he says. "We leave tonight."

"Tonight?" I ask as my world comes slowly crashing around me. "I can't possibly—"

"You can." His voice is firm. "And you will."

***

Eight hours later I'm on Michael's private plane on my way to his home in Costa Rica.

I had tried a few more times that day to argue my way out of going, but everything I said to him fell on deaf ears. None of my reasons made him budge, so I eventually gave up and tried to accept my fate.

When I let Danielle in on the turn of events, she'd been over the moon, doing a happy dance around her office at my predicament.

I wonder if planning a wedding and losing brain cells goes hand in hand. When I asked her that question, she laughed right in my face. In any case, I was beyond grateful for her helping me get out of the office early so I could go home and pack for my trip.

After letting Georgie in on the dramatic turn of events, he had promised to come by my place and help me pack for the ten-day trip. Georgie was just as excited as Danielle and made me swear that I'd at the very least text him with daily updates. He also gave me a piece of advice that I promised to take to heart.

"Just go with the flow, Abby," Georgie said as he walked me out to the car waiting to take me to the airport.

"The flow?" I asked him.

"*Oui*," Georgie said, rolling his eyes. "I want you to enjoy yourself in every way. Allow yourself the freedom, *ma chère*."

"It's more complicated than that," I reminded him.

"*Oui*, it is," Georgie agreed. "But there is nothing you can do about your situation now, is there? And besides, this is everything you ever dreamed of."

His words gave me pause.

Because he was right.

"Don't read into anything," he said, pulling me in for a hug and a kiss. "Just have fun and live each moment as it comes."

Live each moment as it comes.

Even if I wanted to do something different, Michael has ensured that I can't. For the next ten days, I'm completely at his beck and call.

So here I am, sitting in Michael's private plane sipping on a glass of Dom as he talks to the pilots. I'd flown privately with

Dimitri a few times, but none of the planes we had been on were done in such good taste. I've always known Michael has a ton of money but being on his plane now is a seeing it on another level.

The man lives well.

The main cabin is done in mahogany wood, with gold trimmings and white leather chairs and sofas. A wood-lined paneled bar with a large flat screen above it faces a leather sofa and two comfortable looking chairs. There are eight other recliner seats in the back section that are spacious and inviting.

Two attractive flight attendants rush around the cabin making sure everything looks perfect and that our needs are seen to. One of them gave Michael fuck-me-hard eyes when he walked onto the plane but thankfully if he noticed, he didn't let on.

I've got my eye on her now.

I let the other flight attendant top off my glass, and I try my best to keep my emotions under wraps. The flight will take around fourteen hours which means I'll get to sleep for most of the night. Georgie gave me a sleeping pill to take, but I'm hoping the champagne will just do the trick since I don't know how long the effects of the pill will last.

"Would you prefer steak, chicken, sea bass, or the vegetarian dish for your meal?" The flight attendant asks as she sets down a plate of cheese and crackers for me.

"The vegetarian option, please."

She nods before leaving me.

I reach into my bag and pull out Georgie's parting gift for me. A Kindle he bought and filled with what he said was proper reading material.

Before I can look through the catalog of books, Michael makes his way back from the cockpit holding onto a small bag. He's dressed comfortably in black tracksuit pants and a long-sleeved T-shirt that clings to his muscles, looking as impossibly sexy as ever. His hair is still wet from the shower which triggers my overactive imagination, and I immediately begin to picture him naked under hot water.

I can only imagine what a sight it is to see.

Hot.

Every cell in my body responds to his presence and I realize I need to get a grip. I try to distract myself by taking another sip of champagne.

When Michael reaches my side, he holds out the bag to me.

"I thought you might want these. They're pajamas for the flight and a few toiletries you might need."

I take the bag out of his hands and those wonderful fingers of his, that pleasured me just last night, brush up against mine causing goose bumps to run up my arm. My body is more than aware of his proximity.

Torture.

I have a feeling for the next ten days it's going to be my new favorite word.

"You might want to change and get comfortable before we take off," he suggests, casually takes the seat right next to me.

Lord.

The entire plane is empty.

And he's going to sit here?

More torture.

"You can use the bedroom," he continues, completely unaware of what he's doing to my insides.

There's a bedroom?

I'm *so* going to need to take Georgie's sleeping pill.

Why couldn't he have given me a horse tranquilizer?

"I'll be a minute," I tell him as I take the bag and make my way to the back of the plane. The room is a good size and looks very comfortable. It's simple and modern, like a posh hotel with only a queen-size bed and two lounge chairs. There's even a door that leads to a private bathroom with a shower.

I try my hardest not think about how many women he's shared the bed with. With this setup, he's for sure a member of the Mile High Club. And even though his manwhoring around is none of my business, I'm still extremely annoyed. And even angrier that he gave me no choice but to come along on this business trip.

I slip on the silky blue pajamas and they feel like heaven against my skin. I look in the bag and see he's even given me a pair of slippers to wear. Begrudgingly some of my anger dissipates at his thoughtful consideration.

When I'm finished changing, I leave the bag in the corner of the room and walk out to take my seat.

Michael's on his laptop when I reach his side. A glass of whiskey sits next to him.

"I'm glad they fit." His gaze moves over me in appreciation. "I wasn't sure."

"They're perfect," I reply, taking my seat. "Thank you, again."

The Captain's voice comes over the loudspeaker and he tells us our flight time and weather conditions before asking us to prepare for takeoff. A short while later, we're up in the air on our way to Costa Rica.

I press the button to recline my chair and pick up the Kindle, hoping I'll find something to read that will distract me.

Michael takes that moment to close his laptop and lounge back in his chair, turning his big body toward mine. I try to pretend like he's not watching me.

"What are you reading?"

"I don't know yet," I say with a shrug as I stare blindly at the homepage. "I was just going to look through my reading list and see what catches my eye."

Michael holds out his hand.

"May I?"

"Sure." I hand over the device.

Michael clicks the button on the bottom and begins to swipe

through the Kindle. I can't tell what he's thinking as he skims through the different titles.

"This one looks interesting," he says, his eyes lighting up.

"What's that?"

"*Hard Times*," he names the book, his voice sounding serious.

"Uh, yes." I pretend like I know what book he's talking about even though I've never heard of it. "I'm really looking forward to starting it."

"I can see why."

His eyes flicker over me as he swipes again.

"You'll have to let me know what it means to be feminized in jail."

"I'm sorry?" My mouth drops open.

"Paul," Michael continues on as if he's discussing Hemingway. "Apparently the protagonist in this book, Paul, goes through some sort of transformation in jail. A sexual awakening… or at least that's what I gather from this picture on the cover."

Picture?

Oh shit.

"And this book," Michael goes on in a serious voice. "*Submissive in the Bedroom*, a tale of dark delight—"

"Oh my God!" I cry out in horror as I try to snatch the Kindle out of his strong grasp.

I'm going to kill Georgie!

I should have known he'd fill that damn thing with every perverse sexual book he could find time to download.

Michael laughs in my face.

He looks like he's thoroughly enjoying himself.

"*Junk in the Trunk* sounds like a real page-turner," he continues on to my mortification.

He holds the Kindle up high in his hands, and I have to actually unbuckle my seatbelt to reach for it.

"The Kindle is Georgie's!" I cry out in embarrassment as I grab it from his hands. "I swear, he gave it to me before I left my apartment."

Michael can't stop laughing.

"You should have seen your face," he says, wiping his eyes. "It was classic."

"I'm glad you're amused," I reply, trying my hardest to keep a straight face. "I want to kill Georgie."

"He's got the right idea," Michael says, lips twitching.

"*Submissive in the Bedroom* is the right idea?" I tease.

Michael's body goes completely still.

His playful smile disappears, and his eyes are hooded when they meet mine. My skin tingles in awareness as if he's physically touching me.

Damn.

Why didn't I say one of the other funny titles?

One that didn't exactly convey what I want to be for him.

"Have you ever tried it?"

"What? No," I rush out quickly and reach for the glass of champagne. Damnit! There's only a drop left.

"No?" The tone of Michael's voice changes and I know we're about to enter dangerous territory.

"No," I confirm, allowing my eyes to touch his briefly before flickering down to his full, sculpted lips. "I have not."

Michael reacts as though I've physically touched him.

"That's too bad," he murmurs as his eyes lock with mine.

The passion I see in the depths is nearly my undoing.

"I think you'd enjoy yourself," he says with an enigmatic smile.

My breath hitches and I lick my lower lip, searching my mind for something appropriate to say. He watches my response like he knows how much he's putting me on edge.

"Let me know if I can be of assistance." Michael's smile is warm, inviting, filled with promise.

I am so in trouble.

CHAPTER TEN

One sleeping pill, two and a half glasses of wine, and three meals later and we finally land in Costa Rica.

Once we were safely on our way in the air, I quickly realized the only way to get through the flight would be if I were mercifully passed out. So I proceeded to make sure that happened as quickly as possible. If Michael noticed, he didn't let on. He had eventually quit the sexual teases, pulled his laptop back out and began to immerse himself in work. He did generously ask if I wanted to sleep in the bedroom and though part of me didn't want to leave his side, I knew keeping a safe distance from him would be the only way to survive the flight. So after a few hours, when I could barely keep my eyes open, I left him and went to rest in the bedroom.

I'm dead asleep when the flight attendant knocks on the door and notifies me that we'll be landing within the hour. It takes me a moment to get my bearings, and then I look out the window of the plane and remember where I am.

And whom I'm traveling with.

Right. Talk about a reality check.

Fighting off the fogginess from the sleeping pill is a hard battle, but I slowly manage to put myself together, immensely grateful for the privacy of the room. When I finally make my way out to the main cabin, Michael looks fresh and perfect, somehow completely unaffected by the long travel time.

Another reason to be annoyed by him.

I, on the other hand, feel like hell and after staring at myself in the bathroom mirror, am pretty sure I look like it too. I should never have taken the sleeping pill since I'm pretty sure it's half the reason I feel so out of sorts. I can't wait to get to Michael's home so I can shower and freshen up.

"Did you sleep well?" Michael politely asks when I take my seat beside him.

His laptop is open and it looks like he's been working. It's exactly the way I left him when I went to go sleep.

"I did, thank you," I reply, fastening my seat belt.

"Would you like an espresso?"

"That would be perfect."

Michael flags down the flight attendant and asks her to bring me an espresso and fresh fruit.

"Did you manage to sleep at all?" I ask him as I nod toward his laptop.

"Just a few hours," Michael admits with a small smile. "I found it hard to fall asleep."

"The time difference?" I commiserate.

"No," Michael shakes his head. "My mind was just too preoccupied."

Don't ask, Abby.

Don't ask.

"With?"

"The beautiful woman sleeping on my plane," he says softly, seductively. "In my bed. Alone."

I die. Just a little.

He watches me for a moment, observing my reaction.

"Now be a good girl and fasten your seat belt for me." Michael's voice is husky as he turns toward my body and proceeds to reach around my waist to grab hold of the seat belt.

His hands skim across my body, igniting a fire inside with every light touch.

"I can do it. " I try to take the buckle out his hand and end the assault to my senses, but he pushes my hands aside.

"Allow me."

He snaps the buckle in place, and I'm spared from further torture when he turns his attention to the scenery that is visible from the window. I watch as a look of happiness sweeps over his face.

"God, I love it here." His voice sounds wistful.

I follow his gaze and look out the window and stare at the lush tropical foliage that's visible as our plane descends. An excited buzz sweeps over me at the thought of seeing this country for the first time.

The plane lands a few minutes later, and before I know it, we're rushed through customs then ushered into a waiting SUV.

The humidity hits me hard and I peel off my light cotton sweater and stare in awe at the wild and untouched landscape of Costa Rica. Exotic foliage lines the streets as we pass through rural towns. Stray dogs run alongside the roads and locals have small make-shift businesses set up to sell trinkets to tourists.

"My home isn't far from here," Michael explains as I take in my surroundings.

I glance down at my phone and take in the time difference. It's five o'clock back in London, which means it's morning here in Costa Rica.

"This is the local town, Puerto Viejo. There are some really amazing restaurants that you have to try while you're here. I'll have to bring you down a few nights for the local cuisine and nightlife."

"Only if it's not too much trouble."

And just how is eating local cuisine and experiencing the nightlife considered a business trip?

I keep my gaze glued safely out the window and try to focus on the new sights. But now that I'm thinking about the entire trip ahead, I'm not really seeing anything.

"I insist." Michael's voice is husky and filled with promise.

I take in a deep breath and close my eyes, trying with all my power to fight this insatiable attraction I have for him.

Torture.

Here it is.

Again.

The car takes a sudden turn up a small dirt road, jolting me out of my reflection. The terrain becomes rough as we make our way into the jungle, passing white cows grazing the lands. It's the complete opposite of the busy streets of London, and I'm enthralled by everything I see.

The rest of the ride is pretty rough, but it doesn't take too long. When we reach a gate guarded by two security officers, the driver rolls down the window and exchanges a few words with the men.

One of the guards, a pleasant looking man who looks to be in his twenties, leans into the window and gives a welcoming wave to Michael.

"*Hola*, Mr. Sinclair," he says with a smile. "It's nice to have you home."

"Joseph, it feels incredible to be back," Michael greets him warmly. "How are you?"

"Good as can be," Joseph replies. "Caught some killer waves this morning. You came in at the perfect time."

I watch how Michael's eyes light up in pleasure.

"I'm itching to get out there," he admits with longing.

Michael surfs. I never knew.

"And how's school?" Michael continues.

"It's rough," Joseph says with a sheepish shrug. "But that's how it goes."

I sit quietly and watch the two speak.

"And Carla?" Michael asks.

"Driving me crazy," Joseph says, rolling his eyes. "She's nagging me to get serious, and I can't take it anymore. You know how women are, Boss."

I try to cover my amusement, but I fail. Joseph's eyes flash in surprise when he sees me.

"Apologies, ma'am." He sounds mortified.

"None needed," I tell him with a laugh. "I get it."

Joseph gives me a sheepish smile.

"Joseph, this is Abby." Michael introduces us with a smile. "Abby, Joseph is my head of security and surfing partner."

I wait for him to let Joseph know I'm his PA but it doesn't come.

"Nice to meet you, Abby," Joseph says. "Is this your first time in Costa Rica?"

"It is."

"Welcome to our country." Joseph gives me a broad smile. "I hope you'll enjoy your stay."

"I'm sure I will," I reply kindly.

Joseph seems extremely likable and from the brief encounter, I can see why Michael spends time with him when he's in town. His demeanor is so carefree. He's the polar opposite of the guys I went to school with and from the people I know are in Michael's social circle at home.

"Excuse me for one minute," Michael says to me with an apologetic grin before switching dialects and speaking to Joseph in fluent Spanish.

Another ability I never knew he had until now. And Lord is it sexy. I watch them speak for another minute longer before he glances over at me.

"I'm going to take Abby to the house and get her settled in," Michael switches back to English. "I'll catch up with you later."

Joseph taps the exterior of the car before stepping away from the vehicle. We drive down a long pebbled road before pulling up to a giant contemporary hacienda overlooking the Caribbean. The house sits a ways back from the ocean, but you can easily walk there in no time at all.

"Welcome to my home." Michael's excitement is contagious, and I suddenly get a second wind and can't wait to explore the property.

"It's gorgeous," I tell him in awe as I take it all in. "Truly."

Michael grins in pleasure as the car comes to a stop in front of the giant entryway of his house.

"It's my favorite place on earth," he admits with boyish enthusiasm.

I'm touched he brought me here.

To his favorite place.

"I can see why."

"Wait until I show you the rest." He opens the door and hops out of the car, holding out his hand for me.

My heart skips a beat.

Something has definitely shifted between us, and I can only wait and see what's in store for me. After everything he's put me through in the past few weeks, I know I should reject his touch but I can't because no matter how right or wrong it is, I'm craving any kernel of affection he'll give me. I take his hand and it engulfs mine.

And it feels like the most natural thing in the world.

Once I'm out of the car, I expect him to let go, but he doesn't. I pretend like holding hands with him is normal even though my body is humming with electricity.

His tall frame towers over mine when I look up at him.

He looks so impossibly handsome.

Why is he still holding my hand?

"Ready?" he asks.

"Yes," I whisper breathlessly as he slowly lifts my hand and brushes his lips across my knuckles. My skin tingles at the soft touch. His hot gaze traps mine for a second before tugging me along, leading me through the arched open entryway into his home.

An enormous round water fountain flows in the center of the hacienda-style courtyard. Two Buddha statues, which look to be over seven feet tall, flank the wooden doors that lead into his home. A woman, who I gather is a member of his staff, is waiting to greet us. She has dark black hair and tanned skin and looks to be in her fifties. Like Joseph, she has the same relaxed look on her face.

And just like Joseph, she seems genuinely happy to see Michael.

Michael is definitely loved by his employees.

"Welcome home, Mr. Sinclair," she says with a smile.

"Giselle," Michael returns, "It's good to be back."

He turns toward me to introduce us.

"This is Abby."

Again, I wait for him to say that I'm his PA and we're here to work but like before, it doesn't come. Giselle gives me a friendly smile.

"So nice to meet you, Abby," Giselle says. "If you need anything during your stay here please don't hesitate to ask. I live in the guest house on the property so I can be here at any time."

"Thank you," I reply gratefully.

"I hope you and your family are doing well?" Michael asks Giselle as he takes a step closer to me, allowing his body to brush up against mine.

I feel myself involuntarily lean into his touch, hungry for any piece of him I can get. Again, I know I shouldn't allow him the freedom to touch me when I don't even know what's going on between us but I can't seem to stop him.

I don't want to.

Instead, I crave him, greedy for any affection I can get—just like an addict. His fingers rub my hand softly as he and Giselle speak. I wonder if he even realizes he's doing it.

My stomach clenches in response.

"We are good, Mr. Sinclair," she says. "We are all good. And I must thank you again for taking care of Eli's hospital expenses for us."

Michael lifts his hand up, shaking his head.

"Please. Don't even mention it. Eli is a member of the family. How is he recovering?"

"He's doing so much better, like nothing was ever wrong," Giselle says with a laugh. "Here he comes!"

We turn at that moment and a giant dog rushes toward Michael and me at full speed ahead. Michael lets go of my hand and laughs in joy, crouching down to greet the mutt as it hurls itself into his arms.

I laugh in pleasure as the dog throws slobbering kisses all over his face. Michael doesn't seem to mind.

I crouch down as well and pat Eli who turns his full attention to me, smothering me with affection.

"He's such a lover." Giselle laughs as she watches Eli with me.

I hug the dog back as Michael watches us intently.

"What was wrong with him?" I ask out loud.

"He caught a virus," Michael tells me. "It was touch and go there for a while."

"Well thank God you're okay now, Eli." My voice is tender as I rub his body and place kisses on his head. "I'm so happy to meet you. You're such a good boy! Yes, you are. You're just a lover."

Michael stands abruptly, his mood shifting.

"Let's get you settled in your room." His voice sounds gruff.

I give Eli another soft kiss then reluctantly get up.

"He's the best," I tell Michael as I give Eli another big smile.

"Will you be having dinner at home this evening?" Giselle asks.

"We'll stay in tonight and have an early dinner on the veranda," Michael informs her. "With the time difference, it might be too much for Abby the first night she's here."

"I'm all right with whatever you want," I try to argue.

"Trust me," Michael smiles knowingly. "You will hit a wall around three or four o'clock. It's the witching hour for jet lag. It's always inevitable the first few days."

"I guess you know better than me."

"Trust me," he says.

"Well, that settles it then," Giselle says, clasping her hands together. She looks over at me. "Do you have any food allergies, Abby?"

"None," I shake my head.

"Perfect."

Giselle motions toward the house.

"As you requested, I've prepared the two master suites upstairs for you," she tells Michael.

"Thank you, Giselle. We'll be all right on our own now. I'm just going to show Abby around."

To my surprise, Michael grabs hold of my hand again and takes me into his home.

The front doors open up to an enormous space with floor-to-ceiling windows that look out onto the ocean. I can see a huge infinity pool surrounded by lounge chairs and tables, set up in a way to appreciate the captivating view.

The hallways are decorated with teak wood and natural stone. We step into the family room that has a modern white wrap-around couch with dark blue accents. The couch is set in front of a limestone wall that has a giant flat screen television. The furniture is modern but extremely inviting.

"This is the main family room, but there are other lounge areas around the house," Michael tells me as we walk through the home.

The dining room is next to the family room and is also set up for a large number of people—the home was definitely built for entertaining friends.

"It's incredible," I tell him as I look around at the oasis he's created.

He leads me into the kitchen.

It's state of the art and quite impressive with its white limestone countertops and two central islands. The kitchen leads out onto an open-air ocean-view terrace with an intimate dining table set up against a sleek outdoor fireplace.

"There are five bedrooms downstairs," Michael explains. "As well as an office and small theater room."

"I can see why you love it here," I tell him, staring out on the view. I can't seem to look away from it. "I'd never be able to leave this place."

"It is hard," Michael agrees with a smile. "But then it can be lonely here by yourself."

"I can't imagine you haven't come here with family and friends or..." I try to keep my voice light. "Or even a girlfriend."

Michael pins me with his gaze.

"I've never brought a woman here before."

Pleasure.

His words cause a rush of pleasure to sweep through my body, making me feel almost high with joy.

I'm the first woman he's brought here?

Don't read into anything, Abby. Georgie's words echo in my head.

Don't. Do. It.

But it's *so* hard!

"Shall I show you the bedrooms?" Michael asks after an awkward silence.

"Yes, please," I tell him.

We walk upstairs and the wide hallway leads to the two different sections of the house. The house is designed to take full advantage of the gorgeous ocean views. Michael makes a left turn and we walk down a ways before he leads me through two double doors.

"The home has two identical master suites," he explains. "This will be yours. I'm in the other."

The room is impressive. The king-size bed faces the sliding glass doors that look out toward the ocean. I'll be able to open them when I sleep at night and listen to the soothing sound of the ocean. The room has a private sitting area done in the same color schemes as the rest of the house with a couch and two lounge chairs. I even have my own flat screen TV that pops up out of a consul in front of my bed. The master bath is done in white marble and has a huge shower that has an electronic panel to start up one of the five showerheads that fall like rain from above.

"How do you like it?" Michael asks after we walk through the whole room.

I find myself standing by the windows just soaking in the incredible tropical views. This will never get old, I think to myself.

"How do you think I like it?" I jokingly ask him. "Your place is absolutely gorgeous!"

His eyes darken as he watches me intently. I can feel my body react.

There's a knock at the door and we both turn to see the driver bringing in my luggage. He places it in the walk-in closet and quietly leaves us.

Michael turns to me.

"I'll let you freshen up," he says. "I was going to change into my swim trunks and go for a swim if you're up for it."

My mouth goes dry.

"What about work?" I ask him the obvious question. Every activity he's suggested so far sounds more like a romantic holiday than a business trip.

"Work can wait." Michael laughs. "Besides, I'm your boss, and I vote that we have some fun first."

"But that's not why we're here," I remind him.

"No," he agrees with a mischievous grin. "But you've never been to Costa Rica before. I wouldn't be a good host if I didn't show you the country."

He makes it sound so easy.

So innocent. The man is relentless.

Michael takes a step toward me and my heart slams against my chest.

"What do you say?"

Go with the flow... I hear Georgie's words echo in my head.

"Since you're not giving me much choice, then I reluctantly agree." I know my voice sounds nervous but I can't help it.

"Reluctantly agree?"

I meet his gaze with a challenge.

"Is that a problem?" I eye him cautiously.

"Not at all," he says. "As long as you agree, I'll take it."

I lift my eyes to meet his. I wonder what he's thinking. If he's as confused as I am. I doubt that to be the case, given how in control Michael always seems.

"I'll meet you out by the pool once I've cleaned up," I tell him softly.

With my promise to join him, Michael leaves me to get ready for the day.

When he's gone, I send two quick texts to Georgie and Danielle letting them know I arrived and am safe. Both of them respond separately with excited texts back and I respond with a nervous faced emoji.

Next, I unpack my bags and get organized—a quirk I have whenever I travel. Everything has to be put away in its proper place. I'm not one of those people that can keep their things in their suitcase. I'm grateful for the ritual because it helps calm the nerves Michael's successfully wound up so tightly.

After I'm done with that, I shower and immediately feel infinitely better.

I slip into my black bikini, the one Georgie says makes me look sexy, and put on blush and lip gloss to give my pale complexion some color. I don't overdo it because I don't want Michael to think I'm trying too hard. I'm already nervous enough as it is about being half naked around him, I can't do anything that might add to my stress. I stand in front of the full-length mirror and stare at my body for a good long minute, looking for any flaws that Michael might notice.

Surprisingly, it's not so bad.

My waist is thankfully narrow even with all of my recent binge eating, my hips full, my legs are thin and shapely. And I have always been proud of the way my breasts fill out a bikini top. No complaints there. I look good, I think to myself. I throw a black gauzy cover-up on, grab my sunglasses and a bottle of water I found on my nightstand, and head out to the pool. .

I'm the first to arrive.

It looks like Giselle was told we'd spend the day outside because a few umbrellas have been opened up and towels have been placed on the lounge chairs. There's also a full platter of fruit and cheese on one of the four-top tables covered by shade. And Bob Marley's sexy voice rings through the speakers. He's one of my all-time favorites.

It's a scene set up for romance and fun.

I grab a handful of grapes off the platter and pop some in my mouth before making my way to one of the chairs.

As I'm taking my bikini cover-up off, Giselle comes out to greet me.

"*Hola*, Abby," she says with a friendly smile.

"*Hola*," I reply.

"What can I get you to drink? We have many fresh juices and all sorts of tropical drinks. And Mr. Sinclair tells me I make a very good spicy margarita."

The occasion definitely calls for alcohol.

"Your margarita sounds amazing," I say as my eyes light up.

"I will make you one now," she says with a laugh. "Can I get you anything to eat as well?"

"No, that's all right. I'm not really hungry. The fruit and cheese are plenty. Thank you, Giselle."

Giselle nods politely before leaving to get my drink.

I settle into my chair and sigh in pleasure as the rays of the sun hit my skin. It feels like heaven. I let my mind wander, and because I can't help myself, I start obsessing about all of the mixed messages Michael has thrown my way. I recall all of our moments together. The passion we've shared. The things he's said.

Up until the other night, he's been back and forth—like he was fighting his attraction for me. But now, something has changed.

He's holding my hand.

He's openly flirting.

His every action is telling me he's interested. *Isn't he?* I can't be reading into any of this?

But then, there's the other part of me. The part that has to guard my heart against further torment. The part that's afraid to believe that something's different because he's been known to change his mind in the course of a night. It's just so confusing. I don't know how to behave anymore. If I'm supposed to just allow all the intimacies or am I supposed to reject them because he hasn't told me he's ready to give us a try?

Is he? Is that what this trip is about?

I'm not naïve enough to believe he's brought me here to Costa Rica to work. Not after everything that's happened between us.

And honestly, now that I'm here with him, I'm even more in turmoil than ever. A part of me is nervous. A part scared. A part hopeful that this could finally be it for us. All of these feelings just percolating inside my heart as I wonder which emotion is the safest bet.

"Here you are," Giselle says as she walks over to me and hands me an enormous drink. "Let me know if it's not strong enough."

"This looks delicious," I tell her with a grateful smile as I take a sip of the spicy drink.

It's really strong.

"It's just perfect."

"I'm headed out to do some grocery shopping for dinner, but if you need anything, please help yourself in the kitchen."

"I will," I promise her. "And thank you for everything, Giselle. Please don't worry about me."

She leaves, and I take another sip of the drink before putting it down. I need to pace myself considering the alcohol/sun combination will definitely not help with the jet lag.

I slip on my sunglasses, close my eyes, and take in the sun. The rays work like magic and I'm relaxed in no time.

"If you're not careful, you'll burn," I hear Michael say as he comes up to cast a shadow over my half-naked body.

I open my eyes and stare up at him.

He's wearing black swim trunks and a white T-shirt.

I watch as his eyes glaze in desire as they sweep over my body, lingering on my stomach, breasts, and lips before settling on my face.

My body hums with longing.

"I put on sunscreen."

"The sun is killer here," he murmurs. "It catches you before you know it."

"I think I'll be fine for a little while longer and then I promise I'll move in the shade," I reassure him.

His eyes flicker over the drink sitting on the small table by my lounge chair.

"Giselle make you a spicy margarita?" he asks with a knowing smile. "It's her specialty."

"Yes, I know," I say. "She told me."

Michael reaches back over his shoulders and pulls his shirt right over his head.

He tosses it on the chair next to me and I'm left staring at the body I've obsessed about since puberty.

My mouth goes dry.

He's perfect.

Really.

From his slim hips, to narrow waist, and hard-as-nails six pack that is literally drool worthy—he's pretty damn unreal. His legs are powerful, his thigh muscles thick and cut as sharply as the rest of him. His arms are long, sinewy, rippling with every movement like he was sculpted by a master.

So bloody unfair.

I'm staring. Like the kind that is so obvious, there's no way I can deny what I'm doing. I might even be drooling now.

I'd like to blame the improper behavior on my jet lag, but unfortunately, that is just not the case. When I'm finally able to look him in the eyes again, I have New Year's Eve style fireworks going off in my body.

From the look on his face, I think he knows.

"Hungry?" he asks enigmatically.

A loaded question.

"I'm fine," I say with a shaky breath. "Giselle already offered to make me something."

"Let me know if you change your mind." His voice sounds husky, filled with sexual innuendo. "I'm going to cool down and do some laps."

I watch as he does a perfect dive into the pool and begins to methodically do laps across the length. Since I've clearly given up on trying to act uninterested, I lean up in the chair and stare at him as he swims back and forth. The muscles in his arms ripple as he expertly moves through the water. He has beautiful form. Just like an Olympic athlete.

I lose count of how many laps he's done before he stops and leans down in the water until it covers his shoulders.

"You should come in," he calls out to me as he slices water over his head. "The water feels great."

The water does look beyond inviting—especially with Michael swimming around in the pool.

I surprise myself when I get out of the chair.

"I think I will," I tell him as I boldly walk over to the edge of the pool.

I can feel his gaze move over my body as I dip a toe in.

"It's heavenly." My smile freezes on my face when I glance over at Michael.

Heat.

Holy. Lord.

The way he's looking at me. Like I'm the sexiest thing he's ever seen in his life. Like he wants to devour every inch of me. I shouldn't need to see his naked desire. I shouldn't crave it.

But I do.

Every part of my body is exposed to him, my bikini leaving little to the imagination. And for whatever reason, I don't mind. In fact, standing before him like this makes me feel powerful. Like I hold the keys to something he wants and that I alone can give.

And he's right about one thing.

The water does feel incredible against my skin. The temperature is perfect.

I slowly take a step in and sink into the pool, fully aware that Michael's watching my every move. I walk into the water until I'm waist deep. Michael treads water a few feet away from me.

I take a deep breath and dunk my whole body underwater. When I come up for air Michael's moved closer, now only arm's length distance from me.

"You remind me of a mermaid," he says, his eyes appreciatively moving over my face.

"Then you should be scared," I tease. "Mermaids are known to lure young men to their untimely deaths."

Michael's eyes light up.

"There might be something poetic about dying in the arms of such beauty." A grin tugs at the corner of his mouth.

"You're still dying," I say with a laugh and try to brush off his compliment even though my body is humming with joy.

"But what if it's not a real death?" Michael's voice sounds husky.

"What other kind of death is there?"

"*La petite mort.*"

My heart slams against my chest.

The little death.

Or as non-French speaking people know it—an orgasm.

I suck in my breath as the fire behind his words hits me hard.

"Well that would definitely be a much more desirable outcome," I respond as calmly as I can.

Michael throws his head back and roars with laughter.

"I would think so," he finally says.

I offer him a shy smile before I lean down in the water and let it slice over my shoulders. I try not stare at his broad chest or the delicious way the sun hits his skin, casting a golden light.

Michael watches me silently, like he's sizing me up.

"Would you like to play a game?" Michael asks after a moment.

"Depends," I say with a shrug.

"On?"

"What you have in mind."

Michael gives me a wolfish grin.

"Something safe," he tells me. "For now."

CHAPTER ELEVEN

I wait with baited breath for Michael's challenge.

"If I remember from childhood, you're quite good at holding your breath underwater," he says as he looks down the length of the pool.

I'm surprised Michael remembers. When I was younger, I used swim laps across the pool and hold my breath for as long as I could. In retrospect, I think I was trying to disappear from the world. Unfortunately, it never seemed to work.

"I used to be," I say with an embarrassed shrug.

"Let's bet on it," Michael's smile is playful as he explains the game. "Whoever can hold their breath the longest gets to ask the other person any ten questions they want."

"Any questions?" I ask uncertainly, my thoughts drifting over all the possibilities.

"Anything goes." Michael seems amused. "Come on, Abby."

When I hesitate, Michael persists.

"Come on. What do you have to hide?" His voice is sweet and cajoling.

You have no idea.

"Do you hold a title I should be aware of?" I ask with a great deal of suspicion.

"In holding my breath underwater?" Michael laughs in my face. "I'm flattered you think so highly of me."

"It's not flattery," I tell him pointedly. "It's distrust."

Michael barks out in laughter.

"Touché," he says. "Sadly, no. I don't hold any records."

"All right then," I agree reluctantly. "I'm in."

"Perfect," Michael says, sweeping his arm out. "Ladies first."

I walk to the end of the pool, take a deep breath in and sink down into the water. The first underwater lap is not so hard to do, but when I make the turn to come around, I can feel my lungs start to burn. I swim hard and go as far as I can before I emerge from the water more than halfway back.

I'm pretty pleased with myself.

"Nice." Michael sounds impressed.

"Your turn," I call out to him.

Michael dunks his body in the water and begins to swim.

It's really not fair.

He moves down the first length of the pool with such ease you'd think holding his breath underwater is the most natural thing in the world. He turns and begins to swim back another length.

Sensing impending doom, I do the only thing I can—I start to splash around the pool, hoping to distract him and make him pop out of the water.

But he ignores my efforts and goes another length.

Beating me very easily.

But to prove a point, he swims one more length before finally emerging from the water as the winner. He's not even gasping for air.

"That's so not fair!" I yell out and splash water at him for good measure.

Michael seems pretty pleased with himself.

"I win even though you cheated."

He quickly swims over and faces me with a victorious smile.

"Unless of course, you want a rematch?" His eyes light up at the thought. "Double or nothing?"

I flick a bit of water in his face.

"A rematch?" My tone is accusatory. "So you can just beat me again?"

He gives me a smirk as he shrugs his broad shoulders.

"I thought I'd offer," he tells me with a wink. "Feels like the gentlemanly thing to do."

"That's quite all right," I eye him cautiously.

Michael's gaze is hooded as he watches me. His eyes skim over the top of my breasts as the water laps up against my chest. I can feel goose bumps begin to form and I fight the urge to cross my arms.

"So I win," he says after a long minute.

"Yes, you win," I confirm.

"First question?" he asks, studying my face.

I nod uncomfortably and hold my breath. There's no telling where this conversation is about to go.

"I think it's only fair," Michael says evenly, "since you now know my favorite place in the world, for me to know yours."

This is the last question I'm expecting and one I don't hesitate to answer.

"With my father," I admit quietly.

Understandably, Michael looks confused.

"I go the cemetery and visit his grave almost every week," I explain with a sad smile. "When I go there, I feel like I'm with him and it gives me a sense of peace I don't really find any other place."

I'm not surprised I share this part of myself so easily with him. I've always felt like Michael understands me more than the rest of the Sinclair clan. Like he gets me. And understands how lonely I've felt over the years. He's the only one who ever seemed to notice or care about how I was being treated at home. It's one of the reasons I've always been drawn to him.

"I know it might sound silly to you," I rush out when he still doesn't respond.

"Not silly at all," Michael finally replies, shaking his head. "It's beautiful. Like you."

I suck in my breath at the sound of his words. The feeling they give me. He's said it before. That he thinks I'm beautiful. But it's not something I'll ever get tired of hearing.

"I know it was hard for you." His voice is gentle and full of sympathy. "To have grown up without your real father. And to have had to suffer through an existence with Davis."

Hearing the caring in his voice is nearly my undoing. It *was* hard. It was more than hard. It was awful.

"Sometimes it did get pretty bad," I admit softly. "But then I guess I was luckier than most, right?"

"Don't diminish what you went through." Michael's voice is stern. "Just because you had more than most people financially doesn't mean you didn't hurt or feel as much. And from what I know and have seen of your mother, I'm pretty sure she never rushed to your rescue."

I can feel tears begin to form in my eyes and I have to look away from him. The reality of his words hurt. My mother never stood up for me with Davis. Never protected me against his vicious taunts. She was too consumed in her own world to see that her daughter was being tortured every day. It was as if she was blind to the entire situation. Or selfishly didn't want to be bothered with it. So at night, I used to dream about my dad coming down from heaven and saving me.

I would have done anything for that to happen.

But I never had anyone to rescue me.

The only person who ever did was Michael.

I try to blink back the tears that threaten to spill. Michael doesn't hesitate. He pulls me into his strong arms and holds me tight against his chest. His face comes down to rest against my neck, like he's trying to transfer some of his strength over to me. I gladly take what he offers and embrace him, the strong beat of his heart against my ear both calms and reassures me.

"I'm sorry for your pain," he whispers in my ear. "I wish I could take it all away."

My heart stops.

It's everything.

These words of his mean more to me than any gesture or touch.

To know he cares. That he would fight for me. Because it's who he his. A good man. A man I've been in love with my whole life.

And this right here…

This.

This is the reason why.

I don't realize tears are streaming down my face until Michael turns his cheek against mine and begins to kiss them away.

"Don't cry," he whispers to me, his lips resting against my skin. "Please, Abby. They are not worth one of your tears. I promise you, I won't let them ever hurt you again."

His words wrap around me like a cocoon, making me feel safe and cherished.

Loved, even.

Everything I've been denied my whole life.

I pull my face away from him and stare into his cerulean eyes. They blaze down at me. I watch as a myriad of emotions play across his face—anger, sympathy, and what I need to see the most—desire.

For me.

I lift my hands up to cup his handsome face. I fix my gaze on his and allow him to see everything I feel for him. Everything I want from him.

"Abby." My name sounds like it's been ripped from his soul.

I respond to his need and pull his face down to mine so that I can capture his lips.

That mouth I crave.

That tongue I want to taste.

This body I want to be entangled with mine. Pushing into me. Feeding the hunger that I know only Michael can satisfy.

For a second I think he might reject my advances, like he's battling against something in his heart, in his body even—but then something changes and the hunger he's kept in check, the beast inside that he's been able to keep at bay—can no longer be tamed.

And he gives it free reign.

His arms crush my body to his as his hands move underwater and cup my ass, pulling me up against his hard shaft. Michael's tongue sweeps into my mouth, dueling with mine, tasting every crevice as my hands move from his naked shoulders to his rippled back, touching every inch of taut, bare skin I can find.

My legs come up on their own accord and wrap around Michael's waist as our kiss deepens and his hands skim up the side of my body before brushing over the tips of my nipples. I moan in response as they tighten up against his sweet touch.

He rips his mouth away from mine and traces soft kisses down the expanse of my neck as my head falls back to give him more access. His hands palm my breasts, and I moan with need and push against his hard pulsing cock, begging him for release.

"I want to fuck you," he says, his mouth roughly capturing mine again. His admission thrills me, turning the fire he's started in my body into a blazing inferno.

He thrusts his hips up against mine, grinding his hard cock against the thin material of my bathing suit.

Yes.

I let my body speak for me as my hands move over his naked skin, showing him my need—my acquiescence. I reach down and pull his ass toward my hips, rubbing myself against him, answering him the only way I physically can. His hand moves up to tug on my hair, wrapping it in a fist around his fingers as his mouth continues to devour mine. He kisses me so slowly, so deeply—feeding a part of my soul that so desperately needs what he's offering. He pulls back and stares down at me with those brilliant blue eyes of his.

I want him. So bad. It hurts.

If he stops now, I think I'll die.

"Michael," I practically beg, letting him hear my need. To feel the heat. To see the want and desire I have for him. It's all there for him to see. To hear. To know.

He reaches out and rubs two fingers over my swollen lips before his hand moves down to trace a line down my chin, to my throat to the tops of my breasts, leaving a trail of goose bumps in his wake.

"There's no turning back." His jaw is tight as his eyes smolder with desire.

A shiver of excitement runs up my spine.

"I don't want to turn back."

He closes his eyes for an earth-shattering second and when he opens them I know, I've finally won. We're not in a club. We're not in an environment where anything can change. There is no Davis who can show up and ruin everything.

This. Is. It.

Everything I've ever wanted, right now, for me to take.

His eyes slide down the length of my body and I shiver in anticipation of what's to come. I've never wanted anything so badly. Never craved anything so much.

Michael stares at me possessively, like he already owns my body just as completely as he does my soul.

My heart pounds when he reaches out for my hand. I take it and let him lead me out of the pool. He grabs a towel and wraps it around my body before gently picking me up in his arms. I wrap my arms around his neck and let him carry me into the house. He makes his way upstairs, past my room, and enters two doors that lead into his private suite. He pushes the door shut behind him before walking over to the large bed and slowly setting me down at the edge.

The room is charged with electricity.

Anticipation of what is to come.

He leans down in front of me and pushes the towel off my body. I can't help but shiver.

"Are you cold?" he asks, his hot gaze flicking up to mine.

I can only nod my head.

"You won't be for long," he promises me as his fingers brush up against my cheek. Heat shoots through my body, right to my core as I stare at him in anticipation.

Michael reaches out to touch the strings on my bikini top. He brushes the lines of my suit, teasing me with such promise.

"Everything is going to change between us," he whispers to me with warning as his gaze captures mine. "I want you to know that nothing will ever be the same."

"I want you." My voice is direct, strong, giving him no doubt that I want this just as bad as he does.

He lowers his head as his body shudders.

I wait for him to say something. But he doesn't.

When he finally lifts his gaze to mine the desire I see takes my breath away. His hands trail a path up my arms before reaching the straps of my bikini. He slowly pulls my top down, exposing my breasts to his gaze and touch. I remain still, my breath hitched, as his gaze moves over my chest and back up to my eyes.

"God, you're stunning," he whispers hoarsely.

I suck in my breath, his admission giving me the courage to reach out my hand and cup his cheek as I stare at him with longing.

"You don't know how beautiful you are to me," I whisper to him as I trace a line to his lips. "You've been so kind to me. You've given me so much. You make me feel—"

I never finish my thought because Michael yanks me from the bed and pulls me into his arms as he captures my mouth for an earth-shattering kiss. His tongue melds with mine, devouring me, unleashing all the pent up passion he's kept bottled up inside. My legs wrap around his waist, my naked breasts pressed up tightly against his chest as I moan with longing.

His hard body melds into my mine.

Naked skin has never felt so good.

I'm so wet and desperate for release, I can't even think straight.

His hands squeeze my ass as he thrusts his erection against my groin.

"Please," I beg him, pulling my lips away from his and running my fingers through his hair.

"Tell me what you want." His tongue skims over my lower lip.

"You," I pant out.

His hand tangles around my hair and yanks my head back, forcing me to open my eyes and stare up into his stormy, passionate gaze. The savage need in his face takes my breath away.

"No," Michael says roughly, his eyes blazing with need. "What. Do. You. Want?"

I stare up at him, my gaze foggy with passion. No man has ever spoken so boldly to me before. No one has ever told me they want to fuck me. Hard. I'm in a whole new territory now, with someone who's an infamous master in the art of seduction. This is a man whose eyes tell tales of sexual conquest, a man skilled enough to get exactly who and what he wants at any time.

A man who's completely out of my league.

"I'm going to fuck you, Abby." Michael's voice has a hint of warning as he grips my body with a fierceness that makes me forget how to breathe. "And it's not going to be proper with ribbons and bows and everything nice. It's going to be hard. And fast. Until you scream out my name and beg me to give you what you need."

My body trembles with anticipation.

I don't want proper. I've had that my whole life.

I want something new.

Something exciting.

Dangerous.

I want him.

"I don't want nice," I whisper to him.

"What do you want?" he demands.

"Give me the storm."

He pulls back from me, his eyes locking with mine, searching for the truth behind my words.

"I warned you." His voice is low, hungry.

He cups my naked breast, squeezing it before teasing my nipple until it's a tight bead against his palm. Excitement runs through me as he walks over to the side of the bed, holding me tight against his body. He runs his hands along my naked legs before grabbing me by the waist and throwing me on top of the bed. He stares down at me, the look in his darkened gaze one I can't decipher.

He follows me onto the bed and tugs on my bikini bottoms before sliding them off. Michael sits back on his knees so he can stare down at me. I watch as his gaze slowly, but reverently, moves over the length of my body. The ache inside growing with every second that goes by. He's the most beautiful person I know. The most alluring. The kindest.

And I love him.

I rip my gaze from his face and run my eyes down the length of his muscular body. I want to touch every inch of his skin. I want to taste him. I want to drive him as crazy as he's driving me.

I want him naked.

But when I reach for him, he pushes my hands away.

"Do you know what you do to me?" Michael's voice is thick with passion.

I shake my head no, incapable of even saying a word.

He grabs hold of my legs and pulls my body against the edge of the bed as he leans over my body. I suck in my breath as his lips come down to press against my calf. He licks and kisses his way up my leg, his other hand skimming up my body, to cup my breast. My body arches up against his touch.

And then his mouth finds my core, lavishing me with the attention I need more than I need air. Michael's mouth sucks, licks, and torments me until I'm on the verge of exploding. He slips two fingers inside and my muscles tighten around him, trying to hold him in as he continues his assault on my senses.

"Please," I whimper with need.

"Please what, Abby?" Michael's breath is labored as he lifts his body up, robbing me of his touch so that he can look me in the eyes.

His expression is wild, frenzied with need.

"Fuck me," I whisper to him as our eyes lock.

I want to know him.

I want to feel him inside me.

I want to belong to him.

A slow rumble emerges from something deep inside his soul. Hearing my words makes Michael lose whatever tenuous hold he has on his control. He pulls away from me for a second as he shoves his swim trunks off before melding his hard body into mine. It happens so fast I'm not even given a chance to take in that glorious body of his.

But then, it doesn't matter because I have what I've always wanted.

Skin against naked skin.

"Are you on the pill?" he whispers.

"Yes," I all but groan.

He grabs my face between his strong hands as his lips come down to capture mine. We taste each other. We drink each other in. Our tongues battle as Michael fucks my mouth as hard as I want him to fuck my body.

He yanks me into him and crushes my mouth. Our hands grab at every inch of exposed skin. I run my hands over his hard, muscled body, skimming over his broad shoulders, his lower back before grabbing hold of his ass. I've never needed anything as much as I need this man.

Right now.

Inside me.

His erection settles between my legs as his hand palms my breast. I don't know how much longer I can last. How much more I can take.

But before I can even beg him for release, he thrusts into me, filling me to my core. His body shudders as he flexes his full length inside, his shaft pulsing with life. My body adjusts to his large size, craving both the pain and pleasure at the same time.

This is everything.

This moment.

Michael inside me. The things we've both said. Nothing else matters.

Not tomorrow.

Not what this means for us.

Not anything.

I thrust my hips wantonly toward his as he rocks into me with a hard, frenzied need that has me screaming out his name, hoping he sees and hears how the pleasure he's giving me feels. My words are becoming more incoherent as he moves in and out, intensifying his pace.

I arch my body into his, delirious with pleasure as his cock skillfully pumps into me. My nails dig into his back as his mouth captures mine.

"Come for me," Michael commands, easing out of me then plunging back in.

"Michael!" I scream out his name, my pulse racing, his pace pushing me over the edge, giving me exactly what I want.

Need.

His hands grab hold of my hips as he plunges in deeper, stretching my body out until I can't bear any more of the sweet torture.

I explode around him, white-hot heat flooding my body as the orgasm rocks my body. Tremors crash around me as I shudder in ecstasy. A moment later, Michael groans out my name as he joins me in sweet, sweet oblivion.

The first thought that comes to mind when I can think clearly is one that makes me smile…

I can now officially tick Michael Sinclair off my bucket list.

CHAPTER TWELVE

I don't think I'll ever be able to use my legs again.

Michael's breath tickles as he places wet kisses on my neck. He rolls off my body and pulls me into his side, draping a muscled arm over my shoulders, while his other lightly skims over my skin. I trace lines over his taut skin, reveling in the feeling of being able to touch him so freely.

"I've wanted you from the moment I gave you your first kiss." His voice is low, husky from the aftermath of our lovemaking.

His words stoke the embers of hope in my heart.

I lift my head up and prop my chin on his chest so I can look him in the eyes. To see his truth.

"I thought you didn't remember," I admit to him with surprise.

Michael lifts a brow in confusion.

"You were drunk," I tell him with a shy smile. "I didn't hold it against you."

"The last time I was drunk was when I was eighteen," he says with a broad smile. "After spending a night with my head in a toilet, I learned my limits. It has never happened again."

My heart stops as I take in his words. He remembers. Which means he wanted to kiss me. Which means he's wanted me all this time.

Wasted time.

"Then why did you stay away?"

He closes his eyes and sighs.

"I didn't want to hurt you," he admits honestly.

"How could you ever hurt me?"

He opens his eyes and captures my gaze. There's a primal look in his eyes as they flicker over my face.

"You don't know me." His voice has a great deal of warning.

His words take me by surprise.

"Are you trying to scare me?"

"I'm warning you," he tells me.

I stare into his eyes, willing him to say more.

"I'm not easy to deal with. I'm never in one place... my work, it consumes me," he says as confusion flashes in my eyes.

"What's wrong with loving your work?" I ask him as I watch him struggle.

"I've never been good in a relationship. My past speaks for itself," he says almost gruffly. "I'm not what you deserve."

"Why don't you let me decide what I need?" My voice is soft.

I know he's conflicted. I can see it.

"What if this is all I can give you?" he asks quietly, his eyes guarded as he watches my every move.

His words hit me hard and my body stiffens in reaction, involuntarily moving away from his warmth. He doesn't allow me the distance, pulling me back in, his arm wrapping around my waist like a vine, trapping me to his side.

"What then, Abby?" he prods, his voice hard when I still don't answer.

"I don't know," I finally say.

Because I don't.

Can I just be a fuck buddy for him? Fall into bed with him when I need sex and that's all?

Can I handle that?

"I've never just been with a man..." My voice is slow and hesitant. "Only to sleep with him."

For some reason, my comment angers him. His hold on my body becomes possessive. His hand moves to grip my hair, yanking my head back, the look in his eyes proprietary.

"I don't want to hear about any of your past relationships ever again." His voice practically growls. "As far as I'm concerned, none of them existed."

His words are completely ridiculous. I do have a past. Just like he does.

The possessiveness in his eyes, the fire he's spitting from my innocent comment, contradicts what he just said a few moments ago.

"And what about your past?" I counter.

"What about it?"

"How many women have you been with?" I throw out at him.

"Enough to last a lifetime," he answers directly.

Manwhore.

I have the sudden urge to punch him in the stomach.

"Your hypocrisy is astounding," I mutter in annoyance.

Michael growls low in his throat before rolling me onto the mattress so he can lean down over me. His body settles between my legs, his shaft hard again, pushing against my core.

Lord.

A hot shudder courses through my body.

He wants me.

Again.

"Is it?" he asks in a husky voice. The look in his eyes is feral.

"Yes," I say breathlessly. "It is."

"Do you know what I think is astounding?" he asks, tracing his finger along my lips.

I shake my head.

"The way you make me feel," he admits in a rough voice.

The heat in his eyes sets my body on fire.

"You make me feel things…" he continues as his teeth graze my neck. "Things I've never felt before."

There's a fierceness to his touch, a territorial way his hands move over my body as he continues to reveal his thoughts to me.

"That night at the pub, I wanted to rip Stephen's arms away from your body for even thinking it was okay to put his hands on you."

Michael exhales into my neck as my body melts with need. "I find myself jealous of Danielle, of Georgie. Of even the damn dog, Eli."

"Eli?" I whisper incredulously, his words pumping through my system like an erotic storm.

"I'm jealous of the attention you gave a dog." Michael sounds outraged, almost accusatory, like I had intentionally tried to get a reaction out of him.

"Do you have any idea how this makes me feel?" he asks as he tugs on my ear with his mouth.

He grabs both my wrists, imprisoning them with his large hand as he looms before me. Since I'm unable to find the words, I can only shake my head in response to the fire he's started. It begins to burn through my veins and trails its way to my core.

His scorching blue eyes capture mine.

"You make me lose control." His face is clenched with need.

He sits up suddenly and grabs hold of my body, lifting me high up in the air as if I weigh next to nothing and settling me on his lap. His mouth closes over my breast, sucking and licking as if his life depends on it. My head falls back as I moan in longing, my hands holding his head to my chest so he can continue his attention. He expertly teases my flesh, blowing against my sensitive skin, licking the nub until I have no more thoughts left in my head.

His mouth trails a path up my neck, licking and kissing my skin, making me frantic, needing him inside me more than anything.

"I think it's only fair if you feel the same way I do."

I want to tell him I do.

I want to tell him that he has me just as wound up. That it's been my state of existence for as long as I can remember. I want to tell him that I get jealous too. That I can't stand to see him smile at another woman. That I've dreamed about being with him. That he's all I ever want.

But I can't articulate the words.

Because it's too much.

Too soon.

And this right now, the promise of his hard cock inside me, it's all I want.

He yanks me back up against his body, his shaft pushing against my wet sheath as his mouth takes mine with such force that our teeth grind against each other. His tongue moves into my mouth as we devour one another—tasting, licking, and claiming. It's openly carnal. I take his tongue and suck on it, giving back just as hard, showing him what he does to me.

"Please," I beg, ripping my mouth from his. "Let me touch you."

His answer is to lower me down on his erection, slamming into me so fully that I scream out his name. My eyes roll back in my head as I groan in pleasure. My hands bite into his shoulders as my body adjusts to his large size.

I open my eyes and try to focus.

My foggy gaze settles on his beautiful face. His eyes are closed and the look on his face is filled with ecstasy. Little shards of pleasure shoot up my spine as I take in his drunken look of passion.

God, he's hot like this.

Inside me.

Filling me to my core.

The raw need I see on his face.

It turns me on in a way I never thought possible.

As if he knows I'm watching him, his eyes open and meet mine. We stare at one another, the moment so intimate that I don't even want to breathe for fear I might ruin it.

His hands are wrapped around my waist. His cock is filling me to my core. And the look in his eyes tells me everything he's incapable of speaking.

I'm not just a body to him.

A casual fuck.

I mean more to him.

Even if he can't admit it yet.

"You feel so good," he whispers, slowly lifting me up so he can thrust back in. Our moans intertwine as we grasp one another. "You're so wet for me."

"I want to taste you."

Our eyes remain locked. He thrusts inside me again, the vein on the side of his neck pulses with exertion as he shakes his head.

I've never felt such pleasure in my life.

"Not yet."

"Michael!" I whimper, staring into his eyes. "Let. Me. Touch. You."

But he doesn't. The look in his eyes is hard, determined, as he shakes his head with the enigmatic smile I've come to know so well. Our chests are heaving, the electricity between us unlike anything I've ever felt in my life.

"You're mine." The words are rough, his eyes smolder with an urgency that rocks me to my core.

"Say it!" he commands as he lifts me up off his cock, robbing me of the fullness. I cry out in need.

"Please!" I beg him.

His hand tangles into my hair, pulling my head toward his so he can tease me more with those full, sensual lips of his.

My heart races at a frantic pace as my hands move up to cup his cheeks so I can cradle his face against mine.

"Tell me you're mine," he commands in a steely voice, his jaw clenched as he waits for me to give him what he wants.

What he doesn't realize is what he's asking for is everything I've ever wanted. And more. So much more.

I hold onto his face, our eyes locked together, before softly brushing my lips against his.

"I'm yours," I whisper to him with such emotion that there's no way he can't know how much he means to me.

His mouth roughly captures mine as he brings my body back down again on his hard cock. I scream out in both pain and pleasure as he pounds into me with a force that will probably make me incapable of walking properly for another day.

He moves quickly, pumping hard, fucking me like a sexual conqueror. I greedily take in his every thrust, grinding my pussy into his cock, licking his lips, his cheeks, his ear—anything my mouth can find as an animalistic frenzy takes over my body.

Yes. Fuck me. Harder. Faster.

Yes.

The words come out of my mouth in a jumbled mess as he pumps into me with a force that makes my teeth rattle. The wave of ecstasy comes fast, shattering my soul as my hands curl into fists at my side and I scream out my pleasure. Waves of bliss crash over me as I tremble around his cock, and he continues to thrust into me until he throws his head back and shouts out my name.

My body sags around him as he grips onto me, capturing my mouth for another mind-altering kiss that completely consumes my soul. His hands softly move over my body, lightly skimming over my skin as we both come down from our high. He lifts me up, cradling my body against his chest, and walks with me to his shower. Once we reach the glass doors, he sets me down and we walk inside.

Michael fiddles with the electronic panel before warm water spills from above, raining down on us as he picks up a bar of soap and begins to lather my body. The water pounds down on us as he runs his soapy fingers over my skin. The water feels like heaven. His hands lazily trace lines over my body as he methodically bathes every crevice, every centimetre of bare skin that I have. Not one centimetre of my skin is left untouched. I stare at his hard chest, reveling in the power I see in his arms, his muscles bunching together as he strokes my body.

He lathers my hair. Rivulets of water and soap slide down my face as he continues to lavish me with attention. When I can't take much more, I step away from his touch and take the bar of soap out of his hand.

"My turn," I tell him in a voice that leaves no room for him to deny me.

I won't take no for an answer this time.

Michael stands utterly still, finally allowing me to have my way.

I give him a wolfish smile before I take in his perfection.

I watch as his eyes rake over my naked body, giving me a look of pure ownership. It's everything. My heart skips a beat, and I'm mesmerized by the way he stares. Like I'm something fine. Something unbelievably appealing.

Something to be worshipped.

He deserves to know the feeling is reciprocated.

I let my eyes do the talking as I stare at his beautiful, muscled body.

He's cut like an athlete. Every ripple, every line in perfect symmetry. I give myself free reign as I follow the length of his calves, to his rock hard thighs, his thick, long cock that was created to pleasure a woman. His abs are perfect, his muscular chest wide and taut. Those beautiful arms I know firsthand are powerful enough to have his way with me, yet gentle enough to hold me and take away my pain.

His nakedness is the stuff of dreams.

"You're perfect, Michael."

He takes a step toward me, leans down and kisses me so slowly, so completely that I forget how to breathe. But this kiss isn't about sex or foreplay—it's something else. Something deeper.

I pull back from him and take in a steadying breath.

I use the bar of soap to trace my own lines over the length of his body. My hands move over his chest, his arms, around his stomach to his back. I run my fingers over his tight ass, cupping it my hands before bending down on my knees and giving the same attention to his calves, his thighs. I make my way around his body until I'm directly in front of him.

My hands move over his shaft, stroking it, feeling it against my fingers, squeezing softly until I hear him groan in pleasure.

I memorize every inch of him.

I want to remember him like this forever.

His hands move to my head, skimming over my hair and I look up at him, capturing his eyes before I lick the long length. I watch in satisfaction as he shudders in pleasure. I suck his tip before slowly taking him into my mouth. His fingers grip my hair as he rocks his hips, thrusting into me. My body heats up in desire as I watch his head fall back, his eyes half open, pleasure etched over his gorgeous features as he mouth-fucks me. I loosen my jaw, taking him as deep as I can, reveling in the power I have over him.

I feel his cock throb, tighten, before his body trembles out his orgasm into my mouth. His semen is salty on my lips.

"Abby," Michael groans out before pulling me up off my knees and into his arms. He kisses me hard, our tongues melding into one as the water falls around us.

"What am I going to do with you?" he whispers against my lips.

"Anything you want," I tell him as his body shudders against mine.

***

Hours later we wake up wrapped in each other's arms. I open my eyes and find his blue eyes settled on my face as he watches me sleep. I give Michael a shy smile before tiredly rubbing my eyes.

"What time is it?"

"Five o'clock," Michael says to my surprise. I can't believe I slept through most of the day.

"Did you sleep at all?" I ask him softly. "Or have you been watching me this whole time?"

"I like watching you."

My stomach does a little somersault.

"I like watching you too," I whisper to him, reaching out and brushing a strand of his dark hair away from his face.

Michael gives me a tender smile before planting a soft kiss on the bridge of my nose.

"I'm glad." Michael's voice is playful. "I've spent the last twenty minutes willing you to open your eyes. I'm starving."

"You should have woken me up!" I tell him, trying to pull away from him. He rolls over my body again and attacks me hungrily, raining kisses all over my face.

His hands move up to tickle me and soon I'm screaming with laughter, begging him to leave me alone.

He settles his body over mine and begins to kiss me deeply, his tongue lazily lavishing mine with attention like he has all the time in the world.

"You look like an angel when you sleep."

Why does he have to say all the right things?

Most of the time, I remind myself.

He suddenly lifts himself up off my body and places a quick, chaste kiss on my lips.

"Food first," he says.

"And then?" I ask with a raised brow.

Michael gives me a wolfish grin.

"Dessert."

He rises naked and saunters over to his walk-in closet, completely confident with his nudity. I stare at his body in awe. It's absolutely perfect and truly a sight to be seen. I could look at him all day. Michael slips on a pair of gray cotton shorts and walks back over to the bed, where I'm now propped up on my elbow watching his every move.

His smile is playful as he leans down on the mattress and rubs a finger on the side of my lips.

"Am I going to have to drag you out of my bed?"

"I'll meet you downstairs."

"I'm not leaving this room without you."

My pulse flutters.

The thing is, for some reason I'm finding myself a bit embarrassed now to just hop out of bed as naked and confident as he just did. It's silly and completely ridiculous considering he's now seen *and* licked every inch of my body, but now that we're not in the thick of things my shyness has returned with a fury. Proper Abby, as he likes to call me, is about to rear her uptight head.

"You have got to be kidding me," he mutters under his breath.

And then as if he knows what I'm thinking he grabs hold of my hand and pulls me out of bed, not allowing me a moment of hesitation. Once I'm standing naked before him, he stares at my body with longing.

"You're so fucking hot," he says in a raspy voice.

The way he says it makes me confident. Takes away any feeling of shyness I might have let creep in.

It makes me want to dance around the room naked—a feeling I've never ever had with a man before. He grabs me and pulls my naked body up against his.

"I need you to eat," he says with a great deal of force.

"Why?" I ask.

"Because I'm going to fuck you all night long," he says, running a finger down the length of my cheek. "And you're going to need your strength."

My pulse goes into hyperdrive at the thought of the night ahead.

His words are all I need to hear before I move away from his body, grab my bikini bottoms and quickly slip them on. I look around the room and see one of his white T-shirts thrown haphazardly on a chair. I walk over and put it on.

The shirt almost falls to my knees, covering me appropriately enough to walk downstairs and run into any staff that might be milling around. I run my hands through my hair and hope I look halfway decent before turning to him with a smile.

"I'm ready."

The playfulness is gone from his gaze and in its place is an intensity I've never seen before.

"What?" I ask him shyly.

He shakes his head before giving me a sexy smile.

"I like the way you fill out my shirt."

I laugh in response and take the hand he holds out for me.

"But I like you naked more." He kisses my palm and leads me out of the room.

We make our way downstairs to the veranda. The smells coming from the kitchen make my mouth water and I realize how famished I am. Giselle has fixed the table for us and the setting is romantic, overlooking the spectacular ocean view. A bottle of rosé sits on ice next to the table, and Michael busies himself with pouring us both a glass. He hands me a drink before settling down across from me and lifting his own in a toast.

"To your first time in Costa Rica," he says, watching me with a hooded gaze. "I hope to give you many more firsts before this trip is over."

My breath hitches and I give him a nervous smile before taking a sip of the crisp drink.

My gaze sweeps over his chest in unabashed admiration.

"I wouldn't mind giving you a first experience as well," I tell him with a resigned sigh. "But I'm starting to think that might not be possible."

"You already have," he replies cryptically.

I feel my stomach drop through the floor and before I can ask him what he means, Giselle walks out onto the veranda with a colorful tray filled with assorted fish, lobster, and shrimp that could feed a family of five.

"I hope you guys are hungry," she says with a friendly smile as she sets the platter on the table.

"This looks delicious," I tell her appreciatively.

"Giselle is an incredible cook," Michael tells me with a wink.

"I've been trying for years to make her give away her secret recipes, but she guards them with her life."

"You are too kind, Mr. Sinclair." She blushes from the praise. "But I am happy you enjoy my food. Now, if you'll excuse me, I'll go and get the rest."

Giselle leaves us and Michael serves a generous portion on my plate.

"It's so much food," I tell Michael as he continues to fill my plate. There is absolutely no way we will be able to even eat a quarter of this meal.

"I ask for it," he says, giving me a small grin. "We always take all the leftovers to a shelter not far from here. Nothing goes to waste."

If possible, I fall in love with him even more. How can one man be so bloody perfect?

"Everything you do," I say to him in a bit of awe. "All of it... I wish there were more people like you in this world."

"I've been lucky," Michael sounds almost embarrassed. "Giving back to the people and the planet is the least I can do."

"It's still incredible," I tell him loyally. "I know a lot of people who don't share your sentiment."

"It's nothing." Michael waves off my compliment. But that's the thing. It's not nothing like he says. It's incredible. Admirable.

And most of all—it's humbling.

My entire life I've been around wealthy individuals. I've never seen anyone give back the way this man does. And now that I work for him and see it first-hand every day, my appreciation for him and all that he is and has done has only grown.

Giselle comes back out with a large bowl of pesto linguine and a colorful salad that looks to die for. My mouth waters at sight.

"Bon appetite," Giselle tells us. "Please save room for dessert. I made your favorite soufflé."

Michael closes his eyes as if he's in the throes of ecstasy and I can't help but laugh at his boyish enthusiasm.

"God, I missed you, Giselle."

"Enjoy," she says with a wink before leaving us alone on the veranda and closing the door behind her.

I serve Michael some pasta and then put some on my own plate before diving in. Michael is right. The food is heavenly. We're quiet for a few moments, eating in comfortable silence.

"This is delicious."

"The best," Michael agrees, taking another sip of wine. He watches me as I eat and I smile as I motion to his plate.

"She spoils you," I tell him. "She must really love you."

"She's good to me."

"I would venture to guess that you're good to her as well," I say, licking the decadent taste of pasta off my lips.

"Maybe," he says, his gaze lingering on my mouth, his expression ravenous, like he's hungry for more than just food.

I take a deep breath and lean back in my chair, the desire to have him again assaulting my senses.

"I have nine more questions I get to ask you." His head tilts to the side, studying my face.

"You do. What would you like to know?"

"Everything." His voice is fierce with longing, wreaking havoc on my nerves.

"Everything cannot be asked in nine questions alone," I reply teasingly.

"No?"

"Doubtful," I say.

"We'll see about that," Michael returns before jumping right in. "So tell me, Abigail, what's your greatest dream in life for yourself? A secret one that no one else knows."

My heart thumps in my chest as I think about his question.

My secret dream?

You. I want to blurt out to him.

Michael has always been my secret dream. Since I was a child, he was the dream I wished for and held close to my heart. Up until the moment I told Danielle about my crush, Georgie was the only person in the world who ever knew.

"I don't have one," I tell him softly.

"I'm not buying that for a second." He shakes his head. "Everyone has one secret desire."

"Even you?" I ask.

"Even me," he admits with a ghost of a smile.

I sit in silence for a moment and mull over my life. I think about all the dreams I've had over the years, and then I open up to him in a way I never thought possible.

"I wish I knew what I was born to do," I admit candidly. The words seem to rush out of me as if they were locked away in a secret vault for years. "Everyone around me has a purpose. They have a path they're on. And I don't. I never really have. I feel like I've been lost in the wind, just fluttering about trying to find my way. My purpose. Hoping that something will call out to me and I'll just know that it's it—like someone lifting a sign up and saying: Abigail this is for you. This is what you were born to do. And I promise you'll be happy and feel fulfilled by it."

Michael's gaze is enigmatic as he watches me.

"I guess my dream is to feel like you do when you talk about your work," I tell him shyly. "I want to know what that's like. To have that passion and drive for something that I'll just know was for me."

Michael remains quiet when I finish, and I pick up my fork and twist a roll of pasta around, looking for a way to occupy the silence.

I feel more vulnerable than I ever have in my life. More than I did after sleeping with him. This is something different.

I just bared my soul to this man.

"Look at me," he commands in a husky voice.

I lift my gaze and meet his. The blues of his eyes seem to permeate my heart.

"Can I give you advice?" he asks politely.

"Of course."

"I think you put too much pressure on yourself," he says slowly. "I think some people are born knowing what they want and others have to search for a while before they find it. It doesn't make you any less special or wonderful. It just makes your journey more adventurous. You get to try different things. You get to experience life in ways that people who are set and know what they want can't. I think your situation is unique and exciting. And I believe that's the way you should start looking at it as well."

His words give me pause.

I have never looked at my life the way he just painted it.

I've always come from the glass-half-empty side instead of full. I've always been quick to point out my flaws, not my perfections.

"The world is yours to take, Abby. You just have to decide where you want to fly," Michael says as I continue to think about his words.

His advice makes sense, somehow dispelling my insecurities of what I always believed to be my greatest flaw.

"Thank you," I tell him gratefully. "I've never thought about it quite like you just pointed out."

"Because you've always been too busy judging yourself," he tells me knowingly.

"You might be right, " I admit slowly. Because I can't lie. Because he's right.

I have.

Always judged myself. I've never been good enough. Smart enough. Pretty enough. Capable enough. I've allowed myself to be a victim of Davis. A victim of my mother. Of every circumstance in my life.

How horrifyingly awful of me.

Michael smiles as he watches the realization slowly begin to dawn on my face.

"Another first?" he asks rather arrogantly.

I look up at him and meet his penetrating blue gaze. An understanding flickers between us. He gets me. More than anyone I've ever known.

He understands.

And he's not judging me.

"Unequivocally, yes," I tell him with a smile.

Michael looks pleased with himself.

"And you?" I ask him.

"What about me?"

"What's your secret dream?" I prod.

"I didn't lose the game," he returns with a chuckle.

"No, you didn't," I agree giving him a tender smile. "But it's a question I'd really like to know the answer to. I think it's only fair."

Michael is silent for a minute as the light from the sunset illuminates his handsome face. I soak in his perfection, wishing I could stop time and remain in this intimate moment forever.

I wait with baited breath for him to answer.

"I don't have one," he finally admits to my surprise.

"You just said…" I laugh good-naturedly as I shake my head in dismay.

Michael's gaze darkens as it pins mine.

"What if I told you my dreams have been answered?" he asks slowly as my heart melts with desire.

"From what I know about you?" I return as a myriad of emotions flood my mind. "I guess I'd believe you. But still, I'd like to know what they were."

"If you're a good girl, maybe I'll tell you before we leave Costa Rica."

CHAPTER THIRTEEN

Surfing is definitely not on my list of things I want to do ever again.

I cough up salty ocean water as I drag my feet to dry land. Somehow I manage to keep hold of my beginner's surfboard as the water rushes around my sore calves. After a night of unbelievable passion, Michael convinced me to take my first surfing lesson with him this morning.

I hate it.

Like loathe.

Despise.

Never-want-to-do-again hate.

For the life of me, I can't understand why anyone would want to jump on a board and skid on top of the water before being toppled over by an angry wave. What bloody torture. Who invented this sport anyway?

"Abby!" Michael calls out from his surfboard, beckoning me to come back into the water.

I shake my head and shout, "I'm going to just lay out here!"

I need to catch my breath.

Michael gives me a thumbs-up and paddles back out to wait for another wave.

I throw my surfboard on the sand and plop myself on the towels we spread out when we arrived. My body aches all over. I've always thought I was in good shape but from the way my muscles are quivering from the strenuous exercise, I begin to doubt my earlier beliefs. Regular exercise is definitely something I'm going to have to add to my list of activities when I get back to London.

The heat from the sun hits me hard and within minutes my skin is tingling from the strong rays and I feel immensely better. I lean up on my elbows to take a swig of my water and watch Michael expertly catch a wave back in. I sigh in pleasure and wonder if there's anything he's not good at. I'm pretty sure if he puts his mind to something, he can learn to do it better than anyone.

When he reaches the shore, he tips over into the water and quickly runs out holding his surfboard at his side like a pro. He reaches me in no time, his breathing barely labored from the exertion. So unfair! I could barely make my way to the towels.

He smiles down at me as he puts his surfboard on the sand.

"How did you like it?" he asks with a wide smile, his enthusiasm contagious.

"I didn't." I give him a deadpan stare that gives the opposite reaction than I had hoped for as he throws his head back and roars with laughter.

I'm too tired to be embarrassed.

"You didn't have any fun?"

"Not in the least." I am enjoying the current view as I sit back and admire the display of raw masculinity that stands before me.

He hunkers down next to me and leans over my body, the water from the ocean drips on my bare skin causing shivers of excitement to rush up my spine as he stares down at my face, blocking the sun with his wide chest.

"That's too bad," he says with a tender smile as he traces a line down the side of my cheek. "It's my favorite sport."

"By all means, enjoy yourself," I tell him breathlessly.

His lips find mine in a long, satisfying kiss before he pulls back to stare into my eyes. He looks thoroughly amused.

"I had wanted us to enjoy an activity together," he admits with a shrug.

"I thought we already had," I reply teasingly, referring to the sexual marathon we had participated in the night before.

His gaze turns heavy as it flicks over my body.

"How remiss of me," he says huskily, his eyes smoldering with desire.

I lift my hand to cup his cheek. His stubble tickles my skin as he rubs his face against my palm.

"I want to take you to town for dinner tonight," he tells me. "Do you think you'll be able to stay awake?"

He's referring to the fact that I almost fell asleep on my soufflé last night. I had barely gotten two bites in before I felt as though I hit a brick wall and needed to lay down.

"I'll be fine if I can take a nap."

"I might have to let you do that on your own." His eyes lazily caress my body. "I don't know if I can lay in a bed with you and keep my hands to myself."

My heart slams in my chest and I can't stop myself from pulling his face back down to mine to give him another kiss. The things he says. The way he makes my body sing. So far this trip has been too good to be true.

His hand moves up my stomach to palm my breast, teasing my nipple until I moan in pleasure.

"Michael," I whisper in longing.

"Abigail," he whispers back against my lips.

"We're on a beach," I remind him trying my best to remain as modest as possible even though it's virtually impossible with this man. "Anyone can walk by."

He sighs against my mouth before robbing me of his touch and flipping on his back. I immediately regret my words, leaning up on my elbow to stare at his half-naked perfection.

"God, I needed this," he says with his eyes closed soaking in the sun.

"You're a bit of a workaholic," I admit.

"I like what I do."

"I can tell." I trace a line down his stomach. His hand snakes out and stops my onslaught.

"Behave," he says gruffly. "Or I'll forget we're on a beach and have my way with you."

My heart speeds up at the possibility.

As if he can read my mind his eyes slowly open to stare at me. There's a desperate need in his eyes, enough heat in his gaze to light the jungle on fire.

"Don't look at me like that," I whisper to him.

"Or what?"

"Or I'll let you," I admit with longing.

I hear him silently swear before he abruptly stands up and offers me his hand. I stare up at him in confusion.

"I don't want to surf." There's no bloody way I'm getting back on that thing.

"We're not going to surf." A primal look comes over him as he stares down at my body as if he owns it. "We're going to walk back to the house. And then I'm going to fuck you until you don't have any energy left in your body and you can think of nothing else. And then I'm going to tuck you nicely into bed and leave you alone so you can rest up for tonight."

He doesn't have to ask twice.

***

After spending a few hours fulfilling his promise, Michael leaves me so I can take a much-needed nap. I sleep like the dead. When I finally wake up, it's late in the afternoon and I'm feeling refreshed. I take a quick shower and slip into a simple blue maxi dress that falls to my ankles. I leave my hair down and put on blush and mascara before checking my appearance in the mirror. Luckily, I haven't burned and am sporting a golden tan that gives me a healthy glow.

Before I head out, I grab my phone and check for text messages and missed calls. I'll have to sift through my emails later as well. I know I'm probably inundated with work emails I have to answer and

I know I'll have to dedicate a few hours to respond to everyone.

Danielle and Georgie both texted to see how things were going and I write back to both saying everything is amazing, even adding a few happy face emojis to let them know how great it's all going. I know it's late at night and they're probably sleeping so I promise to call them both the following day to talk.

When I listen to my voicemail, I'm surprised to hear my mom has left a message. Since my rather dramatic breakup with Dimitri, a feeling of dread washes over me whenever I hear a message from my mom. It's not like she's had anything nice to say since that moment in my life. Or ever, really. The woman could have a doctorate in how to make your child feel inferior and inadequate. But regardless, she's my mom—the only one I've got—so I force myself to listen to her message and brace myself for the disappointment I will no doubt hear in her voice.

"Abigail." Her voice rings through the phone. "It's your mother. I believe you've forgotten you have one since I barely ever hear from you. But that's not why I'm calling."

Her voice is laced with sarcasm, and I try my hardest not to roll my eyes.

"I believed you couldn't hurt me any more than you already have but as my luck goes, that is just not the case." I hear her sigh dramatically into the phone. "Davis has just informed your stepfather and me that you've been conducting yourself in a way that is so unbelievably shocking I had to call you and hear it from you directly."

My breath hitches as I wait for her to continue.

Even her voicemails to me are long and drawn out, like she has some strange need to torture me more than any human should have to bear.

"He told us that you are having an affair with Michael Sinclair."

My heart stops beating.

Like literally, stops.

Shock waves ripple through my body as the reality of her words

204 | COLET ABEDI

slowly wash over me.

Bloody Davis strikes again!

"Abigail Walters, I sincerely hope this is just a misunderstanding on poor Davis's part," she continues in a stern voice.

Poor Davis?

Poor.

Davis.

Wtf?

More like Davis... the Antichrist!

"You do realize Michael is a forever bachelor and will never *ever* marry you, let alone be faithful." My mother's voice practically sneers with displeasure. "And not to mention, you are related to him through marriage and will never live this affair down if it is in fact, true. Think about what the family will say? Even though you jilted poor Dimitri, who I still believe was a perfect choice for you by the way, at the altar, I honestly thought you had more sense than this. Please call me immediately and tell me that I have nothing to worry about."

I have to listen to the voicemail three more times because I keep thinking I must be dreaming and my mom's one-sided conversation has to be a part of my imagination or even jet lag. But no, on the third go around, I realize it is not my mind playing tricks on me. This is actually a fact.

Holy shit.

As usual, my mother's cold disapproval leaves me feeling help-less and insecure. Like I've done something wrong. It shouldn't matter. It really shouldn't. But unfortunately, old habits die hard, and it does matter.

I sit down on the couch as I allow the reality of my situation to sink in slowly. Well, fuck me. My mom knows. My stepfather knows.

Who else in the family is aware?

Davis can't be that big of an ass, can he?

Who am I kidding?

Yes, he's proved time and time again, that he can.

God, I hate my stepbrother.

Why does he always have to be so cruel? What had I ever done to him?

Since I know the answers to those questions will remain in the black hole of life's eternal mysteries I do the only thing I can to calm myself —I call Georgie.

I don't care what time it is back home. I need my friend to talk me off the edge of the cliff that I'm now teetering dangerously close to and about to jump off from.

"*Oui*?" I hear his groggy voice echo into my phone. "*Merde*! It's three o'clock in the morning, Abby."

"I know." I can't stop my voice from quivering.

"What's wrong?" He immediately reacts to the sound. "Has something happened? Are you hurt?"

"I'm all right," I rush out to him. "I mean, physically yes, but emotionally not so much."

"Talk to me."

I do. I tell him about my mom's message and wait for him to respond.

"Abby." Georgie's voice is uncharacteristically gentle. "A leopard never changes its spots. Your mother is who she is and will be that same person for the rest of your life unless sanity begins to seep into her brain, which I would venture to guess will not happen in the foreseeable future. You cannot live your life in fear of her."

"But what if she's right?"

"About Michael?" Georgie asks directly.

"Yes."

"You knew exactly who you were jumping into bed with," Georgie begins slowly. "You know who he is. He has not pretended to be any other way with you. He has been honest with you from the beginning. Do not allow your mother to suck the joy out of your life.

I told you before you left to have fun and enjoy yourself. The rest of them—your mother, Davis, the family—all of them be damned. This is your life. Start acting like it."

Georgie's words begin to seep into my mind and heart. The truth behind his words making perfect sense.

"You're right," I tell him after a long moment. "You are *so* right. I don't know what I was thinking. Why do I always allow her to second-guess myself? It has to end."

"It does," he agrees.

I smile in gratitude, wishing he was in front of me so I could give him a big hug.

"I'm sorry I woke you up. But I'm happy I got to hear your voice."

"*Je t'aime*," Georgie says.

"I love you too," I say before hanging up.

Georgie's words stick with me and after the conversation I had with Michael last night about dreams and living my life without judging myself, I feel infinitely better. It's none of my family's bloody business what I do or who I do it with. I'm a grown woman. And this is my life to do what I want. All of them be damned. My eyes are wide open and I know exactly what I'm getting into.

And that's all that matters.

I throw my phone back into my purse and head out of the room searching for Michael's whereabouts. I don't see him outside by the pool and wonder if he went out to surf again, maybe with Joseph this time. I walk into the kitchen and find Giselle cutting up some fruit. She smiles in pleasure when she sees me.

"Did you have a good nap?" she asks as she takes in my appearance.

"I did, thank you," I reply, unable to stop the blush that rushes to my cheeks. I'm pretty sure Giselle is aware I'm now sleeping in Michael's room.

"Can I get you anything to drink or eat?" she asks politely as she continues to chop away.

"I'll just have a water."

Giselle puts the knife down and opens the refrigerator to pull out a glass bottle. She sets it on the counter before pulling out a cup from one of the cabinets and pouring me a large glass.

"*Gracias*," I tell her gratefully when she hands me the glass.

"*De nada*," she returns. "Mr. Sinclair let me know you'll be eating in town tonight."

"Yes," I nod. "That's what he told me."

"You'll love the restaurant he's planning to take you to," she says with a knowing smile. "Their food is second to none, and the band is very popular with the locals."

"I'm really looking forward to it."

"Mr. Sinclair was working out here all afternoon. That man never lets himself relax."

"I know," I agree with her.

"Maybe you can convince him to take it easy," Giselle says, giving me a wink.

I laugh off her comment. I really don't believe anyone could ever have the power to deter Michael from what he puts his mind to.

"Do you know where I can find him?"

"His family rang the house earlier and he's been in his office ever since."

"His office?" I ask, thinking how coincidental it is that both he and I received phone calls from our respective families.

"It's the small house down the pathway to the left of the pool," she explains. "Would you like me to take you there?"

"That's all right. I'll just find it myself."

I leave Giselle a moment later and head outside past the pool.

I pause for a moment to take in my surroundings.

The landscape on the property is lush, creating a tropical oasis that is warm and inviting. The pathways are picturesque and I realize I could stay here forever. I might even have to agree with Michael and start calling his home my favorite place in the world.

At the present moment, it is a far more appealing option than returning to London and having to sit my mother down, which I fully plan to do, and have the stay-out-of-my-life-and-start-acting-like-a-real-mother conversation that has been percolating in my head since my talk with Georgie.

I reach the small bungalow that is tucked away in the foliage and knock on the door. When there's no answer, I slowly turn the knob and walk inside. Michael's office decor here is more tribal than the one he has in London, which suits the setting infinitely better. Instead of windows facing the River Thames, he has sliding doors that open up onto a veranda overlooking the Caribbean ocean.

Definitely a preferable working environment.

Michael is seated outside with his legs propped up on a table staring out at the beautiful view. I walk up behind him and place my hands on his shoulders and lean in to kiss his cheek.

He stiffens in response and pulls away.

"Abby." His voice is formal. "You're awake."

I respond to his stiff greeting as if I've been burned and immediately step away from him. I curse myself for being so forward, but then how can I not be after the night and day we've had? I step around to the side of his chair so I can see his face.

Unfortunately, he's wearing sunglasses so I can't even gauge his mood by reading his eyes.

My mother's ominous words ring in my mind, and it takes everything I have not to allow myself to panic over his cold greeting. *It's nothing*, I tell myself.

Don't read into it, Abby.

"I woke up a while ago." I try to smile and push the feelings of doubt away.

"I trust you slept well."

"Perfect. I hope I haven't kept you waiting."

"You haven't."

I wait for him to ask me to sit down but the invitation doesn't come, so I continue to awkwardly stand across from him. I cross my arms to keep myself from fidgeting.

"Is everything all right?" I ask after an awkward minute of silence.

"Why wouldn't it be?" Michael returns in a cool voice.

"No reason," I shrug nervously. "I was just asking."

I wait for him to say something more but it doesn't come, so I turn my gaze away from him and stare out at the ocean.

"Are we still having dinner in town?" I ask after a moment, hating how small my voice sounds even to myself.

"Yes."

I feel a surge of relief at his response. Maybe my mom's message has thrown me more than I know and I'm just reading into things. He has been working all afternoon. Maybe he had a bad work call and is just stressed out?

I turn my gaze back to his, wishing more than anything that I could see his eyes and tell what he's thinking. I force myself to smile brightly.

"When will we be leaving?" I ask, silently begging him to give me some kind of warmth. Anything to appease the anxiety that is slowly building inside.

"In an hour."

Emotionless.

Distant.

The polar opposite of how he had been this afternoon.

I can't help but panic.

I stand there like a fool for a second longer before awkwardly shuffling my feet.

"Then I guess I'll just wait for you in the house," I finally say when Michael doesn't offer me any more.

"Perfect."

I try to hide the hurt I feel from his cold dismissal, but it's hard.

So hard. I bite my lip and nod and turn to walk out of the room.

"I'll see you then," I tell him, my voice raw.

I leave the bungalow as fast as I can and when I shut the door, I could swear I hear him curse out loud. I brush the few lone tears that fall down my cheeks and tell myself that it's nothing. That he's just in a mood. But the fear of Michael the chameleon changing his colors on me again overwhelms me. I can't take it.

I won't allow it to happen.

I won't.

He can't withdraw from me now. Not when we've come so far. I retreat back to my room in the house and do my best to calm myself. I decide to change my outfit into something skimpy and sexy, hoping to entice him and melt some of that icy layer that suddenly formed while I was asleep. For one horrifying moment I wondered if my mom rang him too, but then I shake the thought away.

Even she would not be so presumptuous, at least not until she had spoken to me to find out the truth.

But still... the thought lingers, and I can't help but wonder.

I force the disturbing thought away and slip into a baby doll strapless white dress that shows an ample amount of my cleavage and legs and pair it with high nude wedges. I replicate the makeup Danielle had put on me at the office and am pretty pleased with how I look. I think I do a good enough job and feel confident enough to face anything Michael throws my way.

When I walk downstairs, I find Michael waiting for me in the family room. He's dressed casually in green cargo shorts and a white T-shirt, looking as impossibly handsome as he always does.

If I hadn't been so focused on his reaction, I wouldn't have seen the way his eyes light up in desire when they sweep over my body. The reaction is so quick, like he's trying to hide his true feelings from me. His jaw tightens as he exhales and then the cold wall that met me in the office is back up in place.

I search his face for any sign of the warmth I saw before and it's not there. But I still cling on to hope. I just wish I knew why he's acting like this.

What happened that changed everything?

Was it stress?

Was it something that happened in bed with us?

No, everything about that was perfect.

Too good to be true.

It's something else.

"Ready?" he asks quietly, interrupting my train of thought.

"I am." We walk to the front door and get into the car.

The ride to the restaurant is uncomfortably silent, and I honestly can't wait to jump out of the car and breathe in the open air. I don't understand why the atmosphere around him is so charged now and I'm only hoping the ambiance of the restaurant will help change his mood.

When we arrive, Michael helps me out of the car and issues a few orders to the driver, who leaves us. The restaurant sits right on the white sand beach, and the music from the band can be heard outside. Michael silently escorts me inside and I'm surprised to see Joseph waiting for us by the bar with a dark-haired Latin beauty. His arm is around her waist and he greets us with a warm smile.

"*Buenas noches*," he says happily as he walks over to us.

"*Buenas noches*," Michael and I both reply.

"Nice to see you, Carla," Michael says warmly, leaning in to give her a kiss on the cheek. "This is Abby."

"Pleasure to meet you," I say, shaking Carla's hand.

Carla smiles and returns the greeting.

"They have our table ready outside like you requested," Joseph tells us as an attractive waitress makes her way to us, carrying our menus.

"It's nice to have you back, Michael," she practically purrs as she puts a much too familiar hand on Michael's shoulder.

"Natalia," Michael says with an appreciative smile. "It's good to see you."

I notice the subtle way she squeezes his shoulder and can't help but wonder how well the two really know each other.

Natalia is dressed in short white jean shorts and a crop top that shows off her rock hard abs and a silver belly button ring. Her body is enviable and her sultry good looks would interest a dead man. Her gaze coolly flickers over mine and the female in me can tell she's sizing me up as if I'm her competition.

Instead of shrinking back like I usually would have done, I stand my ground and return her look with just as much icy disdain.

"Follow me," she says as she moves past us and makes her way to the tables outside.

Michael places a hand on the small of my back as we follow Natalia. Fairy lights are hung all around the trees outside, and the deck is filled with occupants eating and enjoying the music and ocean view. Once we're seated, Natalia hands us each a menu and lingers over Michael.

"Jaguar coladas for the table?" Natalia asks Michael with a sexy smile.

"You remember!" He smiles back at her in a way that makes me cringe.

"I remember everything you like," she returns flirtatiously.

I have the sudden urge to throw up. The two are much too familiar with each other. The subtle looks. The way Natalia keeps touching him. I really think I'm going to be sick. Before I can excuse myself from the table and run to the nearest bathroom, Carla reaches out to me and squeezes my arm.

"How do you like Costa Rica?" She tries to distract me from the sexy bombshell that is hanging on to Michael's every word.

"It's great," I reply in a small voice hoping my face isn't betraying what I'm feeling.

"Joseph told me it's your first time here."

"It is," I tell her, wishing I could just disappear.

From the corner of my eye, I see Natalia leave the table and I sigh in relief. Michael turns his attention to Joseph and the two begin to speak in Spanish.

"There's so much for you to see."

I know Carla is trying to distract me from the feeling of misery that has suddenly consumed my heart.

"I'm really looking forward to it," I tell her, wishing the drinks were ready so I could distract myself in any way possible. I know alcohol can do the bloody trick.

"I hear you had your first surf lesson today," Joseph interjects, joining in on our conversation.

"I did," I reply with a flush of embarrassment, thinking about how badly I sucked at it.

"How did you like it?" Joseph asks curiously.

"She hated it," Michael answers quickly before I can.

"Really?" Joseph seems surprised.

I shrug uncomfortably, annoyed that Michael would answer for me.

"I didn't hate it. I've just never surfed before, and it was harder than I thought."

"You'll have to go out again," Joseph says with an encouraging smile. "The first time is always the hardest. And Michael is the best teacher."

"She won't be going out again," Michael returns quickly, his voice hard.

My heart lodges in my throat as I look over at his impassive face.

"I won't?"

"Isn't that what you told me?"

I shrug my shoulders defensively and before I can answer Natalia is back with four large tropical drinks that are just what I need to help calm myself.

She places them in front of us before returning to Michael's side and leaning into him in a way that is completely inappropriate.

I hate her.

"What can I bring you to eat?" she practically purrs into his ear.

Michael gives her a warm smile, obviously enjoying the attention.

"We'll leave it to the chef," Michael says as he hands her his menu.

"Perfect." She collects the menus and gives him another look that makes me want to scratch her eyes out.

Is this really happening right in front of me?

Is he openly flirting with this Costa Rican beauty?

Right. In. Front. Of. Me.

I look over at Joseph and Carla and if they notice, they thankfully don't let on. When Natalia leaves, Joseph grabs his drink and lifts his glass.

"Cheers!" he says as he meets my gaze with a warm smile. "To Abby's first time in Costa Rica."

We clink glasses and I take a long sip from the straw. The drink is delicious and I can't taste any alcohol.

"Careful," Michael finally turns to look at me with an indecipherable look on his face. "These drinks tend to creep up on you."

"I'm a big girl," I return coldly. "You just worry about yourself. I think I can handle myself just fine."

His jaw clenches and he narrows his eyes. I can tell he doesn't appreciate my comment.

I look away from him and smile widely at Joseph.

"Do you give surfing lessons?" I ask him impulsively.

"I do," Joseph says slowly.

"Can I bother you for one tomorrow?" I continue even though it's the last thing on earth I want to do. But Michael's last comment about me surfing has annoyed me more than I thought possible. How dare he?

"Me?" Joseph laughs nervously as his eyes flicker over to Michael.

If possible, Michael's body language becomes more ominous, but I don't care.

"Maybe my teacher didn't do such a good job." I can't help but jab at him with a good-natured smile. Joseph's eyes round in his face and I can tell I've completely thrown him. I know I shouldn't have put Michael's employee in this position, but I can't seem to help myself.

"I think that's a great idea," Carla suddenly chimes in as she looks from Michael to me. "Maybe you were nervous out there with Michael. I know when Joseph tried to teach me I was very uncomfortable so maybe a lesson from someone you don't know might make you change your mind."

Joseph still seems uneasy. He looks over at Michael for his approval.

"So what do you say?" I continue on, completely aware of the angry energy Michael is emitting.

I glance over at him and cringe when I see the ice that blasts from his eyes.

"You're free to do as you please." His voice is cool and emotionless.

If for some reason they weren't aware before, I'm pretty sure Joseph and Carla have caught on to the animosity that's grown between us.

"It would be my pleasure," Joseph finally says with an awkward smile. "We'll go out in the morning."

"Perfect." I take another long sip of my drink.

The last thing I want to do is go out and surf again, but I'll be damned if I let Michael stop me.

"So what do you have planned while you're here?" Carla asks, changing the subject.

"I don't really have plans yet."

"No? Well, you definitely have to go zip-lining and you absolutely must go swimming with the dolphins. You'll love that. It's such an incredible experience."

"Abby isn't like the women here," Michael says casually, leaning back in his chair. "She's posh and won't enjoy anything that might chip a nail."

WTF?

His insult is direct. Cutting. And it stings.

But I'll be damned if I let him know how much it hurts me. How bloody dare he?!

"I think you should let Abby speak for herself." I look at him with icy displeasure. "I would actually love to zip-line and swimming with the dolphins sounds like a dream."

I turn my gaze back to Carla and smile, hoping to dispel some of the awkwardness that Michael is hell-bent on causing.

"If Michael won't take you, I'm more than happy to," Carla replies with a kind voice as she gives me a knowing look. "I have the week off school so it would be no trouble at all."

"Thank you." I shrink back in my seat just wanting to disappear.

Joseph's phone rings and he excuses himself from the table to answer it, leaving the three of us alone.

Luckily a waiter comes over with some seafood appetizers and places them down on the table for us. Unfortunately, none of the appetizing smells whet my appetite and all I want is for dinner to be over so I can go back to my room and nurse my breaking heart. I don't even understand how we got here? What's suddenly switched in Michael's mind?

Carla helps herself to some food as I watch in misery.

"This looks amazing," she says to no one in particular.

"If you'll excuse me." Michael pushes back from the table and heads back inside the restaurant.

I turn to watch him go and notice how Natalia saunters over to him when he reaches the bar. She leans into him and they begin to talk in a much too intimate way—heads bent in close together, bodies almost touching.

I can feel my face flush with embarrassment.

Again, he's openly flirting with her right in front of me.

I really can't even believe it's happening.

I want to die.

Carla grabs my hand and forces me to look at her. I know she can see the pain on my face. She gives my hand a reassuring squeeze.

"Don't let Natalia get to you," she says, her eyes narrowing in anger. "She's a desperate fool."

"He doesn't seem to mind." I try my best to act like I don't give a damn.

"You're obviously fighting," Carla says with a knowing look. "We've all been there, and he's just being a stupid man."

"He is a stupid man," I mutter in return, agreeing with her astute observation.

Carla laughs and I can't help but join in.

"Aren't they all?" She squeezes my hand in reassurance. "This argument will pass."

I shrug my shoulders and look away from her knowing gaze. Carla doesn't know our backstory and I'd rather not get into it with her. She's obviously under the impression we've been together for a while, when that is far from the case.

"Can I tell you something that I could probably get in trouble from Joseph for revealing?" she says as she picks up her drink.

"What's that?" I ask, my interest piqued.

"Joseph says Michael's never brought a woman to his home here before," she tells me. "And he knows he's had plenty of girlfriends. Joseph thinks he's serious about you."

I'm happy I don't have any alcohol in my mouth or I would have spit it out in Carla's face. Her comment actually makes me laugh.

Like, really laugh.

Serious? About me? That's rich.

"What's so funny?" Carla asks in confusion.

"You're so wrong." I shake my head, laughing. "That can't be farther from the truth."

"How can you be so sure? Even though he's mad about something, I can still see the way he looks at you."

"How?" I hate myself for asking, but I can't seem to stop the words.

Carla's smile is slow, sure.

"The way a man looks at a woman he's in love with."

CHAPTER FOURTEEN

"*Buenos noches*!!" the lead singer of the band calls out on the microphone.

The group of diners yells back at him in pleasure as he begins to belt out a song in Spanish. The music is beautiful and sexy and many people get up to dance, swaying their hips in excitement, letting the music be their guide.

I take another long sip of my drink and settle back in my chair to watch the people dancing joyfully. We've gone through our appetizers and dinner and are now just drinking and enjoying the ambiance. Michael and I have both been quiet most of the night and let Carla and Joseph entertain us with their stories. He's refrained from making any more insulting comments toward me, and I've done my best to ignore his presence.

I've also silently obsessed about Carla's conversation with me. I don't want her words to consume me, but they do.

They make me think.

More than that, they give me hope.

Thankfully, Michael hasn't gone back inside the bar to visit with Natalia again, and I've been able to relax if only for just a bit. I'm on my third jaguar drink and I'm definitely tipsy, but I don't care. Carla and Joseph seem to be just as buzzed as I am. Michael, who's had more to drink than any of us, is the only one who seems stone-cold sober. And still in a piss-poor mood.

"Do you salsa?" Carla yells out over the music, clapping her hands in excitement.

"I never have," I yell back at her, shaking my head.

"Come on then." She pulls me up out of my chair and leads me to the dance floor.

She begins to show me a few steps and I copy her movements until I finally get the hang of it. We move around for a bit and Carla smiles in pleasure when a man comes up behind me, his arms circling my waist as he begins to gyrate his hips against my back.

"Dance with me, beautiful," the stranger whispers into my ear as he moves with the music. "Feel the salsa in your blood."

He takes hold of my hand and twirls my body away from him. I follow his steps and before I know it, I'm moving my hips to the beat of the music, grabbing hold of my short skirt and using it as I dance around him. I'm having fun, the music pumping the life that Michael had managed to suck out of me right back in.

I can't stop myself from turning my head to see if Michael is watching.

And he is.

The heat from his gaze makes my heart pound in my chest, and I decide to give him a taste of his own medicine. I move up against the man, emulating every sexy movement I see around me and he holds me close against his body as we dance to the beat of the music.

I can feel Michael's eyes boring holes into my back.

I can feel his anger.

His jealousy.

And if I'm poking a bear, I don't give a damn.

After the way he's treated me, he deserves every bit of this.

But my moment of power is short-lived because Natalia suddenly appears, making her way out between the dancers and gyrating her hips in the most sensual way I've ever seen a woman move. Clearly, she's allowed dancing breaks at her job.

I can't take my eyes off her.

She knows how to move. How to throw her beautiful head to the side. How to lift her hands and sway in order to entice anyone watching.

I sneak a peek at Michael and my heart sinks when I see that his gaze is now focused on her. My stomach becomes unsettled and all I want to do is run away.

I am not going to watch this, I think to myself.

No bloody way.

I excuse myself from my dancing partner and quickly walk away, appearances be damned. I reach the table and ignore Michael, grab my purse, and make my way to the bathroom as fast as humanly possible. I realize with despair that I can't even grab a taxi and go back to his home because I have no idea what the address is.

I'm bloody helpless here.

Unshed tears blind my eyes and I do my best to blink them away. I will not cry because of him.

I. Will. Not. Cry.

Once I'm safely in the single bathroom, I let the sadness I'm feeling rush over me. How have things gone so wrong? What changed while I slept? Was he finished with me? Was this his way of showing me?

He did warn me…

Before my god-awful tears can explode like a bursting dam, the door to the bathroom slams open and Michael fills the frame with so much anger emanating from his body that it takes both my tears and breath away.

My mouth drops open.

How dare he?

How dare he have the audacity to come in here?

"What are you doing?" I ask him in outrage.

His eyes are lit with fury.

"*What am I doing?*" he barks out, slamming the door behind him, locking it for good measure.

His stance is menacing as he slowly advances on me. Since the bathroom is so small, I have no place to go. No choice but to stand my ground.

"Get out," I hiss, my body trembling in anger.

Michael gives me a smile that doesn't quite reach his eyes.

"That's not the way this works." His eyes smolder as he stares down at me. "I give the orders. And you follow them."

"Are you insane?" I yell at him. My hands clench at my side as fury takes over.

"What happened when I went to sleep at the house?" I rant until he's right in front of me. "What happened that's made you act so callously toward me? How dare you treat me so disrespectfully!"

Only inches away.

My eyes rake down his body as my body trembles in anger.

"I think you need a lesson on how things work with me." His voice is silky with promise.

"I think you've already taught me that lesson." I shove past him but his hands reach for my waist, jerking me against his body. "Let me out of here."

God.

He's hard.

And even though it's the last thing that should matter to me right now, knowing he still wants me, makes my pussy throb in response.

His erection pushes against my stomach as he grabs my hair in a fist and yanks my face closer to his.

Desire floods my senses, temporarily distracting me from my anger. I try to push him away. I try to fight the insatiable fire that begins to sweep over me like a blazing inferno.

"You're not going to do this," I whisper to him, even though I'm already wet with longing. Wanting him inside me more than I want to scream at him in rage.

Goddamn my traitorous body!

"Watch me."

His smile doesn't quite reach his eyes, and I know I am in trouble.

His lips crush my mouth, his tongue sweeping into my mouth with brutal force. I try to remain still. To be unaffected. But the assault on my senses is too much to bear. And within moments, I'm kissing him back with as much anger and passion as he's giving me.

Very quickly, it's not enough.

It never is with him.

His hands reach under my short dress and squeeze my ass, pulling my body to his so he can grind his erection into my wet core. His hand moves to the front of my panties and before I know it, he slips two fingers inside, causing me to moan out in longing as I clench him tightly, dying for release.

Suddenly he flips me around. I hear him rustle with his pants, pulling my panties down before plunging into me from behind so fully that I forget where we are—in a public restroom— and only care about him giving me satisfaction. He grabs hold of my hair again and jerks my head back so he can kiss my neck as he pounds into me with a force I need. Crave. More than I need air.

"Look at me!" he commands.

I open my eyes and stare at him in the mirror as he works my body from behind, fucking me harder, faster until my eyes blur in desire.

"You belong to me!" His voice is rough, possessive, his eyes are lit with both desire and anger as he continues to pound into me until I'm crying out in need.

"Say it!" he commands again, slowing down his movements until I'm whimpering for him not stop.

"Michael…" I can barely speak. Let alone think.

"Say it!"

"I hate you right now!" I cry out as he teases me mercilessly with that magic cock of his.

"I don't give a damn." His voice is possessive, his eyes hard, focused, and in control.

He stops moving.

His thick cock settles into my swollen sex, and I try to move against him, but he won't let me. His hold is strong. His grip on my body, fierce.

He nips my neck with his teeth, marking me, making me cry out, cursing him for making me feel this way. Hating him for making me want him so much. Hating him for turning on me.

Loving him for all that he makes me feel.

"Damn you!" I cry out in need.

"Damn you, you little she-devil," he says, his eyes blazing with need. "Did you think you would get away with that display?"

I close my eyes and allow his words to permeate my soul. Whatever was going on with him, whatever battle he was trying to wage against me, it wasn't enough to keep him from wanting me.

When I open my eyes, I let him see it all.

The secret I've kept in my heart for all these years.

The desire.

The need.

The love.

"I belong to you," I whisper.

His eyes glaze over in pleasure. In ownership. And he gives me exactly what I need. He fucks me until I can't breathe or think. Until I don't want to and I explode around him in a mind-altering orgasm that rocks me to my core.

My body trembles in the aftermath as he comes inside me, filling me with his semen, calling out my name again and again until we're both spent from desire.

When my soul enters my body again, my senses become aware of my surroundings. I can hear the loud music from the band outside the bathroom, I can feel Michael's labored breaths against my skin. He is holding me close to his body like I'm the most precious thing in the world.

"You're going to be the death of me," he whispers against my neck, his voice tormented.

He pulls out from me, pushing my panties back in place as my feet settle back onto the floor. My legs feel like Jell-O and I lean up against the sink, wondering if I'll be able to walk out of the bathroom.

"We're going home." His voice is hard.

"Home?" I ask in confusion, thinking he means back to London.

"To my house," he says, rubbing his cheek against mine as he grabs hold of my hand and pulls me out of the bathroom.

We're both deadly quiet on the ride back to the house.

We didn't bother saying our goodbyes to Carla and Joseph and I was grateful because I didn't think I could face them after what had just happened in the bathroom. Michael took care of the bill at the front and texted Joseph goodbye.

When we reach his house, I jump out of the car and rush inside, craving the sanctuary of my room. Needing space from him so I can get my thoughts in order. I run up the stairs, not caring if he's following or not, and make my way to my room. I shut the door behind me and before I even have a chance to breathe easy, the door bounces open.

"What do you think you're doing?" he hisses out at me as I turn to face him.

He's still angry.

My eyes are wide as I stare at his ominous form.

But then…

Hold on…

Why is *he* angry?

I'm the one who should be angry. He should be kissing my ass as far as I'm concerned. His behavior is in question, not mine.

I lift my chin and face him, letting the anger I had earlier sweep over me. Allowing it to make me brave. To give me power over him.

"I'm going to bed," I tell him in a haughty voice. "Alone."

Michael's smile is slow.

"Are you?"

"I am."

"I don't think so." His voice is hard. "I'm not finished with you."

My heart stops in anger. But I won't allow him to get the better of me.

"But I'm finished with you," I tell him as the tenuous hold I have on my temper breaks. "I will not allow you to disrespect me ever again!"

My comment throws him. And for a moment I see the uneasiness flicker in his eyes.

"Natalia?" I snarl at him. "I take it she's served you in more ways than I can imagine?"

Michael has the sense to look uneasy.

"Yes…" I look around for something to throw at him. "I can see from your reaction that she has."

I find a glass vase. Pick it up and hurl it with all my might at his head. He ducks easily and the vase shatters into the door behind him.

"How dare you take me to a restaurant where one of your whores works?!" I shout at him, finding another object to throw at him again.

I'm blind with rage. I can't even see straight as I continue hurl objects at him with all my pent-up anger.

After a moment, I realize Michael's anger has dissipated and he's watching me with an amused expression. Like he's both pleased and shocked I'm so rattled.

I wait for him to say something.

But he doesn't.

"Do you have anything to say for yourself?!" I shriek out at him in uncontrollable anger. How dare he look like he's about to laugh?

"There's an antique statue behind you that was given to me by an indigenous tribe in Colombia," he says nonchalantly. "I'd be upset if you decided to break that too."

His comment takes the wind out of my sails and I shriek like a banshee again as I turn away from him, trying my hardest to calm myself. I look around at the disaster I've just created and am in bloody shock over my own lack of self-control. I have never—*never*—in all of my life lost it like I just did with this man.

"You need to leave," I tell him, my voice trembling.

"I don't think so," he returns with a ghost of a smile. "I've never witnessed anything so spectacular in my life."

"Spectacular?" I whisper out in horror. "Take a look around!"

He does as I say and shrugs his shoulders.

"Objects that can be replaced."

"Objects that can be replaced?" I ask in confusion.

"That's what I just said." He gives me a wicked grin.

"You're insane," I whisper.

"A bit," he admits. "But from the look of things, I do believe I'm in good company."

I throw my hands up in anger and stare at him like he's lost his mind.

"Up until an hour ago you were treating me like I was an infectious disease," I remind him.

"You're definitely contagious."

"You're making me crazy."

"Sweetheart, I think you were already there." He smirks. "But I must admit I find your temper terribly attractive. Who knew proper Abby was capable of such…"

He looks around at the disaster I've just created.

"Destruction."

"Was this intentional?" I ask him with narrowed eyes.

"What part?"

"All of it."

"Not quite." His eyes dance with mirth. "Though I would love to take credit for making you finally lose it."

I did just definitely lose it. I take a deep breath in and count to ten. The man is going to make me crazy. What am I thinking? He *is* making me crazy!

"What changed?" I ask him as I cross my arms. "I went to sleep thinking…"

I stop myself from talking.

"Thinking?" he asks slowly as he takes a step toward me. "Finish your thought, Abby."

"That everything was finally happening!" I shout out at him.

"Finally?" he asks, lifting a brow in confusion.

"Come on!" I explode. "Stop pretending like you've never known how I've felt about you! You bring me on this trip. You make love to me. You show me kindness. You make me feel things... and then you throw it all away with your mercurial mood—and then if that's not bad enough, you flirt with that woman right in front of me! How dare you treat me like this?! I'm not some common woman who can be yo-yoed around!"

The tears begin to fall before I can stop them.

"I won't be toyed with!" I cry out to him, my emotions blinding me. "I have feelings. I'm human, goddamnit!"

I don't know how he gets to me so fast but one minute I'm a quivering mess of tears, and in the next, he pulls me into his arms. Kissing my head, my face, the tears away before I can even muster the strength to push him away.

"I'm an ass," he whispers into my ear. "I'm so sorry for making you cry. I never want to be the one to cause you any pain."

I let him hold me for a minute longer, needing the comfort he's offering more than anything. But then sanity kicks in, and I remember everything he's put me through and I push away to look into his eyes.

"Then why did you hurt me?" I ask him softly, feeling more vulnerable than I ever have in my life.

Michael's pained gaze meets mine and I see the struggle in its depths. He closes his eyes and leans his forehead down against mine not saying a word. His breath is slow, labored.

"Michael?" My voice is uncharacteristically forceful. "Answer me."

When he remains silent, I move out of his arms, giving myself space.

And wait.

"Abby…" His voice sounds tormented.

He turns away from me and silently curses before looking back at me with his bright cerulean gaze.

"I told you I'm not good at this," he finally says.

"No." I shake my head, not buying it for a minute. "That's not it. There's more, and you owe me an explanation."

"Clayton called," he says to my surprise.

"Clayton?"

"Yes," Michael says as his gaze meets mine. "That ass of a stepbrother you have has been talking…"

I curse out loud, loathing my stepbrother more than humanly possible. After I speak to my mother, Davis is the next target on my list.

"And Clayton disapproves?" I say the obvious, feeling almost deflated.

"Yes."

My heart sinks in dread and the feeling of anguish that comes over me is almost too much to bear.

"Of course he does," I whisper back as tears begin to sting my eyes again. Michael's admission hurts more than I thought possible. I've always loved Clayton and looked up to him. I was a champion of his relationship with Sophie. I wanted him to find happiness. I always thought he felt the same way about me. Did he not think I was good enough for his younger brother?

"It's not what you think," Michael rushes out quickly when he sees the look on my face.

"No? Then what exactly is it?"

"Christ, Abby," Michael mutters as he closes his eyes. "It's not about you—it's about me."

"You?"

"My past. The way I am. My entire life, goddamnit! I've never had a steady girlfriend. I've never wanted anything serious. I've never even felt more than passing affection for a woman. Never."

Icy dread spreads through my heart as I eye him cautiously.

"And you." He throws his hands up in despair. "You're not just some woman… you're—"

"I'm what?" I prompt when he's silent.

"You're *you!*" His jaw tightens as he exhales. "You're sweet, Abigail. Innocent. Fragile. You're not the kind of woman I would ever think to pursue. And I did. Knowing goddamn well what all the consequences would be."

A feeling of helplessness sweeps over me as I allow his truth to seep into me. He's being honest. As hard as it is to hear, I can't blame or fault him for it.

I wait for him to say more but he doesn't. So I push him for the answers I need to hear.

"Then why did you?" I finally ask.

He opens his eyes and meets my gaze head-on, the desire he has for me there to see, burning into my heart.

My soul.

"Because I can't stay away!"

He holds my gaze for a second longer before looking away, a look of disgust sweeping over his face.

"And now here we are," he practically growls, his emotions as volatile as a simmering volcano.

I watch him for a moment and feel like I'm having an out-of-body experience. Like a voyeur looking in on a scene that has nothing to do with them. And I see it all for what it is.

A strange feeling of calm comes over me as I let the reality of the situation set in. He's sexually attracted to me. He wants me physically. But the rest…

"What did Clayton say?" I ask calmly.

Silence greets me again, but I wait. I want to know.

Everything.

And I won't let him leave until he tells me.

"He was angry." Michael's gaze flares as it sweeps over my face. "Rightfully furious with me. My brother loves you and doesn't want to see you hurt again. And he believes I will do just that."

No one knows Michael more than Clayton. The two have always been close. More than anyone in the world, Clayton would know what his brother was capable of, or not. I stare at Michael and will him to say something to make me feel better. Something to make me feel safe.

But he doesn't.

The energy shifts into something somber.

He hasn't bothered to deny his brother's thoughts. He believes Clayton is right. That breaking my heart is an inevitable outcome.

"And I guess, I just realized he was right," Michael voices the words that make my heart twist in pain.

After another awkward moment of silence, I find my voice.

"Thank you for clarifying our situation," I reply softly, unable to mask the hurt I'm feeling.

"Abby! Don't look at me like that. It's killing me," Michael pleads. "You're not cut out for a life with me, a relationship even."

His words throw me.

"Cut out?" I question, not understanding what he means.

"You're posh."

There it is again.

I decide I hate that word.

And I hate him for using it over and over to describe me.

"I find that observation incredibly insulting," I tell him harshly.

"It's not meant to be." His voice sounds unapologetic. "It's just the truth."

"You act as though you weren't raised the same way I was." My voice is hard as I attack him right back. "You had much more than I did growing up. Look at your life now. This house. Your multiple homes around the world. Your driver. Your plane. It's astounding... I'd really like to know what your definition of posh is."

Michael watches me intently before shaking his head.

"You're misunderstanding me," he says. "It's not about money —"

"Then what?"

"The places I go," he begins to say. "The things I do—"

"Because I didn't particularly like surfing?" I cut in angrily. "I'm sorry I didn't realize that not enjoying a sport would cause you to label me as a vapid, insipid woman consumed with the finer things in life."

"That's not what I'm saying..." His voice is harsh, eyes narrowed fiercely as he stares at me.

"Then what are you saying?"

"You would never enjoy the life I like to live," he says grimly. "You would never survive it."

"That's incredibly judgmental of you, Michael," I reply coolly. "And it hurts. You're the last person in the world I'd ever think to cast opinions about me."

"Maybe I am judging you." Michael's voice is hard. "But I've also known you since childhood. I've seen you out at parties and in social settings. I saw the man you picked to be your fiancé for god's sake!"

I blush in shame at the mention of Dimitri. If there were one thing in my life I could change, it would be that damn decision to ever get engaged to that man.

But I can't take it back.

"That was a mistake." I hate my voice for trembling, for sounding weak. "Dimitri was just a foolish, foolish decision on my part."

"Then why did you do it?" Michael's eyes narrow as he stares at me in anger. "Tell me why."

"My mother—"

"Fuck!" Michael curses before turning away from me and running a hand through his hair. "You let your mother dictate your life? You let your goddamn mother decide who you were going to marry?"

He jumps to his own conclusions. Ones that are not far from the truth, as demoralizing as it might be.

"What do you want me to say?! I made a mistake! I'm sure you've made plenty in your life. And maybe I was trying to run away from it all—my life at that moment! I don't know. But I'm not going to go back in time and defend myself to you, defend how helpless I felt. It happened. And it's done. If that was the life I wanted, I would have gone through with the wedding. But I didn't. I realized it was the furthest thing from what I wanted."

"What do you want?" Michael asks, taking a step toward me.

His stance is forceful.

My mouth goes dry as I stare up at his handsome face. It's almost painful to look at him.

You. I want to shout out at him.

You are all I've ever wanted.

But after everything he just said, I can't.

I shake my head instead.

"You're not being fair," I whisper to him. "You have no right to judge me. You have no right to jump to conclusions about who you think I am. You can just be honest and say that you don't want to be with me. You don't have to do or say all of this."

When Michael is only a foot away from me, he stops. We stare at each other. Close enough to touch one another, but now separated by so much more than just physical space.

Michael's stormy gaze meets mine and deep gut-wrenching anguish comes over me.

Is this it?

This can't be it.

I'll die if it is.

"I never said I don't want to be with you." His voice is soft, husky. "I said you wouldn't fit in my world. And I don't want to hurt you. I can't stomach the thought."

Hot tears begin to fall down my face as I stare into his eyes. I don't even care that he can see how much he's hurt me. My emotions are raw and I don't know how much more of this I can take.

"Then that's it." I'm finally able to speak. "There's nothing more for us to say."

He watches me with a ferocity that makes my breath catch and for a minute I think he's going to pull me into his arms and tell me he's wrong, that he's going to give us a chance. But when I see the cold wall sweep up over his face, I know that's not going to happen. He's made up his mind, and from what I know of him, he will not budge.

"I'd like to be alone now." The words are even painful to say because it's the last thing I really want.

"Are you sure?"

"Yes." My voice is filled with the finality of our situation.

He nods curtly before swiftly turning his back to me and walking out of the room.

When the door shuts, I crumble to the floor in anguish. I sob until I have no more tears to shed. Until I'm raw and have nothing left.

I feel completely empty as I realize the truth.

When Michael Sinclair left the room, he took my heart with him.

CHAPTER FIFTEEN

My eyes are swollen from crying all night.

I wasn't able to sleep at all, reliving the evening over and over like a broken record. For one blissful moment in the morning, I thought I had I had a bad dream, and it didn't really happen. But no, reality sunk in and the misery and devastation I felt the night before hit me as hard as the sun's bright rays.

I shower quickly and then pull out my computer to book a ticket home. The earliest flight I can find leaves that evening. After I finish, I pack up my things and reply to texts from Georgie and Danielle. I don't tell them I'm coming home, figuring I'd fill them in on my heartbreak when I get back to London.

I change into a sundress and decide to head downstairs to find Joseph and ask if he can help me find a driver to take me to the airport. When I make it down the stairs, I see Giselle straightening out the family room. She gives me a welcoming smile.

"*Buenos días*, Abby," she says kindly. "What can I get you for breakfast?"

"I'm not hungry, but thank you."

"No?" She frowns as she takes in my appearance.

I know she can tell I was crying, my eyes are so swollen it would be hard not to notice.

"Are you all right?" Her voice is gentle and nearly my undoing. Sympathy is the last thing I need right now. Sympathy will only make me feel sorry for myself and bring on more tears.

"I'm fine. I was actually wondering if you could tell me where I can find Joseph?"

She watches me for a minute longer before giving me a sympathetic smile.

"I saw him out front of the house. I think he might still be there."

"Thank you," I say gratefully, making my way past her.

I step out the front doors and look around the courtyard for any sign of Joseph. Luck is finally on my side as I see him next to one of the cars, bent down low, waxing the wheels.

I walk toward him and he turns to face me when I approach, giving me a sheepish smile.

"Are you ready for that surfing lesson?"

"No," I say with a small laugh. "That's not why I'm here."

Joseph looks almost relieved.

"Then what can I help you with?"

"I was wondering if you could help me organize a car for this evening?"

"Do you want to go shopping in town?"

"I'm leaving tonight," I tell him softly. "And I need a ride to the airport."

Joseph's eyes round in surprise.

"You're leaving?"

"Yes. I think it's for the best."

Since Carla and Joseph were witnesses to the tension between Michael and me last night at dinner, I'm pretty sure he knows why.

"Does Michael know?" Joseph asks curiously.

"I haven't had a chance to tell him yet. But if it's not too much trouble, I was hoping you could help me."

"Of course." His response is immediate. "I'll take you myself."

"Thank you," I say gratefully. "My flight is at seven o'clock so I'll have to be at the airport a few hours before. But I'll go whenever you can take me."

"We'll leave at four."

"Perfect. I'll be ready then."

I leave Joseph and head back inside. I'm grateful Michael is nowhere to be found. I head back upstairs and slip on my bikini, grab a towel and head back down. Since it's my last few hours in Costa

Rica, I'll spend the day on the beach and enjoy the ocean. As I make my outside, I find Michael waiting for me in the family room.

My stomach drops at the sight of him and another wave of heartache sweeps over me.

I take in his rugged appearance. He's dressed in black swim trunks and a white T-shirt. From the look on his face, I can tell he didn't sleep at all. I do feel some satisfaction in knowing he is just as affected as I am.

His blue eyes meet my gaze, turmoil swirling in their depths.

"Abby." His voice is husky.

"Good morning."

"I spoke to Joseph," he says to my surprise.

That was fast. I nod my head in acknowledgment.

"You want to leave?"

"I do. There really is no need for me to be here any longer."

"You haven't seen much of the country."

"No, but hopefully I'll come back one day."

Michael watches me silently, and I wish I could tell what he's thinking.

"You're here now," he replies. "And there's really no need for you to go."

"After last night, you know I can't stay." I swallow the lump in my throat.

Michael sighs loudly and stands up to face me. It almost hurts to look at him, but I bravely meet his gaze.

"If that's how you feel. I won't try to stop you."

"It's how I feel."

"Since your flight doesn't leave until late tonight, I'd like to show you something."

"Michael…" I shake my head. I don't want to do anything with him that will confuse me more.

"Please," he pleads. "I promise you'll enjoy where I want to take you."

The last thing either of us needs is to spend more time with each other. It will just hurt too much.

"Let it be my gift to you." He continues talking when he sees my hesitation. "Please. I want to share this with you. Please don't say no. It will only be a few hours."

There are a million reasons why I should say no.

A million.

For my sanity. For my heart. For my self-preservation. But like someone hell-bent on torturing themselves even more than humanly possible, I crave him.

Crave his company.

Because I realize this could be the last time I'm ever alone with him again.

"All right," I finally say and watch how his body relaxes when I answer yes. "But I have to be back by four."

"I'll have you back in time." He smiles.

A tremor rushes through me as we continue to stare at each other. Our eyes locked as memories of all that we've shared bounce between us. What's a few more hours? One more moment with this man to have locked in my mind forever, keeping me company on the lonely nights I know I'll have ahead without him.

"Where are we going?" I finally ask, breaking the silence between us.

"It's a surprise."

***

An hour later, we're speeding across the Caribbean in Michael's motor yacht. His crew met us at the dock and saw to our comfort once we boarded. The yacht is really beautiful, with three bedrooms, a living area, and kitchen. The front deck has an L-shaped couch with sun chairs to take full advantage of the view and the sun.

A member of his staff offers me a glass of champagne that I

gladly take as I sit on the lounge chair and take in the ocean around me. When we arrived at the yacht, I made Michael assure me again that we would make it back in time for my flight. He told me I had nothing to worry about and I believed him.

Michael sits next to me with a beer in hand.

I have my sunglasses on and sneak a peek when I think he's not looking. Once we were on our way to the surprise destination, Michael took his shirt off and is now bare-chested, sitting casually in front of me. Even though I try not to, I admire his physique.

"Are you hungry?"

"No." I can't even stomach the thought of food. A first for me, since it's always been the way to comfort myself in the past.

"You didn't have breakfast," he says, and I realize Giselle must have talked to him this morning as well.

"I'm really not hungry. Maybe something later."

He props his feet up on the table and studies me. I can feel his gaze burning into me and I curse myself for saying yes to this little day trip of his. I'm so wound up I can barely relax.

"So where are we going?" I ask him, breaking the silence.

"It's a surprise." Michael smiles. "It won't be long before you see for yourself."

"Can I get a hint?"

"No. You'll see shortly. I promise you won't be disappointed."

I take a sip of the champagne and lean back into the cushioned chair, tucking my legs underneath me. I close my eyes and let the ocean breeze move over me. I can feel his eyes on me. Watching my every move.

"What's your favorite flower?"

I open my eyes and look over at him.

"I'm sorry?" I ask in confusion.

"I have eight more questions."

Right. The bet.

"Tulips."

"What color?"

"Purple."

"Is that your favorite color?"

"Yes," I reply, quickly pointing out, "you only have five more questions."

Michael laughs good-naturedly.

"Now you're counting."

"I am."

"All right," he says with a smirk. "I'll take that."

"Finally," I mutter as I scoop out a strawberry from the champagne glass and pop it in my mouth.

"Finally?" he repeats, tilting his head to the side in question.

"We finally agree on something."

Michael stares at me pensively.

"I think we've agreed on more than that."

"Really?" I ask impatiently. "What would that be?"

"Your stepbrother being the world's biggest ass." His voice is biting and filled with loathing.

His comment makes me laugh.

"All right," I say. "I'll give you that."

"I hate the way he's treated you." Michael's voice is gentle, and my traitorous heart responds to the sympathy I hear.

"He's terrible," I agree.

"He's more than that. He's an awful human being. And I can't imagine what your life must have been like growing up with someone like that. I wish I had smashed his face in at the club. He deserved to be put in the hospital."

My heart responds to the protective tone in his voice. I know he means what he says. And I love him even more for it.

"But then you'd be in jail," I point out the obvious.

"It would be worth it. I might even pay him a visit when I get home—"

"Please don't." Even after everything that's happened, I couldn't bear the thought of Michael getting in trouble on my behalf.

Or worse, getting hurt.

"He's not worth it," I tell him.

"Protecting you is worth any price I would have to pay."

My breath hitches and I silently curse, wishing he would stop talking. I don't want to hear him say these things. It's only going to make leaving even harder.

"It's kind of you," I say as my emotions wage war.

"I'm not feeling kind right now. I'm feeling just the opposite."

My stomach twists in knots and I force myself to look away from him and not prod him to continue. This is not a conversation I want to have.

"Are we close?" I ask, changing the topic.

"About fifteen minutes out." He finishes his beer and stands up. "I'll be back."

When he's gone, I let out a sigh of relief. I can finally breathe again. It takes all my strength to distract myself from the turmoil that is churning in my stomach. All of this, the way he's behaving now, this is why I've loved him for all these years. And to know, after last night, that I can't ever have it is devastating. I try to remember all of the things we said to each other. The reasons why it can never be. The reasons he told me himself. And I still want to cry out in frustration and ask why. I grab my phone out of my bag and look at the time.

Only four more hours, I think to myself. And then I'll be on my way to the airport. The torture finally over... and a new kind of torture waiting for me on the other end. I didn't want to think about everything else that would come after, what I'd do at the office with him, all of the uncomfortable moments that were sure to come—at least not yet. There was plenty of time for that.

Michael returns a short while later with a platter of cheese and crackers and places it on the table between us.

"Something to snack on. You'll need your energy."

I smile gratefully and take a cracker. He watches me carefully.

"Does your mother know?" he asks to my surprise.

"Is that your next question?" I ask him with a raised brow. "You'll have only four left after." ·

"Touché. Yes, it is."

"Yes." I give him a simple answer.

"What did she say?" Michael prods. "I know I'll have only three left after this."

I shrug uncomfortably before leaning in to grab a piece of cheese.

"As you can imagine she wasn't too thrilled."

"Specifics," he insists. "I get to have more than that."

"What do you think she said?" I sigh. "She is furious with me. She thinks I've embarrassed the family even more and of course, it's all about her."

"Embarrassed the family?" Michael repeats quietly.

"My mother is well aware of your reputation," I point out to him, not caring if I hurt his feelings.

"My reputation?"

I look at him and watch as he takes off his sunglasses. I can tell he's not very happy with my comment but if the shoe fits...

"Your vast experience with the female anatomy and your philandering ways," I tell him with a sweet smile. "You were quick to point them out to me last night, so I wouldn't look so shocked."

He stares at me with an inscrutable look.

His face is so handsome, I think to myself. I wish more than anything I could lean over and pull those philandering lips to mine and have another taste of them.

God.

I want him again.

Manwhore that he is.

Incapable of settling down. Incapable of emotion. Incapable of giving me what I want.

And yet I still want him.

Life can definitely be cruel.

"There are advantages in having my vast experience," Michael says, his eyes darkening.

"Really?" I laugh off his comment.

"I think you've experienced them firsthand."

My stomach flips at the thought of the pleasure he's given me. Yes, there were definite advantages.

"Haven't you?" he prods huskily.

"Is that your next question?"

"It is."

"Yes," I whisper, taking another nervous sip of my drink.

Before Michael can continue his tortuous line of inappropriate questioning, the boat slows down and I hear the crew begin to call out to one another. Michael stands and looks out the bow. A smile sweeps across his face.

"We're here."

Since I've been so consumed by his company, I hadn't even taken note of everything going on around me. I stand up and look out on the ocean and the sight that greets me takes my breath away. Hundreds of dolphins swim around the boat, playing in the water, jumping out as if they are putting on a display for us.

"Oh my God!" I whisper in awe, setting down my drink and grabbing my phone to take pictures.

It's one of the most beautiful sights I've ever seen.

"This is incredible!" I tell him in excitement, soaking in the sight.

"It really is," he agrees as he comes to stand next to me.

We take in the joyful scene and I'm beyond grateful he brought me here to see this. I lean over the railing to soak it all in. I turn to give him a happy smile.

"This is everything!" I tell him. "Thank you for bringing me here."

"There's more." His eyes sweep over my face and linger on my lips. My body reacts to his hungry look and I force myself to look away.

"Come with me," he says, grabbing my hand and leading me to the back of the yacht.

Two members of the crew are waiting for us at the back of the boat with snorkels and fins. I turn to look up at him in excitement.

"We can go in?" I ask giddily.

"Yes," he says with a warm smile. "This is the best part."

I quickly pull off my sundress and rush to grab the snorkels and fins from the waiting crew. Michael laughs at my enthusiasm.

"Wait for me," he cautions.

I slip on the gear and turn to him and watch as he does the same.

"Ready?" he asks, giving me the thumbs-up sign.

"Yes!"

One of the men helps me to the side of the boat where there are steps that lead out into the sea and I jump in, easily treading water as I wait for Michael to follow. He gets in quickly and we bob in the water together.

"Follow me," he says, dunking his head in and swimming toward the mass of dolphins.

I do the same and the underwater display that greets me is spectacular. There are dolphins everywhere. Swimming playfully underneath us, calling out to one another as they gracefully move through the water. I could stay here forever.

Michael takes my hand and leads me out as we both swim around and take it all in. He squeezes my hand and points out different pods and I look on in happiness as I watch the dolphins. They watch us curiously, turning to their sides and swimming around us, allowing us this secret look into their habitat.

We spend what feels like hours out on the ocean.

And I never want to leave.

When Michael tugs on my hand and motions for me to come up

out of the water so he can talk, I'm reluctant to take leave of the sight.

We both emerge at the same time and I take off my snorkel and shake my head in happiness.

"This is unreal!" I tell him in pleasure.

"It is," Michael agrees smiling back at me with as much joy as I feel. "But we have to go in now."

"Why?" I ask, wanting to take more in.

"Lunch. Then we'll come back out."

"But I'm not hungry. You can go in—"

"No." He interrupts me sternly. "I don't want you out here without me. We'll go back in, I promise. You have to eat."

Since I know he won't let me argue the point I reluctantly follow him back to the waiting boat.

Once we're back on deck, I can't stop myself from throwing my arms around him in a wet, slippery hug.

"That was truly incredible!" I tell him happily. "I'm so glad I came."

He holds onto my body, his strong arms curving around my hips as he crushes me to his chest. Our eyes meet and something electrical passes between us. He leans down and before I know what's coming he kisses my mouth softly. Later, I will tell myself it was the excitement of the moment. My adrenaline is pumping through my body, making me feel more alive than I ever have before. That's what I will tell myself.

I kiss him back, not caring about the audience around us who busy themselves with cleaning up the deck.

I kiss him with the gratitude I feel.

With the joy I have in my heart at this moment because he is giving me another first experience. Another experience I never thought could be possible.

His mouth becomes more forceful, his body insistent. His erection is hard against my naked belly as his tongue sweeps into my mouth, holding me close, taking what I willingly offer him.

After a long minute, he pulls away from me, leaving me breathless with longing.

And then he leans down, picks me up in his arms and carries me into the yacht, through the living area, into one of the bedrooms. There are so many reasons why I should say no, why I should deny him—deny myself—this moment, but I don't want to.

I want him.

I want this.

We reach for each other with a frenzied need. Ripping off our bathing suits, our naked bodies coming together like our lives depend on it. He lifts me up and places me on the bed, his body never leaving mine as we kiss each other deeply, passionately. His hand moves over to palm my breast, teasing my nipple until it's a hard nub while I rub myself against his cock, craving him inside me.

"You're so beautiful," he whispers against my lips. "So goddamn beautiful."

I respond to him the only way I can—kissing him, licking his lips, rubbing my hands down the length of his back before my hands cup his ass, begging him for the fulfillment I know he can give me.

"I want you," I tell him hungrily as my mouth covers his face with kisses.

He leans up on his elbows and pulls away so he can stare down at me. His eyes, bright with passion, sweep over my face.

"I can't get enough of you," he admits softly, letting me see the confusion he's feeling in his depths.

He moves his shaft to press up against my wet core, the tip teasing me mercilessly as my emotions rage in desire. I buck up against him and watch as he growls with desire.

"I'm not going to let you leave me," he whispers harshly, his eyes feral with longing.

I try not to think about what he's saying, what it even means and only focus on this moment.

"Michael…" I say with longing, begging him with my body.

"No." His blue eyes are on fire with such deep emotion. "I won't let you."

"I'm here now," I whisper back, my hands pulling his mouth back down to mine. But he won't budge.

"Take this chance with me." His voice is hungry with longing.

My body stills at his words.

The implication of what he's asking vibrating through my heart and soul. He wants to try. Is that what he's saying?

"Abby," he groans as he leans down and kisses me again, with more force and urgency than I've ever felt from him before. "I need you."

I close my eyes in bliss as I allow his words to crush the fragile wall I had put up to protect myself. *I need you is not I love you.*

But it's something.

It's an opening.

It's hope.

"Look at me," he commands.

And I do. And then I tell him the words that have been locked in my heart forever. Because I realize, he should know.

"I love you, Michael Sinclair," I whisper to him as my eyes fill with unshed tears. "I love your kindness. Your generosity. Your heart. I've loved you from the moment you protected me against Davis when I was a child. I love—"

He doesn't let me finish my words.

I hear him groan in passion as his mouth takes mine and his cock plunges into my body. I scream out in need as he moves inside me, giving me the fulfillment that I'll die without.

But this is different.

Something about the way he touches me. The sweet words of passion he whispers in my ears. The tender way he cups my face as he kisses my mouth. Everything about it is different.

It's filled with love.

We both come at the same time.

Exploding and calling out each other's names as our bodies tremble in ecstasy. It's a long time before I can move. Before I can think. Before I can breathe easy again. He rolls to his side and pulls my body to his as he rubs my hair, my back, his hands touching my naked skin as I let the beauty of the moment sweep over me.

Neither of us says a word.

We don't have to.

And I let myself close my eyes and fall asleep, feeling safe and utterly loved in his arms.

***

"Try this shrimp."

We're sitting across from each other on his bed with a giant platter of food between us. I'm wearing his T-shirt with nothing else and he's bare-chested with boxers on, both of us spent from the passion we shared and the time we spent in the ocean. I've never felt more comfortable or happy in my life.

I take the food he offers and lick his fingers for good measure, watching the way his eyes light up in desire.

"It's delicious," I tell him, smiling in pleasure over the way he's staring at me.

"You're so sexy."

"So are you," I reply, letting my gaze move over his rippled body before settling on his mouth.

"Fuck," he groans, leaning over the platter to kiss me lazily.

I playfully pull away from him and try to focus on the food in front of me.

My appetite is back with a vengeance.

"Don't distract me," I tease him.

"Food didn't interest you before," Michael says, raising a cocky brow.

"That was before."

He throws his head back and laughs as I shamelessly gorge on the food, not caring a lick if it's ladylike or not.

"What would your last meal be?" he asks as his eyes dance with mirth.

"You'll have one more question after this," I tell him flippantly as I pop a piece of sushi in my mouth.

"I think I'll get more questions after I'm done," he says rather arrogantly.

He's probably right.

"Spaghetti Bolognese, Margherita pizza, and a giant chocolate cake." I close my eyes in pleasure just thinking about it. "An entire one, of course."

Michael roars with laughter.

"You couldn't eat an entire cake if your life depended on it."

"Try me," I tell him with a wink. "Sugar is my weakness."

"I'll keep that in mind," Michael says, his eyes alight with pleasure.

"And you?" I ask as I lick my fingers, savoring every taste.

"Allow me." Michael grabs hold of my hand and proceeds to lick every single one.

My body begins to throb with need, and I try to pull my hand away, but he won't let me. When he's finished, I'm wet with desire, the food completely forgotten.

He smiles knowingly before dropping hold of my hand and picking up a piece of sushi, knowing full well how turned on I am.

"What would your last meal be?" I stare at that mouth of his and think about all the pleasure that is about to come.

He plops the sushi in his mouth and casually leans back on his hands as his gaze lazily runs over my face.

I wait for him to respond.

"You would be my last meal." His voice is husky with desire.

It's all I need to hear before propelling myself into his arms and giving him exactly what he wants.

***

"Tell me what you're thinking," Michael whispers into my ear later in the day, after we're both spent from the afternoon of love-making.

"Is that your last question?" I return with a teasing grin.

"It is."

"I'm thinking I love you," my voice is strong.

He squeezes me tightly and pulls me against his naked body before kissing my mouth. I pull away so I can stare into his eyes. He's still scared. Unsure. I can see it. But whatever he was fighting against, I know he's finally given in.

To me. To us.

To the chance of what can be.

"Abby…" His voice is tender, hesitant.

"I just wanted you to know," I tell him, bringing my fingers to his lips and smiling into his beautiful face.

Michael stares at me, an enigmatic look in his eyes.

"I want to be with you. More than anything I've ever wanted in my life. Do you know I stalked you at the coffee shop for a week before I finally found the courage to come in?"

My eyes widen in shock. "I don't believe you."

"It's the truth," he admits with a rueful smile. "I was fighting myself and then I saw you from the window looking adorable in that hat and apron and I couldn't stay away."

My heart pounds in happiness. His confession means everything. Everything.

"I'm so glad you did."

"Me too."

I stare at his ruggedly handsome face. One I've dreamed about my whole life. I realize this is all I've ever wanted. To be with him.

For him to give us a chance. I'm going to put my heart out there and gamble everything just for him. The air is electric between us as we stare at one another. Both of us afraid. For different reasons. But willing to take a chance.

"This is all we need right now." My voice is tender as I stare at him with all the love in the world. "The rest... let's just see where it takes us. I can wait..."

"Wait?"

"For your love."

His face is strained for a brief moment before he closes his eyes. When he opens them, my heart stops.

My dream...

He's just given me my dream. And it's all there in his eyes for me to see.

"You've always had my love," he says softly.

A myriad of emotions wash over me as I close my eyes in pleasure, allowing myself to soak the moment in. I'm so overcome with joy I can't even find the words to speak.

"I love you, Abby." He finally gives me what I've longed to hear my whole life. I can hear him say it a thousand times and I wouldn't get tired of it.

After an emotional few minutes of declaring our love for one another, Michael pulls my body to his so I'm laying on his chest, giving me full access to be able to stare down at him and look into his eyes.

"I want to take you to Africa."

"When do we leave?" I ask quickly.

He gives me a smile.

"After Costa Rica?"

"If my boss will give me time off work," I tell him with a shrug. "He's a bit of a tyrant though..."

"Shall I talk to him for you?" he asks with a teasing grin.

"He's pretty stubborn," I reply. "But maybe there's something I can do to sway him."

I rub my breasts against his chest and watch how quickly Michael's eyes light up with desire.

"It might work," he says in that sexy voice of his.

I smile playfully.

"And after Africa?" I ask teasingly. "Where are we going then?"

"I want you to come with me to see my brother and Sophie."

His voice is so solemn and the look in his eyes so intense that it takes my breath away. Michael taking me to see his brother is more than I thought would be possible—at least, just yet. And it speaks volumes.

"Yes."

His strong hand cups the back of my head and pulls my mouth down to his and he kisses me with such passionate tenderness that it brings tears to my eyes. When he finally breaks the kiss, I pull away to stare into his eyes again.

An understanding moves between us.

"Tell me again," he whispers to me, his gaze possessive.

"I love you, Michael Sinclair."

EPILOGUE

"You are the most beautiful bride I've ever seen," Sophie says to me as she takes in my appearance.

I look over at my friend and smile in gratitude. Sophie's glowing in a way that only pregnant women in love do. Since her marriage to Clayton last year she's been my constant companion. Lucky for me, the two moved to London and live close to Michael and I. We've become inseparable and have even taken on the lead to chair a few of Michael's causes to help endangered wildlife.

"Thank you," I reply gratefully as she squeezes my hands in excitement.

"Not feeling the need to run away this time?" she asks with a raised brow, referring to the time we met and I was about to make the biggest mistake of my life.

"Not in the least," I reply with such passion that she bursts out laughing.

"I'm relieved to hear it."

"Can you believe it's finally happening?" I ask her, referring to the whirlwind engagement and wedding I let my mother plan in less than three months time.

Michael hadn't wanted to have a long engagement and insisted we be married by Christmas. My mother had balked at the idea and had even tried to sway him, but once Michael put his mind to something... well, it was never to be deterred.

She had begrudgingly gone along with his orders and had actually planned a beautiful event that she was beyond proud of. I let her have it, all things considered.

"Wait until you see what your mother has put together," Sophie tells me, her voice in awe. "The grounds look like a magical fairy garden."

Michael had insisted we marry in Bath, on the estate his brother was buried on, wanting him to be part of the day. His poignant request was not one I could or would ever deny.

"I can't wait to see," I tell her as I smile in excitement. "And you look stunning, Sophie."

"I look like I'm about to pop," Sophie glowers, putting her hands on her giant bump. "And if that's not bad enough, having Clayton follow me around like I'm about to trip over something at any minute and hurt myself or the baby isn't so fun. Trust me."

We both share a laugh. It's astounding really how much Clayton has changed since Sophie's come into his life. There's a glow about him that was missing before and such happiness he exudes that it's made everyone think Sophie put some magic spell on him.

"He loves you," I say the obvious.

"I know," she admits with a dreamy sigh. "That's the only reason why I'm putting up with it."

"Have you seen Michael?"

"He's holed up in the guest house with Clayton and some of his friends from school. From the hangover Clayton had this morning, I know they must have had too good of a time last night."

"I'm glad," I tell her.

There's a knock on the bedroom door and we both turn to see my mother enter, looking as regal as ever, carrying a small jewelry box in her hand. Sophie quickly excuses herself, leaving us alone.

I face my mother and smile as her gaze sweeps over me. I'm more than surprised when I see tears glistening in her eyes.

"You look breathtaking," she tells me, her voice filled with emotion. "Absolutely breathtaking."

"Thank you," I return, suddenly overcome with emotion.

"I wanted to give you this," she says, holding out the black velvet box. "Your father wanted you to have it on the day of your wedding."

My eyes water at the mention of my father and I reach out to shakily take the gift.

"They belonged to his grandmother and they're now yours." Her voice is soft as she watches me pop the box open.

I gasp when I see the beautiful sapphire earrings staring back at me. They glisten against the light and I admire the delicate beauty.

"Let's put them on." Her voice is filled with emotion as she helps me with the sparkly studs.

I force myself to blink away the tears that threaten to fall.

"He would be so proud if he could see you now. Of the woman you've become."

"He's here. I can feel him."

She takes a step away and stares at me. She nods her head sadly in agreement.

"Yes, my dear," she says. "I know he's here."

We stare at each other for a long moment. I see her for who she is. Because of Michael, I've finally been able to accept her with all the flaws and attributes.

"Thank you," I tell her softly.

"For what?"

"For putting all of this together," I say. "I know you didn't approve—"

"I never wanted you to get hurt," she admits. "I wanted you to have a wonderful, safe life. I know it didn't seem like it a lot of the time, but I promise you that's all I ever desired for you."

"I believe you."

I take a step forward and pull her into my embrace and let her feel the love I have for her.

"I'm finally happy," I whisper to her. "I love him so much."

"And he loves you." My mother pulls away from me and wipes the tears from her eyes. "It is a good match."

"It's a perfect match."

She smiles in pleasure and nods her head before heading to the door.

"Are you ready to marry the man of your dreams?"

"I think I've been ready forever."

***

The ceremony was beautiful. The reception was second to none. According to my mother, people would be talking about it forever. But for me, only one thing mattered.

Michael.

Walking down the aisle to him. His handsome face staring at me with all the love in the world when we said our vows. His mouth crushing mine when we were done.

Dancing in his arms for the entire night. Holding his hand. His words of love. Of joy. And encouragement.

Looking down at my ring finger and knowing I was Mrs. Michael Sinclair.

Forever.

Later, when the party was over, we spent a night of love and incredible passion in each other's arms, with him holding me close to his body as he always did, and me getting to look into his eyes and see the love that was all mine. Forever.

"I love you," I tell him softly as his bright blue eyes stare into mine.

"I love you," he replies tenderly. "So much."

"I'll never get tired of hearing you say it."

"I'll never get tired of saying it."

I lean up to kiss his soft mouth and sigh in pleasure. Who knew proper Abigail Walters would ever tame Michael Sinclair?

Dreams do come true.

THE END

ABOUT THE AUTHOR

Colet Abedi is a television and film executive based in Los Angeles. She had her first taste of living her dream as head writer and showrunner for the FOX-owned MyNetworkTV serials, American Heiress and Fashion House. She is the creator and executive producer of Unsealed: Alien Files. She is the co-author of young adult fiction novel, FAE. FAE was optioned by Ridley Scott & Giannina Scott.

Colet is a native of California, graduated with a B.A. in English literature from the University of California at Irvine, and currently lives in Los Angeles with her husband and three dogs.

Find Colet Abedi on the web at
http://coletabedi.com/
https://www.facebook.com/coletabedifan/
Tweet me: https://twitter.com/ColetAbedi
Follow me on Instagram @coletabedi

ACKNOWLEDGEMENTS

My special thanks to Nina Grinstead for her overall awesome-ness and amazing attitude. Nina… I wish there were more people like you in the world.

A special thanks to Christine Estevez for all of her help.

To my friends. Thank you for being the best support group ever and putting up with all my crazy.

To my husband and my family. I love you all more than you know.

I'm a lucky girl.

And how can I not thank the hot man on the cover of Tame? Erik....I love you forever.

Keep reading for a sneak peek of

MAD LOVE

1

I am in complete darkness.

I panic for a moment, forgetting where I am. The quick jolt of turbulence instantly reminds me. Right, I'm thirty-two thousand feet in the air on my way to a vacation that people only dream of. The Maldives. One of the world's most beautiful and remote destinations. I try to get excited. But right now the feeling is nonexistent. I grimace as reality starts to wash over me like a tsunami. Try to be grateful, Sophie, I silently snarl to myself. Who wouldn't trade places with you right now?

I flip the eye mask off my face and stretch out in my seat. The cabin is darkly lit and a quick look at the television monitor tells me that we are still a few hours away from Male. I click the button on my chair and move from the flat bed to a seated position. Yes, I know I'm lucky. To be in a window seat in first class and not crammed in coach is a blessing. I used to appreciate these kinds of moments more, but now I'm just bone weary. I feel older than my twenty-three years. But then, so much has happened in the past few weeks. So much has changed in my life. Some for good, some not so great. I try not to dwell on negative thoughts, but it's hard. I can't seem to help myself.

I force myself to think about the self-help and spiritual books I've read and downloaded on my iPad to help me become a more well-rounded person. There's The Power of Now by Eckhart Tolle, who teaches you to live in the now, which I personally find really hard to do. I mean honestly, who can always be present besides Buddhist monks in remote villages in Thailand? I realize my cynicism is getting the best of me. I need to be fair. I used to believe you could live in the now. Maybe you can. Try now, Sophie, I think to myself. I take a deep breath and focus on the seat I'm sitting in, the television screen in front of me, the sound of the plane humming through the sky. That's the now, right?

Then my inner voice chimes in. This vacation is costing you a fortune, it says. And, I ask myself, your point is? The point is, Do the math. Your bank account can't handle this.

Whatever!!

Okay, so living in the now is really not working at this moment. I continue to mentally flip through the catalogue of books. What about Don Miguel Ruiz's The Four Agreements? That's a good one. What are the agreements again? Oh yes, Never Make Assumptions, Do Your Best, Be Impeccable with Your Word and Don't Take Anything Personally. Well, shit. I'm sitting here right now because I've taken everything in my life personally. And if I consider the rest of Mr. Ruiz's agreements, I've definitely made a lot of assumptions. According to my parents, I'm not so impeccable with my word, and I can't honestly say that I've always done my best. Umm, that's zero out of four.

Yikes. I clearly need to do some spiritual work on myself.

I sigh and grab the remote for the television. I'm just so tired. When did this happen? How did this happen? I'm only twenty-three, for the love of God. I shouldn't feel like I'm carrying a five-hundred pound weight on my back. I expected this general feeling to occur later, when I'm married with four kids and have a mortgage I can't afford and am drowning in credit card debt. I fidget in my seat in agitation.

There is just so much going on in my head, so many different problems I need to sort through. This vacation is supposed to be my saving grace, my salvation from all the real-life drama I've faced in the past few weeks. My family is angry with me for becoming "a stranger overnight," as my mother so dramatically said. First, I broke up with Jerry—the man they wanted me to marry—because he never kissed me with the passion that I'd read about in romance novels. And then I dropped out of law school to pursue a career in art. Lord Almighty, just thinking about it makes me break out in a sweat. No wonder my mom tearfully told me that she was going to disown me, that she didn't know who I was, and that I had disgraced the family.

I hit the call button for the flight attendant. It's a good time for a drink, right before panic starts to envelope me. In a second the flight attendant leans over me. I can't believe she looks so good after fourteen hours in the air. But then I was told that Singapore Airlines has the best looking and most accommodating flight attendants in the world.

"Gin and tonic, please," I whisper in a voice, slightly embarrassed that I'm asking for a drink at what is breakfast time in Los Angeles. If she disapproves, she doesn't show it. She simply nods and hurries off to get me my drink.

I guess if I'm going to have my own eat, pray, drink vacation, I think with some amusement, I should do it with a bang. I used all my precious air miles to book the first-class ticket. I even cajoled my best friend and his boyfriend to join me on my extravagant vacation —except they didn't need to max out their credit cards to find themselves, my mind annoyingly reminds me. I'm instantly angry with myself for going down this dark path. I hit the button on the remote to find a movie.

"Did you just ask for a gin and tonic?" Erik asks me as he rolls over on his flat bed to look at me. He pushes the blanket off his body and runs a hand through his thick hair.

"Yep." I can't help but smile at how gorgeous he looks.

His blond hair is slightly tousled and his big blue eyes are earnest in his handsome face. Why can't he be straight, I ask myself for the thousandth time. He moves his seat into an upright position and studies my somber demeanor.

"Are you going to cry again?" He's clearly afraid of my answer.

"No," I say, but my voice wavers. God, I hope not. The amount of crying I've done in the past few weeks should be a crime.

"Honestly, Sophie, if Orie and I are going to have to cajole you out of bad moods the whole vacation I'm going to be really pissed off."

I laugh. His candor is biting, but real. Okay, borderline offensive, but what can I say? I love the guy.

"It's not like I don't have anything to cry about," I say a bit defensively.

"The only thing you should be crying about is that outfit you have on." Erik checks out my pajamas, courtesy of Singapore Airlines.

"What's wrong with it?"

"There's a reason they're free. And given to you in a small plastic bag."

"Oh, please. They're comfortable. And besides, who's seeing me on this plane?"

Erik turns his overhead light on and looks straight at me.

"First of all, I'm seeing you. Second of all, and almost as important, you should dress every single day, every single outfit, as if you're going to die in those clothes."

It's hard not to laugh out loud but I want to be considerate to the sleeping passengers. The funniest part of the conversation is that Erik is dead serious.

"Trust me when I say you wouldn't want to be caught dead in

that." He points at me and turns the overhead light back out.

"You're obsessed."

"And? You're the girl who was wearing boot-cut jeans until last year. I found jeans in your closet that you used to wear in high school. The only reason you don't have them on right now is because I threw them out!"

"If you love me you won't talk about those four years of hell." The thought of high school makes my skin crawl. I so didn't want to relive Sophie Walker's Wonder Years. Because seriously, there really wasn't anything wonderful about them.

"If you didn't want a reminder of how completely uncool you were, why keep the hideous jeans?"

"I loved them," I tell him honestly.

"Sophie, that offends me. On every level."

I lose the battle to stay silent and burst out laughing. Erik is a stylist to the stars in Hollywood. He's considered to be one of the best, and every celebrity he works with instantly falls in love with him and can't get enough of him. I don't blame them. He lives and breathes fashion. His love for clothes, handbags, shoes, and accessories comes a close second to his love for Orie. And sometimes, depending on what designer he has on, he might even love the outfit more.

Before I can answer, the flight attendant brings my drink.

"May I get you anything else, Miss Walker?"

"This is great, thank you," I say politely.

"I'd love to have one of those as well," Erik asks her with a smile. She nods and walks away.

"Are we drinking our sorrows away?"

I stir my drink and shrug. "Maybe."

"Sophie, your parents are assholes." Erik just rolls right into it. I know what's coming next so I take a giant sip. "Instead of supporting their daughter and her dream of being an artist, they act like pricks."

The thought of my parents makes me sick to my stomach.

"I mean, look at you. Not at this moment, of course. I'm talking in general. Your parents should be so proud of you. Of how brave you are. Of being so confident in your ability as an artist. I mean, it's your choice if you wanna be poor," I almost smile. Erik looks so indignant. "Your mom should support your artistic endeavors. She was a dancer for God's sake! Your dad is a stiff lawyer, but your mom? She's got a lot of nerve to be pissed at you."

I bite my lip and hope my face doesn't betray the pain of his words. I wish I made my mother proud. Instead, I'm the cause of her anxiety and heartache. But then I could never be as perfect as her. When my father first set eyes on my mother she was a ballerina in Swan Lake—of course, she was the swan queen. He watched her perform and was instantly smitten. He had to meet her, so he bribed his way backstage and came face to face with my mom. They both say that when they set eyes on each other they knew instantly that they were meant to be together forever. And to this day, they are still madly in love.

They compliment each other in every way. My mom is small, petite, perfect. My dad, a former football player in high school, is the epitome of the all-American, with his wholesome good looks and easy smile. My mom quit the ballet company and followed my dad to Los Angeles, where he was enrolled in law school at USC.

Now he has a successful criminal law practice and my mom is his rock. She has dedicated her life to him. They never had any other children so all they do is focus on me. Obsessively, I think. They expected me to pursue a career in law and take over the family business. And being the pleaser that I am, I dutifully did as I was told and applied to law school—in Los Angeles, because my parents couldn't bear the thought of me leaving them. I got into my dad's alma mater and was on my way to following in his footsteps. That was the plan. Was being the operative word.

And then there's Jerry. Perfectly coiffed, immaculately dressed, and knowledgeable about everything, he is the perfect man. And he looks like George Clooney. I've known him since I was five years old; we played hide and seek when we were kids. He taught me how to ride a bike, spit like a man, and catch frogs. We drifted apart in high school because of our three-year age difference, but we always talked and always remained friends. When Jerry came back from Harvard Law—where else?—he started working for my dad's firm—of course.

I interned there almost a year ago, and one night when we were both working late, Jerry looked at me seriously and said, "Should we just give it a go?"

"Give what a go?" I had no idea what he was talking about.

"Us." He smiled at me, showing perfect dimples. "It seems kind of natural, huh?"

My heart dropped. What was I supposed to say to him? We were friends. I didn't want to lose that. ·

"I don't know—"

He leaned in quickly and kissed me softly on the lips. I was frozen.

"We're perfectly matched. Our families know one another and like each other." He shrugged as he brushed his hand across my cheek. "It just feels—comfortable."

Comfortable? Huh?

Before I knew it, I was in a comfortable relationship with comfortable kisses, comfortable handholding, and nothing uncomfortable about it.

Two weeks ago. Erik made me see the light. I may not have been ready to have sex with him, but I at least wanted to know that the man I was going to marry at least wanted to. I tried to break up with Jerry via text, I was so chicken shit. But Erik made me do it in person, and even drove me to Jerry's house. He waited down the street while I took a swig of vodka from a flask, a first for me, and walked up to Jerry's house at three a.m.

I rang the doorbell and after a moment Jerry opened it, his hair disheveled from sleep but still looking good in sweat pants and a t-shirt. He was immediately concerned, which made me feel even worse.

"Sophie? What's wrong? Do you know what time it is?"

"I'm breaking up with you," I blurted it out like projectile vomit.

It took a moment for him to register this piece of information. Then he said, "What?"

"I hope we can remain friends," I said and turned around to run straight back to Erik's car, but Jerry took my arm.

"What is wrong with you? We are not breaking up!"

"Yes, we are, Jerry." I pulled my arm away and mustered up what little courage I had. "You can't really tell me that you want this for the rest of your life." I pointed at my body for dramatic effect. I knew I was insulting myself but I didn't care.

"I do. I want you."

"No, you don't," I told him, shaking my head emphatically. "You can't even bear to kiss me! Am I going to stay a virgin forever?!"

I'll never forget the look on his face. He was mortified by my question, but then I was humiliated that I even had to ask.

"I was trying to be considerate."

"Considerate?" I practically shouted at him. "Do you know how completely horrible that sounds to me?" He's Just Not That into You popped into my mind. Clearly I could have been a case study.

"Yes! There's a family relationship here, Sophie. I'm being respectful. Try to get a grip and understand."

But I felt like sex-starved nymphomaniac.

"There's no passion between us."

He looked so offended by my words that I felt even worse than before.

But for once, Jerry was quiet. How could he deny it? There was no way he could.

"You know I'm right," I rushed out. "I love you like a brother. And if you're honest with yourself, you only love me like a sister."

That was about all I could handle before turning around and running to Erik's car like a bat out of hell. This time, Jerry didn't try to stop me.

The next battle, my parents. I didn't want to disappoint them, but it was inevitable. Jerry is what my dad likes to call "a rising star." He says Jerry exhibits this in his social life and in business. Unfortunately for me, they adore him even more than what the average person would deem normal.

My mom was so upset by the break-up that I think if she had to choose between us, she would have chosen Jerry.

The night I told them, I went home to their place in Brentwood for dinner. I walked through the front door and felt the familiar feeling of home and security, as I always did when I entered their cozy domain. The house is a traditional Cape Cod and my mom had designed the interior as if it were in the Hamptons. As was our ritual, she greeted me at the door.

She always looks so good, never a hair out of place, always

immaculately dressed. She's like a little porcelain china doll.

"Where's Jerry?" she asked as she looked over my shoulder.

"He's not coming," I managed to say through my dread.

"Oh? Is he working late, dear?" she asked as she wiped her hands on her apron.

I tried to muster up as much courage as I could.

"Mom, Jerry is never coming with me to this house again." There it was. Out in the open.

"Whatever do you mean, dear?" My mom stopped in her tracks to turn and look at me, a brow raised in surprise.

"I broke up with him." I felt relieved.

My mom was quiet for a moment, then she shrugged and said, "Lover's quarrel. You'll make up."

I hadn't expected that. I needed to be clearer about this. Brutal. It was the only way to get through to her. "No, mom. We are never making up. I'm not in love with him."

"Yes, you are."

"No, actually I'm not."

"Yes, you are."

"Are you really trying to tell me how I feel? I don't love Jerry!" I told her. I couldn't believe we were even arguing about it.

"Oh." I could tell my mom was devastated. She didn't say any-thing else, but walked to the bar and poured herself a healthy glass of scotch. She downed it in a second, like a pro. I was impressed.

"Are you upset?" I asked as I watched her pour another drink, tap the bar with the cup, and take it down in one swig.

"Why would you think that, dear? It's your life, your choice." I knew she wanted to add your mistake.

"Well, thanks for understanding, Mom." I tried to keep the sarcasm out of my voice, but I hoped that my innocent comment would make her feel bad.

"Of course, dear. You know we'll always support you in every decision you make," she said as she headed into the kitchen. I thought I was home free, almost at the finish line, but then my mom can't ever seem to help herself when it comes to me. "Even if you'll never ever find someone as kind, intelligent and handsome as Jerry," she said over her shoulder before disappearing into the kitchen.

Nice.

I chose not to respond with an equally biting comment because I knew that if the two of us started down this road it would end in tears —only mine, of course—and in my mom inevitably convincing me of the error of my ways.

I'm sure she wonders sometimes if I'm really her daughter or if the hospital made a mistake and swapped me for her real child. If you really analyzed us you would notice that the only similarity we have are our toes, and even those are questionable.

"Speaking of your mom, where did she come up with name Sophie? It's not like she's French. She should have named you Maria or Monica." Erik brings me back to the moment in a second. I'm so glad for him.

"I'm named after my dad's mom."

"I always wondered," he says as he pulls out a Chanel face mist. He gives himself three sprays then holds it out to do my face.

"Close your eyes." I do as I'm told. The mist actually feels great on my skin.

"Thanks." I open my eyes and smile gratefully at my friend.

Erik stares at me for a long moment. He knows me well. He has sat with me through endless tirades about my family, about Jerry, about my desire to be an artist, the many nights all blurred into one, giant, alcohol-induced haze.

"So what's on your mind? Why can't you sleep? Please tell me you're not thinking about Jerry the fairy." He says the last part with a great deal of animosity.

I snort out loud. "He's not—"

"So is. The man never ever tried to have sex with you—"

"Lower your voice!" I hiss at him in agitation as I look around the cabin." He says he was being considerate."

"Considerate?" Erik pauses for a moment. "Do you believe the lies he tells you?"

"Whatever."

"Oh honey, there is so much you have to learn." He pulls a lip balm out of his Goyard make-up bag.

I finally ask out loud the question that has plagued me since the moment Jerry and I started dating. "Maybe he didn't find me attractive?"

"Spare me the mental anguish! Have you looked in the mirror lately?"

I look away from Erik. "You're my friend."

"What I find so damn puzzling about you is how you can be so strong and confident about certain things and so insecure about your own beauty." He shakes his head at me in disappointment.

"Strong and confident because I don't want to live a lie? I can't stand law. I'm just so done with doing what my parents want. I want to live my own dream. Nothing makes me happier than painting. Nothing."

"Exactly. You walked away from law school in your second year and then you dumped the man your parents wanted you to be with because it didn't feel right in your heart. That's confidence, babe. That's someone who knows what she wants and won't settle. And yet you don't see the hot woman looking back at you when you look in the mirror. I'm at a goddamn loss."

"Hot? Please." He's right about the confidence part. But come on, hot? Me? That's not an adjective I would ever use to describe myself.

Erik looks like he wants to strangle me.

"You're a knock-out. You've got an amazing body. You have perfect brown hair, which happens to have its own natural highlights. Most women pay a hair stylist a lot of money to get that color. You're blessed with great skin, beautiful green eyes, spectacularly long, naturally curly lashes. If you were five inches taller you could have been a model."

"Thanks, I think." I laugh again.

"What? Five feet four inches isn't so bad." He leans over and whispers, "Maybe I can look into those surgeries that stretch people out. I think they do that a lot in Asian countries."

The flight attendant arrives with Erik's drink.

"Thanks." He says and takes a sip.

"I'm totally serious about the surgery, by the way."

"I know you are. But I'm completely okay with being average height."

"Actually, it's called petite, babe."

Erik looks over at his sleeping boyfriend. His jet black hair peeks out from underneath the blanket he has draped over him. "Orie could use a few inches. Maybe we can get a two-for-one deal."

"You're terrible." I shake my head at Erik as I look on the sky map.

Only three more hours to go.

2

My eyes are closed again and I'm stretched out in the waiting lounge of the W Spa and Resort. After we landed, we were ushered here by the welcoming committee, which would take us out to the resort in a seaplane. I changed from my plane pajamas into loose pants and a tank top because it's really hot. Orie, who happens to be a famous hairdresser, has braided parts of my hair and artfully pulled it back, a look he tells me will make me blend right in with the island girls. I just go with it.

It's early morning in the Maldives and all I want to do is sleep. Jet lag sucks. I'm using my carry-on bag as a pillow, and Erik and Orie are to the left of me chatting away, completely adjusted and okay with the time difference. They look good. Really, really good. It's unfair. After almost twenty-four hours of flying they look fresh and flawless. Orie's black hair is perfectly combed back from his good-looking face and Erik looks immaculate. On the other hand, it'll take a good scrub and a nap to make me feel like myself again.

I hear voices and know that more guests have entered the resort's private waiting room. I assume they'll be on the seaplane with us to our destination. The guys are quiet for a moment and I know they're checking out the new arrivals, evaluating the other people who'll be at the resort. I decide to take a quick peek myself. I'm instantly glad I have my sunglasses on to conceal my blatant appraisal of the guests.

Wow.

Let me rephrase that. Holy shit.

A vision of a perfect male specimen is in the room. He's standing in a corner and talking to what I assume is one of his friends. He has light brown hair and cerulean blue eyes that are so bright they make my heart skip a beat. His lips are full, sensual, and he's got a straight, perfect nose. His face is utterly masculine and hot. He's tall, really tall, well over six feet, broad shouldered, and is sporting a natural tan that hints at a life spent out in the sun. He looks like he's in his early to mid-thirties and he exudes worldly sophistication. I stop breathing. I can't help it. I think I even might have forgotten how. He is the most good-looking man I've ever set eyes on. He literally looks like a walking piece of art. Erik puts his hand on my leg and squeezes hard. He sees what I see. I ignore him.

But Erik's movement catches the gorgeous man's eye and he glances over him at me. His gaze slowly moves along my outstretched body, lazily assessing me, from my sneaker-clad feet to the top of my head. He stops at my face, staring intently, almost like he can see through me, and I hold my breath again. Does he know I've been looking at him? He can't, I tell myself. He isn't Superman, he can't see through my shades.

But his gaze remains fixed on me, staring so intensely now that it makes me incapable of movement. It's the kind of look Daniel Day Lewis gave Madeline Stowe in Last of the Mohicans, when he literally devoured her with his eyes right before he dragged her off for the epic love scene. It is still one of the best love scenes of all time. I used to imagine what it would be like to have someone give me that Hawkeye stare. And now it's happening, for the very first time, from the drop-dead gorgeous stranger.

Erik has a death grip on my leg, clutching it so tight that I think I'm losing circulation. Clearly, he's witness to this most incredible moment, so it can't just be my jet lag or runaway imagination.

The stranger's bright gaze moves to my lips and they part of their own accord.

He smiles.

Oh my God! He knows I'm staring. I close my eyes and try to control the mortification that comes over me. How embarrassing!

I count to ten then open them again.

Shit. He's still looking.

...

Made in the USA
Columbia, SC
14 September 2021